THE DARK LABYRINTH

by Lawrence Durrell

THE DARK LABYRINTH

by

LAWRENCE DURRELL

A Dutton **dep** *Paperback*

NEW YORK

E. P. DUTTON & CO., INC.

1964

Library of Congress Catalog Number: 62-7808

For
MARGARET, GERALD
& LESLIE

LAWRENCE DURRELL, a British citizen of Irish parentage was born in the Himalaya region of India. His first ten years were spent in India. After schooling in England, he decided to become a writer. Throughout the 1930's Mr. Durrell devoted most of his talents to his poetry which has won much acclaim. His first novel, *The Black Book,* was published in Paris in 1938, and was cited by T. S. Eliot as being one of the great hopes for modern English fiction. *The Black Book* was published in the United States for the first time in 1960.

World War II temporarily interrupted Mr. Durrell's literary career. During the war years and for some time thereafter, he served Great Britain in various official and diplomatic capacities in Athens, Cairo, Rhodes and Belgrade.

The publication of *Justine* in 1957, and the subsequent appearance of *Balthazar* (1958), *Mountolive* (1959), and *Clea* (1960) as parts of the same magnificent series called "The Alexandria Quartet" devoted to an examination of the various aspects of love, immediately caused Mr. Durrell to be recognized as one of the greatest and most important writers of modern times.

THE DARK LABYRINTH was first published in England in 1947 and in the United States in 1962.

Contents

THE DARK LABYRINTH

The Argument

During the early part of June, 1947, a small party of sight-seers found itself trapped in what was then the newly-discovered labyrinth of Cefalû, in the island of Crete. They had penetrated the network of caves and corridors with a guide from a tourist agency, their intention being to examine the so-called "City in the Rock"—whose discovery early in the preceding year had set a seal upon the long archaeological career of Sir Juan Axelos. By a sudden and unforeseen accident, the guide in charge of the party was killed. Falls of rock separated several members of the party from the main body, and it was only the sheerest chance that led one of them, Lord Graecen, to find his own way out.

Where a novelist might find it necessary to excuse himself for the choice of so formal a theme, the journalist feels no such inhibition. This extraordinary story found a welcome place on the front pages of the London papers. As representing that part of Truth which is stranger than fiction, it found a no less welcome place in the American Press, where the final piquant note was added by sub-titles reading "Lord Lost in Labyrinth". *The Times* took the opportunity to call attention once more to the brilliant discovery by Axelos of a labyrinth so long believed to be purely mythical. The words "Labyrinth" and "Minotaur" occurred in the *Daily Mirror* crossword puzzle on the fifteenth of the month. The Greek Press of Athens, while it was unable to afford the expense of a special correspondent, reprinted the accounts given in the American Press. In one of these, a correspondent went so far as to say that the Labyrinth was still inhabited by some monstrous creature—a minotaur, in fact—which had been responsible for the death of a number of innocent villagers. With a definitive story from Lord Graecen himself, in which he described the accident and the luck he had had in finding his way out, the incident was all but closed. The young American drank his fourth cup of tea and closed his notebook. He was still a little awed by the childish dignity of Graecen, and the bulky figure of his friend Axelos, who sat upon the sundial in the grounds of his lovely house, idly smoking and appearing to give no heed to the young journalist's questions. The air was very still, save for the clap of shears along the thick hedges. "Cefalû" was a large white stone house, set back from the sea in a grove of oleanders. In the twilight the young American could see the sun touching the snow-tipped summits of the White Mountains. He sighed.

"Well, Lord Graecen," he said. "I guess that's all." He shaped a sentence in his mind which was to compliment Sir Juan on the exquisite situation of his house and grounds, but he somehow could not get it out. Axelos was a forbidding figure, with his bandy legs, sickle nose and bald head. His eye had a reptilian slowness and torpor. He was sitting on the edge of the sundial smoking a cigar. "I guess I'll be going," said the young American. The car was waiting for him in the village. It was a long drive to Canea. He allowed Lord Graecen to shake his hand with a dazzling condescension. "Thank you, sir," he said as he made his way down the pebbled path on to the mule-track which led to Cefalû. It wasn't much of a story.

He had left his notebook behind on the tea-table. He retraced his steps, taking a short cut across the terrace and the pebbled drive. Axelos was sitting in a deck-chair. He had just selected a peach from the plate on the table. Graecen sat with his arm round the back of a chair, and one leg thrown over the other. They looked up as the young man's step sounded upon the gravel. He excused himself and took up his dog-eared article.

"Mr. Howe," said Axelos in his coarse deep voice. He had started to peel the peach with a small silver penknife. His insolence of voice was superb—and unintentional. Nature had combined in him the features of a degenerate pope and the torpor of a crocodile, and to these had added a voice of unconscionable harshness. When he smiled the young American saw at once that he had not intended a rudeness. "The entrance to the labyrinth has been blocked by a fall of rock. Until it's clear there probably won't be any more news of the others. I feel I ought to advise you not to go messing about in it, eh, Dicky?"

Graecen's face wore its customary air of childish pomposity. He nodded benignly. "It's extremely dangerous." The young American felt the vague irritation that always came over him when he had dealings with the English. "It's disturbing, sir," he said, manipulating the r's until they curled on his tongue like golden syrup, "that you can't tell me exactly how many people were in the party. The reports conflict. For example, you gave me the name of a Mr. Campion."

"Oh, yes. Quite definitely. Rather," said Graecen. "He was there all right."

"He's not on the passenger list of the *Europa* at all. On the other hand, Captain Baird . . ."

"Captain Baird is here," said Axelos. "He did not go into the labyrinth."

"Well: the purser of the *Europa* has his name down as one of the original party."

"An error."

"It's very confusing."

He pocketed his notebook and hurried off to the village, climbing the steep and stony road with long strides. The car was where he had left it, and, climbing into it, he was driven slowly down the side of the mountain towards the plains. At the last bend in the road he told the driver to stop. The sun was falling, dense with its own golden weight, towards the sea. He looked back once more at Cefalû and caught his breath. It was a fantastic locality; a huge cone of conglomerate rising a thousand feet into the blue Cretan air. On the one side it ran clear up from the sea as if it had been sheared out by some insane architect. The sides were weathered and lightly covered in holm-oak and myrtle. On the very crown rose a tuft of green cypresses and olives. Half-way up the cone stood the village of Cefalû, its houses with their child's-paint-box colours glowing pristine and ingenuous in the waning sunlight. The mountain ran straight up from this little circle of cultivation, into the sky. He could see the avenue of small cypresses that led to the mouth of the labyrinth. Then, below the road, he could look down to the lovely house that Axelos had called Cefalû. It was built in a fault of the rock which gave it access to the sea. A white sailing boat lay like a breathing butterfly against the white mole. From this last bend he could look down on to the lawn and watch the two figures, foreshortened but quite clear in the bluish light.

Katina had come out in response to Axelos' call, bearing the chessboard and the box of pieces. She placed a candlestick upon the table and a box of matches. "What do you think of her, Dicky?" said Axelos with his slurred pronunciation. She was dressed in blue with a yellow head-dress: superbly built, and with a dark hawk-featured face. Axelos passed his hand lazily across her buttocks as she bent forward to remove the tea-tray. "Dark as sin," he said, depressing the corners of his mouth and stroking her—as a man might pass his hands over the smooth flanks of a deer. Katina seemed not to notice. Graecen looked nervously round him, aware of the sardonic gaze of his friend. "She's superb," he said with a well-bred discomfort. Axelos opened his lips and expelled some air in a mock-laugh.

"Katina is the product of an idiorrhythmic monastery," he said. "She is a widow—or was. That is what makes her so idiorrhythmic. So uncompromisingly idiorrhythmic, eh, my dear?" The girl carried the tray into the house. "As a term of endearment the word is unbeatable . . . my little idiorrhythmic nun, eh?" Axelos began to set out the pieces upon the board. "My dear Dicky," he said, "do not look as though I was letting the white man down." Graecen made one of his ineffectual little gestures in the air, disclaiming the implied criticism—a "far-be-it-from-me" gesture. Axelos enjoyed his discomfort. He took his chin in his fingers and once more depressed the corners of his mouth in a smile. "My Arabic mother and my Greek father," he said, "gave me a clear insight into the Mediterranean world where they value people for their . . . idiorrhythmicity, shall we say? Apart from the unhappy accident of a nationality my father thought would be useful to me, I have little enough in common with the products of the high table. And Dicky, after thirty years you still look abashed."

Graecen sighed. "Silenus," he said, using the nickname that Hogarth had bestowed upon Axelos when they were in their first year, "Silenus, you'll come to no good."

"She has a little sister who is even prettier and more idiorrhythmic if you'd care to . . ."

"Now," said Graecen primly. "I've been teased enough, Silenus. On guard."

Axelos lit a candle; they sat now in a golden puddle of light while all round them the bluish airless evening closed into nightfall. The girl reappeared and placed glasses near them and a decanter. "I suppose Baird will stay the night up at the monastery," said Graecen abstractedly. Axelos put his cigar out and opened the game resolutely. "I've noticed that all Hogarth's patients leave hurriedly for monasteries: or become monks: or accept a deaconate on Athos: what is the old devil up to with his analytic game? His last book was unreadable, I thought." Graecen stroked his eyebrow and murmured something abstractedly.

"Baird was in charge of some guerillas," he said, having moved, "during the last war. He says he knows parts of the labyrinth well. It's funny he didn't come upon your temple—and do you out of it." Axelos suddenly fixed upon him an eye as round and bright as a button. He gave a chuckle, a deep and ineffable chuckle this time. "Of such are the kingdom of heaven, Dicky," he said. He seemed about to say more but checked himself. Then he drew a breath.

"Dicky, you're an expert—you saw it."

"Yes," said Graecen, with a startled and defensive air. It alarmed him to be called an expert.

"The sculpture I sent you for the Museum, and the relief—would you pronounce them genuine?"

"Of course," said Graecen.

"They're not. If Baird never found the temple when he operated from the labyrinth it was because it wasn't there. *I built it.*"

Graecen had a limited range of expressions at his command. He looked pained now rather than surprised. Axelos could not help smiling at the mixture of pain and disbelief that flitted across that serene round countenance. "The stone is from an old dig near Castro," he said. "The temple I assembled from fragments of marble fished out of the ancient mole. The plinth and the bas relief were done by an old monk here. The sculpture by me." He laughed until his eyes disappeared completely and his nose almost touched his chin. It was the face of a Greek tragic mask, thought Graecen. It was most disturbing. But then, one could always count upon Axelos for some such ponderous hoax. As a man who took antiquities seriously he felt extremely annoyed. "That was why you warned me not to . . ." he said unhappily. He remembered the brilliant sunlight leaking through the slit in the roof on to the great bas relief. Axelos said: "It sets a seal upon my career, Dicky, does it not? A triumph of scholarship. I had to wait until the monk died before I could tell the world about it—'The City in the Rock'." They sat looking at each other across the chessboard. Graecen sighed and shook his head. Axelos said: "By the autumn the hoax will have been going a year. I then propose to tell the Press the true story. It will underline in uncompromising fashion the two principles in which I believe: that experts know nothing and that archaeology has developed into a science as dull as theology. It's your move."

"But your *reputation*," said Graecen, reflecting, as he did so, that the whole of Axelos' life had been cast in this mould. As fast as he won honours he threw them away; not exactly as if he did not relish them, but as if some perverse quality in his nature denied him the enjoyment of them. There had been first of all, that brilliant speculative reading of Nugatius while he was still in his first year. The Trinity Fellowship had gone down the drain, too. His tutor had said once, "He's brilliant all right—when the facts fit his fancies." And now he was being beaten by the same enviable, skilful unorthodoxy at chess. Or perhaps he was not paying attention? One of Hogarth's funnier imitations had been of Mullins, the scout, leaning breathlessly over his bed, whispering "White chapel today, sir" and adding "Mr. Axelos came in, sir, and told me to tell you he was in trouble again, sir, and don't know which way to turn, sir."

As if he had divined the thoughts passing in his friend's head, Alexos laid down his glass and said: "It's no use you shaking your head over me, Dicky. I'm incorrigible. On a thousand or two a year one can afford to be. But you've been living on short commons too long to realize the inadequacy of our intellectual amusements for a man who wakes up one day with the Platonic fire in his guts."

His face looked sad now—the face of a ruined pope, in the light from the single candle. He was unhappy, Graecen saw, and his ready sympathy was at once kindled. He sat there staring at Graccen as if he wasn't quite seeing him, the large, rather feminine hands at rest in his lap. "Check," he called and blew out the candles, before taking his friend's arm and leading him slowly into the lighted house.

Five miles away, the American reporter took out his note-book and the various scraps of paper on which he had jotted down items of interest about the affair. He always found it difficult to read his own shorthand. By the light of a pocket torch he steadied the papers on his knee, and, bracing himself against the jolting of the old car, tried to compose his dispatch. There were several interesting notes which would help to give his cable colour. For instance, Sir Juan had several times notified the authorities that the labyrinth was unsafe, that conducted tours should be discouraged. The British Consul himself had tried to dissuade the captain of the *Europa* from letting his passengers embark on the excursion. Then there was the interesting fact that several expeditions had disappeared in the labyrinth. He had the dates: 1839, 1894, 1903. They were all unofficial bodies and no trace of them had been found. Sir Juan estimated that the ramifications of the labyrinth might cover an area of several square miles. There was a peasant legend to the effect that a large animal of some kind lived in the heart of the labyrinth.

At Canea he was settling down to a cheerless dinner when he received a telegram from his office in Athens giving the passenger list of the *Europa*—or rather the names of those tourists on it who had set out for the labyrinth.

> Mr. O. Fearmax.
> Mr. V. Truman and Mrs. Truman.
> Miss Virginia Dale.
> Captain J. Baird.
> Lord Graecen.
> Miss Dombey.

The name of Campion did not appear. He ticked off Lord Graecen's name and that of Captain Baird. They had both been accounted for. The others he presumed dead. He wondered what the chances were of any of them finding a way out. After all, a mere twenty-four hours had passed. Should he stay on a while and see whether time could put a better story in his way? A glance at the forbidding darkness of Canea decided for him. He would catch tomorrow's plane back to Athens. The rest of the tale, he thought, must be followed up in London. His head office might unearth something of interest by sending reporters round to the private addresses of the victims. He contemplated the list once more before turning out the raw electric light that hung from the bug-ridden ceiling on a length of dusty flex. The name of Fearmax seemed vaguely familiar. . . .

At this time the liner *Europa* with the rest of its holiday-makers, lay in the port of Alexandria. The Captain and the purser sat in a stateroom and contemplated the latest telegram from the Company offices in London. Most of the questions contained in it were easily answered. For instance, why had the Captain not organized a search party to rescue the victims? It was a question so stupid that it annoyed even the purser, whose profession had given him the character of a lamb and the omniscience of God. First of all there was no transport to take a rescue party a hundred miles across Crete; secondly, the mouth of the labyrinth had been blocked; thirdly, the *Europa* was on a schedule, and had to consult the wishes of several hundred other passengers. "That's terse enough," said the Captain angrily as he read through his own reply. "What do they think we are?" The purser took up the telegram and retired to his own quarters. He unearthed a passenger list and an indelible pencil.

As he put a line through each name it seemed to him that he was exorcizing the shadow of the accident which seemed to be lying heavy on the minds of the remaining passengers. Death and holiday-cruises, he thought, were things that no amount of explaining could reconcile; and he remembered how nearly he himself had been tempted to join the party that had set off from the ship's side on that fine spring morning. The word "labyrinth" suggested something at once terrifying and enticing. What was it? At the old Wembley Fun Fair there had been a water-labyrinth. You sailed through the darkness in a small boat, passing at last through a corridor of mirrors and lighted panoramas.

The circle of enquiry was all but closed. There remains to be recorded only the documentation of the Travel Agency in charge of organizing the cruise. Extracts from the Captain's log, newspaper-cuttings and the personal effects of the missing people were posted on to London for the benefit of an alarmed insurance agent. There was little enough in all this to interest anyone. The clearing out of the cabins fell to the lot of an Irish stewardess. In the Truman cabin there was an old trunk containing several cheap and badly-cut dresses, several large hats —two of which were trimmed with feathers: a hot-water bottle: several packets of letters tied up in ribbon: and a couple of knitted sweaters. The stewardess tried on the dresses and found they did not suit her. One of the sweaters, however, was of a thick rope-stitch and suited her admirably. She kept it for herself. The letters she placed carefully in the trunk, together with the rest of the articles. She was tempted to read them, but her upbringing had been such as to instil in her a respect for private correspondence—if not for private property. The Trumans had been rather a nice couple, she thought, as she pocketed a comb and a packet of unopened cosmetics from the bunk-head. Elderly and quiet, and perhaps a little eccentric. Not like Miss Dombey with her freckles and red hair and peremptory voice—Miss Dombey whose cabin was an arsenal of religious tracts and Church Society pamphlets. She had a particular dislike for Miss Dombey. No sooner had she come

aboard than the bell rang and there stood Miss Dombey at the
door of her cabin with her arms on her hips, waiting for her to
help her unpack. "Come on," she had called in her brassy
assured manner. "Hurry up." And then, what? You would
never guess. She asked her her name and, thrusting a little
book into her hand, said, "Here, read this when you have
time." The book was called *The Way of the Cross*. It seemed
absolute gibberish to her, and day in, day out, Miss Dombey
would question her. "Have you read it yet? Is there anything
you would like me to explain?" And then there was that beastly
little dog of hers messing everywhere: she had brought it
aboard in defiance of regulations, and no one was able to part
her from it.

As she turned over Miss Dombey's effects, which, apart
from the bundles of tracts, were few, the stewardess remembered another incident which had surprised her. She had recounted it later in the voyage to the purser who seemed to find
it very droll. The bell rang and there was Miss Dombey standing outside the cabin door, her red freckled face contorted
with anger. Without a word she turned and led the way to the
private bathroom which was attached to her saloon. Pointing
a quivering finger, she said, in tones of outrage, "And what
might this be?" She was pointing at the *bidet*—for the *Europa*
was one of those French liners which had changed hands after
the war. "That ma'am?" she had said, with a dreadful feeling
of being personally responsible for the outrage. "That's a
biddy." It was enough for Miss Dombey. She turned on her
heel and bowled out into the corridor. "I am going to see the
Captain," she said. "It must be removed at once." She actually
fought her way on to the bridge to see the Captain. What she
said to him was not known, but when they came down off the
bridge they were both red in the face. The bidet stayed where
it was, but an arctic coldness sprang up in Miss Dombey's
manner whenever she passed the Captain on deck. The

Captain was not one to be put upon by such behaviour.

Mr. Campion had taken all his things. He had, however, trodden a certain amount of paint into the floor, and had forgotten a small folding camp-stool. There was a paper bag full of walnuts under his pillow and a small dirty comb. A dozen roped-up canvases stood in the corner tied together with a rubber band and label. The label bore an address in Marseilles. Mr. Campion was rather too familiar with her. "A penny for your thoughts," he had said on one occasion; and when she did not reply: "No? Well then, a pound for your body." It was hardly the way to speak to a decent girl—even if she wasn't a lady. Mr. Campion had also left a beret on the wardrobe. He always wore a beret and an open-necked shirt. Perhaps he had more than one beret. She tried it on and thought she would keep it; it would look quite nice after a dry-clean. The walnuts seemed to be mostly bad.

Who else was there? It always gave her a pleasant feeling of superstitious fear to go to Fearmax's cabin. It was rather a gloomy one on A deck. It was in a fearful mess. There were a number of books lying about, clothes hanging out of suitcases, and several bundles of envelopes done up with string and sealing-wax. She touched them softly, as if she were afraid that some of the medium's magnetism might remain in these belongings of his. There was the short cloak he wore for the ball—it suited him over his evening clothes. A box of cigars and a rosary lay beside his bed. She turned over some of the envelopes in her hands. On one was written in a spidery hand "*Press Cuttings, 1941–48*", on another "*Articles to The Medium*", and a third, "*My last Will and Testament, O. Fearmax*".

The steward came in to help her sort the belongings which littered the cabin. She commented on the quantity of things Fearmax had left behind. "He was going on to Egypt," said the boy. "All the others were going to stay for a while in Crete and took their things." Was that true, she wondered? Miss

Dale had left an evening-frock behind. "That poor Miss Dale," she said. "So quiet and gentle." She oiled her spitcurl in the mirror and twisted it round her finger. The boy gathered up the books into a bundle and dumped them in a suitcase. "He's not left any money about?" he asked suspiciously. She folded the suits and placed them one on top of the other. "Didn't have much to leave, I expect," she said.

In Baird's cabin they found a pair of khaki shorts, and, in Graecen's, a shaving-mirror which was propped at an operational angle by a half-crown. "You could tell he was every inch a Lord," said the stewardess pocketing the coin. Who else would use money to prop up a shaving-mirror?

Miss Dale's cabin was not as empty as they had at first glance imagined it to be. "There—you see? Careless," said the steward reprovingly. He had been particularly fond of Miss Dale with her sad blonde appearance, and her being too timid to ring for servants because, as she said, "she wasn't used to them." She had spent all day in a deck-chair, wrapped in rugs, convalescing from a serious illness. Latterly, Lord Graecen had been seen reading to her. "Ah well," said the steward with a sigh to himself, "Romance, that's what it was." The stewardess noticed his sigh and shrugged her shoulders.

The miscellaneous periodicals they gathered up found their way at last into the purser's hands as he stood on C deck, talking amiably to a friend and spitting into the oily waters of Alexandria harbour. "Thanks," he said. "I could do with some light reading." He talked as if he had been wrestling with heavy books of reference all day. The bookshelf above his bunk was crammed with yellow-backs. He took the bundle of papers, put them under his arm, and continued his conversation. He was describing to a friend the tragedy that had overtaken the party in the labyrinth. After having extracted the fullest possible pleasure from this he went and sat in a deck-chair aft, lit a fresh pipe and glanced through the papers. He wondered for a moment which papers had belonged to which passengers—one could hardly imagine these *Bystanders* belonging to Fearmax. Fearmax had rather awed him. He looked like a minor prophet—a gaunt and vehement character. He had refused to give a séance in the first-class saloon, pleading that he was in poor health. And yet he talked like a volcano in short and crisply-articulated sentences. He wore soft black bow ties with drooping ends—such as were fashionable in Belgravia towards the end of the last century. His face had the charred finely-lined character of the later Rudolf Steiner portraits; under his eyes there were deep smudges of black which seemed violet in the harsh lights of the first-class deck. He walked about the decks for hours with his hands in his pockets, like a monomaniac.

For a short while the purser played drowsily with these fugitive recollections, before dropping off to sleep. He noticed that some of the portraits in the society papers had been decorated with moustaches in pencil and wondered whether Graecen had been guilty of the impropriety. The sun was sinking behind the jumble of masts and hulls and a light wind had sprung up.

At Toulon they had all been ashore, and the Truman couple had arrived back rather drunk in the pinnace. He had seen Miss Dombey sitting opposite them with that suffused and swollen look—that redness of the wattles—which always came over her when she was outraged. Mr. Truman's hat was over his ear and his arm was round his wife. They were singing "When Irish Eyes are Smiling", with a care that seemed a little over-scrupulous to the more sober members of the crew who watched them from the rail. Graecen had made some remark to Baird and they had both laughed. It was obvious that Miss Dombey was not enjoying their company. She kept her gaze steadily averted and wondered how these disgusting people had managed to travel first-class. As the boat came in to the *Europa's* side she had caught Truman's eye and, to her horror, after a second's patient, indulgent, and glassy scrutiny, he had winked at her. "That man," she hissed to Baird as she came up the gangway. "He's drunk."

The purser had liked the Truman couple. He was short and thickset, with a good deal of grey hair and a clipped moustache. His manner was extremely good-natured and he appeared to suffer from no sense of social inferiority whatsoever in travelling first-class: "Money," he said whenever he had to produce any at the bar. "It means nothing to me. I never had any use for it. Here, take the lot." He was reputed to have won a fortune on the football pools. Miss Dombey found him infuriating because she could not condescend to him; he was alert, civil, and very faintly mocking.

Mrs. Truman was a good-looking woman but a trifle sluttish of dress. Her rouge was nearly always unevenly put on, her deck-shoes rather grubby. Between her husband and herself there existed a sensible bond of ordinary humour; they were accomplices in the criticism of the world around them; a world which threw up people so irresistibly funny as Miss Dombey or as pleasant as Graecen. They were particularly pleased at any speculations as to how they had managed to acquire their wealth; as a matter of fact they had just fifteen pounds of their savings in hand. Truman had won a competition in a weekly paper which had offered him a choice between a pound a week for life or a holiday cruise. The choice was characteristic of them. "Mother," he said with a calm good-humour, "the pound a week I can make myself, but a holiday cruise we shall never afford if we don't go now."

They were obviously very much in love, and Miss Dombey could not forgive them for their private jokes, the way they whispered into each other's ears, and walked hand in hand about the wet decks like schoolchildren. The stewardess's, in qualification of her liking of them with the suggestion that they were perhaps a little eccentric was due to a conversation she overheard one night when they were undressing in their cabin. The door had been left ajar while Truman cleaned his teeth—which he always did with a gusto and uproar quite out of proportion to so elementary an operation. You would have thought that a horse was being curried in its stall. He added to the noise by trying to hum snatches of song as he brushed. One night as the stewardess passed the door she heard this customary performance broken off abruptly and the sound of weeping, subdued and rather unearthly in the corridor which was silent now save for the furry noise of the fans. "There, Elsie," Truman was saying, "I know things would have been different if it hadn't died." After some further conversation she heard Mrs. Truman's melodious voice, recovering its steadiness, say: "I know it's silly, but I can't help feeling I killed it, John."

Later that evening she heard Truman cursing the narrowness of the cabin: "Making love in these bunks is like making love in a matchbox," he said with his comical north-country accent, with its flattened vowels.

But perhaps the seal was set upon their eccentricity when one day the stewardess found them sitting naked, side by side on the bunk, playing noughts and crosses. "Come in, dear," Mrs. Truman had said with pleasant unconcern, and then, seeing her consternation, "John, out of sight with you." She heard Truman laughing immoderately as he struggled into a shirt. She confided this adventure to the steward, asking him very seriously whether old people like that still made love: it seemed faintly indecent. They were old enough to have children. The steward stifled a smile and said he didn't know—they were probably eccentric. She was thoroughly satisfied with this proposition. Eccentric, that's what they were. But they were good-humoured and undemanding, and she had a little wave of pity in her heart as she packed the ill-fitting cheap dresses, the old wire-hair-brush, and the copies of *Tit-Bits* in the trunk which, according to the metal stamp, had been made by a Mr. Stevens in Peckham Rye.

It was not till some days later, when Graecen's escape was announced in the Press, that the purser discovered that he was a poet. *"England's Foremost Poet-Peer,"* said one paper and gave a brief outline of his history, his Scottish title, his M.C. and Mention, and his brilliant batting for the Gentlemen *versus* Players at Lord's in 1936. Everyone felt that they wished they had known at the time; he had been so quiet and unobtrusive—so like a middle-aged stockbroker. It is true that he had once been seen sketching in a book, and that he read to Miss Dale once or twice on A deck—but whether it was poetry or not they could not tell. It seemed, however, no less than poetic justice that he should be saved. Later still the purser was to see in *The Times* the poem of Graecen's, beginning: "When death like the sundial casts his shadow." The lines were, he noticed, dated April, 1947, several weeks before the incident of the labyrinth, but they read to him like a premonition—as many, that is to say, as he could understand. He read them over several times, cut them out with a penknife and transferred the cutting from his grubby fingers to his pocket-book for future consideration. And here the circle of speculation closed.

Ariadne's Thread

It was in the middle of May that Graecen for the last time closed the little makeshift office which had been built around the Cefalû statue while it was being cleaned, and started to walk, with his deliberate soft pace, across the Graeco-Roman section. Twilight had come—that strange marine twilight which only seems to come to Museums—and the long cases reflected his sober figure in subaqueous tones as he passed them. Today was the end of a ten-year term in a life devoted entirely to them, he was reflecting, as he descended the long staircase step by step, and ten years was a long time. He was trying to invest the episode with some sentimental significance, but in truth he felt a little empty and negative. He tasted the damp air from the gloomy corridors of stone and glass around him. It must be seven. The light was fading fast outside; neutral, grey London had seen no signs of spring as yet. He breasted the tide of scholars emerging from the great library, flowing through the central doors and dissolving into the grey hinterland outside, and handed over his key with a sigh of resignation, a little surprised that it did not hurt more. As he was collecting his hat and coat, Swan, the attendant, hurried up to him.

"Is it true that you're leaving us, sir?" he said. It was true, of course; but the eager self-indulgent emotion in the old man's voice struck no echoing spark in Graecen's heart. He stood on one leg, flushed. In his neat black clothes and preternaturally shined shoes he looked very much a gentleman covered by a gentleman's confusion. "For a time, Swan," he said, "I hope to be back soon." The blush lit up first his face and then the little bald spot on his crown which always made him look like a saint in a halo. Blushing was a habit he tried to cure without success. He saw that Swan's rheumy eye was marking the blush as it travelled steadily upwards and round towards the nape of his neck. He put his hat on, and pressed a ten-shilling note into the old man's hand. "I shall see you very soon," he said as he passed down the hall and through the swing-doors.

He halted for a moment on the marble steps, experiencing a sense of aimless emptiness which must, he thought, be such as prisoners feel, who, after a long sentence, hear the prison gate close behind them. It was a leave-taking peculiarly without any positive sentimental bias, and as a sentimental man he regretted it. "I've resigned," he told himself aloud, and, looking round, found that the pock-marked elementary Easter Island carvings were staring at him with their familiar cruelty from the porch.

Museum Street looked drab. So did Great Russell Street. Drabness multiplied by drabness. The last suds of light were running down behind St. Pancras. London was drawing up the darkness like a blotter. *Syrinx* was out, however. He saw that it was in several bookshops. A few notes on the scrannel for a Spring that was, as usual, late. "Ah well," he said, and took off his hat to feel the air upon his brow. He bought a *Times Literary Supplement* and a packet of cigarettes at the corner. It was no good reading the reviews in the left-wing papers—they always upset him with their ill-bred shrillness. As an afterthought he stole into a bookshop and bought himself a copy of *Syrinx*: as usual he had given all his complimentaries away. It was absurd to feel guilty and panic-stricken, for he was still comparatively unknown as a poet. *Syrinx* was his seventh book and he did not expect more than the usual mede of literary lip-service for it. He had long ago resigned himself to the fact that his verse was neither very experimental nor very exciting. But at least it got published: and he adored publishing. He had all the author's vanity in the appearance of a new book, and

Syrinx was really very pretty, very pretty indeed. The cover was bright, and yet refined. The pan-pipes, the reeds, the rather mouldy-looking swan—they all, he felt, admirably expressed the nature of the poems. They, too, were a little mannered, a little old-fashioned, perhaps a little threadbare. ("Lord Graecen's Muse, turned housewife, once more beats out her iambics like some threadbare carpet": that was the kind of thing he found so unkind.)

Enjoying the feeling of the little book under his arm he turned into a tea-shop to look it over once more. The review in *The Times* would be, as always, sepulchral but kind. Old Conklin admired his work, genuinely admired it. He avoided the corner where old Sir Fennystone Crutch was devouring buttered toast. His skull-cap and slippers made him a familiar figure in the reading room. He hated being disturbed at his tea —which was the only real meal he had during the day. Graecen had once done so and had been severely reprimanded. "Go away," the old man had said, "Can't you see I'm eating?" An all-consuming passion for Sanscrit and buttered toast—did that give one the right to be rude to people, Graecen wondered? Nevertheless he had learned his lesson; he squeezed past the old man in a hurry and fitted himself into one of the dark wooden alcoves, ordering tea, toast and a boiled egg. He opened the paper.

For over an hour now he had forgotten what had been haunting him for several days; well, haunting was too strong a word. He sought in his mind for something with a little less value. His round innocent face puckered as he searched the columns of the paper, leaving one-half of his mind to indulge its capacity for fear, and to play with metaphors for death. It was like having a cavity in a tooth—one simply could not keep the tongue away. Death, of course, was a cavity considerably larger and more exciting. After all, he reminded himself, it was not *certain* that he might die during the next few months. It was merely the opinion of certain medical men—an unreliable faculty at the best. The thought had been, of course, sufficient to dislocate his life to a degree—and yet there need have been no reason. After the first day the expectation of death had assumed a kind of uniform greyness; he referred back to it as he had, when a schoolboy, referred back to the expectation of a thrashing scheduled for the next day. There was an element of pleasure in it too; at times it gave him a sense of isolation and detachment from the rest of the human race, and then he was forced to remind himself that they were also going to die. They, however, were not disturbed by the accent upon a particular time. Yet the idea, which he had confided to nobody, *was* disturbing. At times he felt almost ashamed of the knowledge—as if it were a disease that should be hidden from his fellows. That was really why he had resigned. It would be somehow awful to die in the Museum. "It might happen quite suddenly," the doctor had said, adding, "Pop, just like that." Graecen had been impressed by the phrase. He had found himself saying absently to an assistant curator apropos of a badly-arranged terra-cotta. "It might fall down and break—pop, just like that."

And once more logic began to intervene with its clearer assessments. Just look (he had invited himself for the last three mornings running) at Sir Fennystone Crutch. He could not go on for ever. No sane medical man would give him more than six months to live. Toothless, buried in his Sanscrit, forgetting his lunch-hour every day and leaving a jumble of gnawed crusts all over the reading-room floor. He could have no delicacy about the idea of dying at his desk, could he? What would they do if he did? Graecen decided that they would put him on the trolley—already groaning under tomes of Sanscrit—and lay his carpet-bag, skull-cap and slippers beside him. Then they would wheel him away. Would they go through the North Library, and so avoid the main entrance?

Graecen became exasperated with himself for wasting his time like this . . . Following up these fatuous chains of possibility. What the devil did it matter which way they wheeled him? He pictured them wheeling the old man's body across the Graeco-Roman section. Young Stubbs would obviously be the one to wheel him. . . . He frowned at himself and drew his mind back to the task in hand.

All this time his eye had been travelling across the sedate columns of the newspaper searching for a review of *Syrinx*. He was eating buttered toast, his face growing more and more innocent and childish as he felt the butter trickle to his chin. He got out a handkerchief and started absently to dab it. Could he say that life had gained in value from the possibility of its extinction? He knotted his brows in a scowl and cracked the top of the egg. In one way, yes. Everything had been thrown into dark relief—as though he had woken one morning and found the whole world inked in at the edges by a fall of snow. It had informed his critical sense—that was rather an awful phrase. And yet his feelings neither rose nor fell at the idea. Why?

Even his poetry—had it shown any inclination to strike a deeper note? No, it was just the same. He remembered that his work had been described by a young critic in a little review as "pre-atomic, non-radioactive, non-conducting bilge". It had annoyed him considerably. "Lord Graecen sticks to the rut of *rentier* poetry", was another phrase from the same article. Was he honestly so bad?

> When torpid winter covers
> The city and its lovers,
> The cold finality of snow
> Whitens the signs and clear defines
> The way mortality must go.

It was all of a range, but he liked it. Of course the demonic element he admired so much in Emily Brontë, that was missing. But was it, as the young men said, cake without currants? It seemed on the contrary rather full of plums. At any rate Yeats had printed one in an anthology; and old Lord Alfred had once invited him to Hove where, he said, he would teach him the elements of the sonnet. It was rather condescending of him, really, but Graecen had thanked him profusely.

"Ah," he said, for his eye, travelling slowly down the penultimate page had struck the title "England's Cricketer-Poet". There it was to be sure, written with all the overflowing admiration of old Conklin. He noted the usual references to his title, his scholarship, and his cricket. Conklin did not like his poets effeminate. With a certain indignation, however, he read: "It has become increasingly clear that a new Gordon Bottomley is amongst us. Lord Graecen is definitely in the great tradition of Lord Alfred Douglas, Roland Tuft, Canon Alec Smudge, and Loyola Tipstaff, any of whose lines are worth a bookful of today's harsh clangour, which, to the uninformed, passes for poetry." Graecen made an irritated gesture in the air and spilt some butter on his tie. "Here!" he said plaintively, addressing Conklin, "you can't say that." It was obviously crass. One hated adverse criticism—but could one bear to be damned by *this* sort of praise? He read on, however, with growing bitterness——

The bell on the outside door clinked and he saw Hogarth enter, stooping low in his baggy grey trousers, his arms full of books. "Hogarth," he said delightedly, "Hogarth." The newcomer lowered his grizzled taurine head and started towards him, with all the caution of a big man who fears that he will overturn something. "Well," he said, "I was thinking about you—wondering why you hadn't rung me up." Graecen was childishly delighted to see his old friend. "Sit down, my dear fellow," he said. "It's very nice—dear me—very nice indeed."

Hogarth sat down slowly, battling, it seemed, with something like the centrifugal force, and unloaded his books on to the table, placing his stained pork-pie hat on top of them. He regarded Graecen with sardonic affection. His small keen eyes took in Graecen's appearance: the buttered toast in one hand, the handkerchief in the other, the book open on his knee. "Richard," he said sternly, "you are reading your own work again." Graecen blushed like a girl. Hogarth always adopted a tone of savage irony for the sheer pleasure of teasing him.

To do him justice, Graecen's character demanded something more barbed than the conventional responses; and Hogarth, whose dominant character was almost the exact antithesis of his, found himself to be almost complementary in feeling and outlook. They got on admirably; fulfilling indeed Hogarth's theory of psychic union between two essentially polar types. He had named them "dominant" and "recessive".

He sat now, regarding his thumbs for a moment, and got his breath. It was obvious that he was a little out of breath. Graecen cherished him with his glances, for he had not seen Hogarth for several weeks. The familiarity of the picture pleased him. Hogarth's large shoulders were clad in an old tweed coat patched with leather at the elbows. His grey trousers had shrunk in the wash, and their nether ends exposed his thick ankles whose socks hung down about his shoes. His face was like one of those carved Austrian pipe-heads—large bony features which were only kept alive by the small pointed eagerness of his eyes. They were rather fine and changed their colour, the eyes; they were engaged on a perpetual enquiry. When Hogarth laughed they disappeared into small commas like the eyes of pigs. When he opened them very wide, as he did when there was a question to ask, they seemed to become younger, to shine with a beauty and candour of their own.

"Well," he said, ordering tea, and starting to charge his great blockish pipe with tobacco, "I've been running to get away from Boyd."

Graecen registered a rather fussy interest. Boyd was a friend of his. He was wondering how much he should tell Hogarth. "Boyd wants me to do the preface for his book on psycho-analysis and art. He takes both seriously." Hogarth sounded gloomy and irritable. "The book is farcical. There is an analysis of Poe's *Raven* which would make your hair stand on end. You know the Freudian tie-up between the symbol of the bird and the penis?" Graecen did not, but he blinked and nodded rapidly, moistening his lips with his tongue. "Well, the *Raven* with its mournful 'Nevermore' is a terrible confession of Poe's impotence." Graecen said "Dear me" twice, with sympathy. He knew nothing about psycho-analysis, but he could never bring himself to be disrespectful about anything. Hogarth lit up with seven gargantuan puffs. "He has traced a strong interest in masturbation running through Dickens; the choice of names like Mr. Pickwick and Sam Weller are only thinly disguised symbols . . . Dicky, what's the matter?"

Graecen felt suddenly unhappy again; he had remembered the sentence. "I've resigned from the Antiquities," he said in a small voice. He had a desire to confide a number of things in Hogarth—among them even old Conklin's article; but they had all got jammed together at the entrance of his mind and he did not know which he could get out first. His face looked round and ingenuous. His lower lip trembled ever so slightly.

"You're run down," said Hogarth.

Graecen nodded and handed the paper across the table to his friend, pointing with his finger to the offensive passage in the review; yet before Hogarth had time to read it he add~ out of breath, "I'm supposed to have only a fe live." It sounded absurd. They looked at each oth~ and both laughed, Hogarth gruffly and Graecen in a high boyish register.

"Of all people, me," he said, suddenly feeling almost jubilant.

"I don't believe it."

"Oh yes, it's true," said Graecen eagerly. He was all of a sudden anxious that the trophy should not be taken from him by mere scepticism.

"Of all people—me. Dicky Graecen." He had the rather irritating habit of objectivising himself in the third person, as children do. "So what does old Dicky Graecen do?" was a phrase that appeared unfailingly in all his stories of his own doings. He saw himself, as he said it, childishly far-off and remote, as a sort of wayward young man. Young Dicky Graecen. In this case it was young Dicky Graecen who was going to do the dying—he himself, his alter self, was going to live forever; well, if not forever, for at least another fifteen years. By association this brought him back to *Syrinx*.

"My new book is out," he said with a certain pleasant coyness, flushing again. Hogarth looked at him steadily, his eyes still laughing. Whatever happened to Dicky was funny—even the idea of him dogged by a premature death-sentence was funny. One's compassion was stirred for him through one's humour. He was holding up the book of poems for inspection.

Graecen never sent Hogarth his books because the latter professed no interest in poetry or the fine arts. Hogarth however always sent him his own books, however ponderous and smudgy they were. On the flyleaf he always wrote "Dicky— push this round among the nobs. Good for trade."

Graecen felt faintly irritated by this suggestion, that he was, at best, a social tout for Hogarth's clinical work; but the long friendship and affection, dating back to their university days, always won the upper hand, and he swallowed his chagrin.

"There is no reason", said Hogarth turning over the book in his paws, "why you shouldn't die. All of us will have to. And I'm not sure I wouldn't prefer to be warned. I like to get myself in order before a change."

This was not quite the style of thing Graecen liked. He did

not want pity or commiseration, but he did feel. . . . "Well," he said, "I've locked up the flat, sent Garbett on a holiday, and made my will. I'm as free as the wind. And look." He flourished the travel-company's ticket before Hogarth, who was slowly turning the book of poems over and over, as if it were some puzzling potsherd whose function he could not decide.

"Cefalù," said Graecen, enunciating clearly but softly the word which seemed to have come out of a W. J. Turner poem.

"Cefalù," repeated Hogarth without any emphasis one way or the other. His interest had now moved on from the book to the ticket. The name of the ship was the *Europa*, "Baird is going to Crete too," he said. "A patient of mine. You'll be travelling together, and will see. . . ."

"Silenus," said Graecen with the air of a conjurer bringing off a trick. "I shall tell him everything."

"You won't need to," said Hogarth sardonically. "He'll probably tell you, that old Phanariot intriguer. What is all this about the labyrinth? I saw it in the paper."

Graecen fished a letter out of his pocket holding up an excited hand to prevent Hogarth saying any more until he should deliver himself of his news, "A letter from Silenus," he said. "Look."

Hogarth saw the familiar vermilion and the little drawing on the letterhead, of a village perched upon the side of a high stone cone. "Read it," he said. He knew that Graecen loved to read aloud, having a conceit of his voice. "All right, I will."

Graecen sat back and put on his story-book voice—the voice reserved for reading of his own work on the radio.

"The sun", he read, "comes up every day like the naked flash of a cannon. I am sitting in the garden writing on a fallen block of marble. The roses are doing well and so, as you have heard, is the archaeology. Further to my last, the labyrinth has produced a stone inscription—pre-Minoan? At any rate another script I cannot tackle, part hieroglyph. The Museum say they will send for you if I wish? My dear fellow, of course I wish. A summer in Cefalû would do you good. I need company. Bring anyone you wish. But please follow these instructions implicitly: Do not in any way, in print or by statements to the Press, commit yourself to a belief in, or knowledge of, the New Era (we hope) I've stumbled on. Got that?" Graecen broke off in confusion and found Hogarth's steady eye upon him. He wrinkled his brows. "Now I wonder *why*," he said plaintively.

Hogarth admitted a wrinkle to his left cheek and shook out the burnt top of his dottle. "Why not guess?" he said. Graecen looked at him innocently.

"Dicky," said Hogarth, "you know what our dear Silenus is. It's just possible that the New Era is——"

"Faked?" said Graecen in alarm.

"Well, it's a proposition," said Hogarth easily. "It surely wouldn't be hard to do."

"But the lovely statue," said Graecen.

"I should have a good look at it," his friend advised.

Graecen looked confused and put the letter back in his pocket. He thought hard.

"How do you tell the age of a statue anyway?" said Hogarth, "apart from guesswork or typology?"

Graecen was too busy thinking to answer. He could easily get Firbank and his beastly chemicals to come along and test the stone; "but I don't want to start any suspicion about Axelos," he said.

"Chemicals?" said Hogarth. "Take some along with you when you go."

"I will," said Graecen fervently. "I will."

He ate a rejected crust off his plate and seemed lost in thought. The statue was exquisite.

"Now then," said Hogarth paying the bill and building a pyramid of books before taking them up. "I want you to meet a young man who is travelling on the *Europa* with you. He's waiting in a pub in Shaftesbury Avenue."

As usual Graecen had a thousand and one things to do. He took out his little leather notebook. Hogarth must really come to lunch or to dinner; but as usual he was booked right up. Tomorrow he was taking Mrs. Sanguinetti to the new Disney film. There was a dinner at the Savile in the evening. He read breathlessly through his engagements. Hogarth noticed that death hardly intruded upon Graecen's daily life; it was assumed that he would not die before Saturday, when the *Europa* was due to sail. He lowered his crest like a bull and dragged his protesting friend to the corner of Tottenham Court Road. When Graecen showed signs of breaking away Hogarth anchored him successfully by giving him some of his books to hold. In this way they made their slow way down to the little pub in which Baird sat, reading a newspaper over his beer.

Later, as always happened, Graecen found that he was too late to keep the scheduled engagements for the evening, and found himself taking Hogarth out to dinner at the little Spanish restaurant in Old Compton Street, whose pimento-flavoured rice they had enjoyed together for so many years. Baird in his tactful way slipped off and left them together.

"How is it", said Graecen when he left, "that that normal-looking young fellow should turn up in your consulting-room, Hogarth?" How indeed? Hogarth considered the question fairly for a moment. The reason for Baird's journey to Crete was fantastic enough in its way. Cefalû was to be the answer to more than one problem. "By jove," he said, "I almost wish I was going too, to help him dig up Böcklin."

Over dinner he told Graecen the story.

Portraits

The portrait of Baird which emerged over the grubby table-cloth in Old Compton Street was of formal proportions; as a history it was uneventful, and only the calm force of Hogarth's description made it of interest to Graecen. Hogarth was tirelessly interested in his own patients; and he could communicate his interest when he pleased. And yet, thought Graecen so often, while he listened to him, Hogarth was so much more interesting than any of his patients could be. His peculiar reticence, for example, had preserved a wall between them for a third of a century. At the University Hogarth had been a monosyllabic misanthrope, working in his own fashion —chiefly during the day with his blinds drawn and the little electric desk-lamp on. Later he had accepted a fellowship to a German University, where he spent some ten years in talking philosophy and walking in the mountains with his students. He had returned to London with a German wife whom Graecen had never seen. Hogarth lived in Herne Hill, of all places, doing some miserably-paid work as analyst for some Government Department. During this time they met fre-quently, but Graecen was never invited to visit his home or meet his wife. By accident he found out that Hogarth had a son—but when he asked him about it he received a blank stare. Hogarth neither denied nor corroborated the story. Yet some-how, in some fashion that Graecen could never understand, their friendship remained unimpaired by all this. Later still he was surprised to see Hogarth's name in the catalogue of an exhibition of oil-paintings at the Leicester Gallery. The paint-ings were powerfully-executed landscapes, owing nothing to influence or training. Hogarth had dismissed them lightly when he mentioned them. "I did them in Germany during my student days," he had said, without either interest or self-depreciation. That was all.

Later still Hogarth appeared on the scenes in London as a consulting psycho-analyst with a small consulting-room in Harley Street. He seemed to be immediately successful, and had written one or two rather queer books, expounding some sort of philosophy of disease that Graecen had not been able to understand. He had read one of the books, hoping perhaps that he might be able to review it for Hogarth, but it was frankly beyond his powers to understand it. And now Hogarth was busy at work at analysis—he referred to it ironically as "half-soleing the souls of the half-baked"—and into his web people like Fearmax and Baird seemed to be wandering in increasing numbers.

Baird was an only son. His father was a member of the landed gentry displaced by fortune and endeavouring to keep up standards in a world which every day found them less comprehensible or necessary. He was a Justice of the Peace in Herefordshire, a capital horseman, a regular contributor to *The Field*, and the author of several books about birds. Baird's mother had died when he was three and his father had never married again. In the stone-roofed house with its neat topiary hedge and green lawn running down to the river, his life had been a quiet and a happy one. His well-regulated youth was calculated to offer him an education and an outlook fit for the inheritance his father was to leave behind; a tradition for mildness, good-breeding, and cultivation rather than culture. In those days it seemed that the genteel might inherit the earth, and that Baird might be among them.

At Charterhouse and Oxford he learned all that his father could not teach him, except by precept. He was averagely good at games and achieved some distinction by winning a music prize. At seventeen he became interested in literature and began a novel about public schools, which he was never destined to finish. At the University, like all young men, he passed through the distemper of Communism and emerged from it unscathed. He rode to hounds with unremitting ardour and shot with style. His sympathy for the working classes, while it had not completely foundered, had given way to an acceptance of the order of things. His father was an admirable companion—interested in everything—and the two of them explored places and subjects together in perfect friendship. Their taste in books and paintings differed widely, but the precept of tolerance was so well ingrained in him that he let the old man have his way in most things. He was a dutiful son.

For a time he lived in London, on a small allowance left to him by his mother, and seriously intended to "commence author". The phrase sums up his choice of models admirably. At Oxford, Pater and Ruskin had followed hard on the heels of Marx and Engels; the nineties offered one a tremendous latitude for mannerism, and it was mannerism that informed his writing rather than manner—for he had none of his own. A member of the *Wine and Food Society*, he once or twice wrote essays upon the French Rally for A. J. A. Symons, in which he devoted a critical terminology, with fine discretion, to the description of hard-boiled eggs in Worcester sauce—and other matters of equal weight. During this apprenticeship he was considered rather promising; it was an opinion he himself was inclined to share.

While he could not afford to belong to clubs, his tastes led him to meet a number of artists and musicians so that he never seriously lacked for company; and he contrived to be at every cocktail party given between the Seven Dials and Hammersmith. He was, in fact, always there, a modest and handsome figure in a well-cut lounge suit, dissecting art with artists, music with critics, and life with young women of varying ages and tastes. It was during this period of his life that he had run into Campion at a cocktail party given by a publisher. Campion was quite unknown then, but quite as forthright as when they met again on the deck of the *Europa*. "How I abominate, how I loathe and distrust and fear all this society back-slapping," he had said to a rather surprised Baird. He was a small, strongly-built little man with a lot of curly yellow hair coarsely pushed inside a beret. He wore sandals and an open-necked shirt. "Listen to them," he said fiercely. He was eating rapidly as he talked. Baird looked at the party and could not for the life of him see what was so offensive about it; there were several distinguished people present. Mincon the musician was standing at the mantelpiece. He thought perhaps that Campion might be suffering from some obscure class-inferiority, and asked him pleasantly if he would care to meet the French composer, whom he knew quite well. "God, no," said Campion in horror, "I could not be nice about his work." This had rather shocked Baird. Mincon had been accepted everywhere as a genius. "Don't you like it?" he asked. Campion gave him a long sober look. "Music for the credit titles of a Hollywood film," he said quietly. "And as for these other people." His contempt was boundless. Baird asked him why, if he disliked this kind of thing so much, he accepted invitations to parties. Campion once more gave him the cold steady look and answered: "Because of the food—can't you see? I'm starving." A little later he had left, and Baird had transferred his attentions to someone more pleasant—someone to whom he might confide his burning desire to write the novel of the age.

He met Alice Lidell in the tea-room of the Tate Gallery and fell in love with her at sight. She was tall and beautiful and her fine blonde hair picked up the reflected light from the long mirrors, twinkling as she combed it. Her diffidence and breeding were charming. They were immediately friends. He admired her long shapely fingers and fine northern colouring.

She was, he discovered with a thrill, an art student at the Slade School and keen to be a painter herself. Their friendship survived even her description of Whistler as a "bemused sentimentalist" (a phrase he had heard a friend of hers use) and her defence of Picasso as "the only painter alive". However, he weathered these intellectual storms and took her to lunch with his aunt—a recognized preliminary to any announcement of his engagement. His aunt approved. Alice found her collection of jade enchanting. She was equally successful with his father, who spent hours showing a rather bored Alice how to hold a gun. By this time, of course, she had decided that she would really like to marry him—he was so personable, so intelligent. His origins and antecedents were unexceptionable. Her own parents were in India and offered no objections. They were married after a short engagement, and retired to a Tudor cottage ten miles from his home, where she proposed to paint, and he to write a book on aesthetics.

This latter idea was suggested by Alice herself, who held rather unorthodox views about the current literature. "The novel is a dead end," she told him. "The only thing left is to map out the aesthetics of the new Age." She believed strongly in some undefined New Era of art which was being ushered in by Dadaism. Baird listened patiently. It seemed to him to be extremely important and necessary that a great critic should arise in England to take the prevailing ideas in hand and synthesize them. He was also secretly rather glad to put off the projected novel, which he felt quite incapable of handling. "The novel is a dead end," he told his friends, "the only hope is to direct the currents of aesthetics from a vantage-point." What exactly the vantage-point was he himself was not very clear. At any rate he felt vaguely important and pleased to be doing something, and read industriously in the British Museum every day while Alice painted.

After their marriage they moved to the cottage, where a

small car, books and friends confirmed them in their happiness, and in the importance of the work each had to do. It was during this time that Baird had chanced upon a book by Hogarth and had been struck by a passage in it upon the sensibility of the artist. Alice thought it was rubbish.

"Art is a dangerous thing to play with, since it demands self-examination and self-knowledge, and many people do not really wish for either. Its true function, after all, is to insist on the existence in us of unused faculties for experience which custom has staled—or compromise to intellectual order of the society in which we find ourselves. The artist does not invent or discover; rather does he, by making himself unusually receptive, be discovered and re-created. We tend to measure artists by their powers of transmission, but even bad artists suffer of the sense of displacement and anxiety which we see recorded in the lives of the great. Benjamin Haydon and Van Gogh are equals in suffering if in nothing else. Each was lost in the labyrinth of his own spiritual discoveries."

Alice wrinkled her pretty nose as she closed the book and handed it back to him. No, she said, in response to his question, it was just another attempt by these psychologists to put the artist in the strait-jacket of a clinical definition; she did not want to admit that the individuality of the creative man was not by its very nature beyond definition. John must find some way round the problem or he would find his book on aesthetics a study of the artist in one set of terms. This, of course, was precisely what John wanted to do, but his respect for Alice made him defer judgment until he had read through the whole of Ruskin once more. Several summers and winters passed in this pleasant frivolity. John wrote the best part of his *New Aesthetics* in clear workmanlike prose, but found that the book had turned out rather a frost. Several friends criticized it in typescript, and it became obvious that it was simply another of those productions by young University men which earn them, at the best, a column in a weekly journal. There was no harm in publishing, but John Baird was determined to publish something first-class or remain silent. Alice thought this very wise. She in the meantime was busy painting and reading books about painting. Less critical and far less self-conscious than her husband, she allowed her work to be shown on more than one occasion, and was known to derive comfort from criticisms written about her in the *Burlington Magazine*. At this time there was almost no sacrifice too great to make on behalf of her art—so strongly was she under the influence of Vincent (as she called him). She even thought that they might have a baby. "I do not feel fully awakened," she told an astonished Baird one evening in May, "and I notice I'm painting nothing but Madonnas with infants-in-arms. My subconscious must be getting interested in pregnancy." It was the High Renaissance of Art in England at that time—a Renaissance that was to come to an end in Sloper and Frampton—and people were in the habit of talking like that. Baird was rather taken aback by her sense of proportion, which, it seemed to him, did little credit to a married woman of several years' standing, but he said nothing. Indeed there was nothing to say. There was no reason why they should not have a child. They were comfortably off. "You could have one by February," he said after a brief calculation on his finger-ends. But then it was discovered that this would interfere with their yearly trip across the Channel, and the idea was temporarily shelved. Alice had been promised an introduction to Picasso (she still imagined the artists bore more than a superficial resemblance to their work) and would not trade that for a subconscious gratification.

Their life was a happy one simply because no obstacles presented themselves; but it could not last for ever. After several years John became troubled by a sense of failure, and even she felt an incurable staleness creeping into her work. They did not seem to have advanced a step towards their objectives. T. S. Eliot was not yet overthrown, and, try as she might, Alice found it impossible to make much headway. As the young man in the Oxhead Gallery said to her: "Frankly, you know, dash it all, taken by and large, as it were, everyone's gone non-representative now. I mean to say, in England, mind you, a lot have even gone heterosexual in a desire to keep up, as it were." It was a true if sad proposition. If it hadn't been for the *Burlington Magazine* Alice would have utterly lost faith in herself. Specially as John was so gloomy and sat about all day by the river, tearing up his manuscript and repeating in hollow accents, "What the hell is the meaning of it all, anyway?" His father had given him the *Parmenides* for a birthday present.

They travelled briefly in France and Spain, and the sun woke them up a bit. Everywhere they moved along the charming and romantic landscapes with the sense of having found at last their proper environment. They thought of taking a house in Venice, but gave the idea up as expensive and impracticable. The little English cottage cost a lot to keep up. In Madrid they had, enjoyably enough, a terrific quarrel—the first they had ever had. Alice had some trouble over her period and imagined that she was going to have a baby. Instead of being pleased for the sake of her unawakened subconscience, its very idea threw her into a panic. Now it seemed to her that a baby would threaten not only her art but her freedom too—the self-indulgent effortless years of conversation, travel and friendship which lay ahead. Though she still wanted the child the thought of losing both freedom and figure at one blow was too much. She became rather hysterical and, of course, John was to blame; he, for his part, found her rather tiresome as a travelling companion. After a brief passage-at-arms in which Alice broke a plate over his head, he retired to sulk in a nearby hotel until she should come to her senses.

They had both of them been staying in a villa belonging to Coréze, the little South American Jew whose brief run of glory many will remember, and whose acrobatic leaps from style to style had amazed and delighted Alice. "Bounding vitality", she had told John, "written over every canvas." It was written all over Coréze's little Semitic face too. Coréze was for some time a fiery little pace-maker for the Cubists, and had impressed them both with his tales of the great men he knew. His impersonation of James Joyce writing in chalk on a blackboard was impressive to a degree. He even gave the impression that parts of *Ulysses* would never have been written if he, Coréze . . . The story of Picasso and the Pernod, too, never failed to bring the house down. His imitation of the way the Master had put the glass down and said: "Tiens—un Pernod quoi?" was funnier and more expressive than Fernandel.

When John walked out of the house, after carefully leaving the name of his hotel (so that Alice could go round and apologize), Coréze was full of sympathy and sadness. He had been flattering Alice a good deal, and had even bought a couple of her line-drawings to hang on his walls. He had prophesied great things for her. It was only natural that what had begun as a flirtation of minds should now go a step forward—at least so thought Coréze. Alice was not unwilling to bring John to heel, and what could be simpler than to pretend that she was falling in love with Coréze? As a matter of fact she was not quite sure at this stage what she felt about anything. Coréze was charming, so considerate and gentle. He took her in his arms as she was doing a pencil sketch of him and said: "Don't let me fall in love with you, please don't let me. It hurts too much." There were tears in his eyes. It was rather exciting and not a little touching. "I have been so hurt by love," murmured Coréze, getting his hand under her skirt, "it can't happen again, it mustn't." His passion was very convincing. "Say you won't make me," he almost shouted and covered her mouth with his own before she could promise that she wouldn't.

She wrote a note to John and asked for a final interview.

Rather alarmed by this he hurried back to the villa from the terrace of the hotel. He was received in a dramatic and steely fashion. She had, she said, a confession to make. She was going to leave him for Coréze. He could not help finding her touching and pathetic as she made this confession; people (an irrational part of his mind kept interjecting) are products of their experience. Alice was now behaving rather like Lilian Gish in—what was the name of the film? For a moment John was tempted to say something extremely forcible to Coréze, but the latter had removed himself to Barcelona for a few days to be out of reach. He had a long experience of Latin husbands and did not propose to find himself once more scuffling in the fireplace over a girl he did not really want. He had excused his departure in a short heartbroken note on the grounds that he could no longer stand Alice's presence unless she crowned his flame.

John Baird was really too lazy to get angry. He took a plane for Paris and left Alice fuming. Characteristically, the only reproach he had offered her had been of a social rather than a personal nature—for he was more outraged in his social vanity than in his feelings. "People", he said, "simply do not behave like this. We are not Bohemians, after all." It was this that made Alice wonder whether she really could love him or not. If only he had shown violent jealousy and determination—who knows? She might out of pity have renounced Coréze. But no, he treated her with the haughty disapproval of guardian for the erring ward. His worst reproach was, after all, to be a case of English sulks. S'blood!

John left and Coréze returned. As a matter of fact he had only retired to the house of a friend in the suburbs to pass a Jewish feast in self-examination and purification, leaving this little affair, so to speak, on the hob. Alice's letter took a week to be forwarded on from the address in Barcelona. It gave them both time to review the situation.

Alice found in the meantime that she was not going to have a baby after all; but things had progressed so far with Coréze that she did not feel able to draw back at this stage. Besides, Coréze was always teasing her about her youth and inexperience, and this would only give him more ammunition. He would consider her naïve and irresponsible. She felt more than ever that she should show herself fully emancipated, and yet. . . . But John had carried off all their travellers' cheques by mistake, and there was no way of evading a decision. After all, there *was* the faintest hope in the world that she was going to enjoy it all.

She did not. Coréze made love to her with an art and industry which would have to be described to be fully appreciated. Her pride, her self-respect went out of the window in the short space of forty-eight hours. In the same length of time she succeeded in borrowing the price of a plane-ticket to Paris from the Consul. How bitterly she regretted the whole business. So that was what Lawrence meant with his filthy old gamekeeper with his shirt-ends tied round his neck. She would never, she felt, be much of a success as a wife again, and as the aircraft nosed over the Pyrenees she clasped her cold hands together, thinking darkly of broken faith and nunneries.

To John, sitting innocently on the *terrasse* of the Rotonde it seemed that some pronounced attitude of mind was called for on his part—but precisely what? How did one react to the debauching of one's wife by some unchristian foreigner? Here again he found himself, in an obscure way, more angry because the act had offended against the laws of hospitality rather than because his personal love was deeply wounded. He discovered with a shock that he himself had disposed with sex as a problem some long time since. Its only relation to himself now seemed as a subject for conversation with lady novelists. Perhaps this was because he had achieved a certain amount of "intellectual detachment"—as he was pleased to call it. Coréze's behaviour, he thought firmly, was unpardonable in a host. Things like that were not done in England. Or were they?

The little pile of white saucers rapidly grew on the table before him. Should he attempt a gesture of some sort—drink himself to death or ring up Chloe?

Drinks only gave him indigestion or made him sleepy. Besides, his love for Alice was so deeply and comfortably based in habit and interest, that he found it hard to bring to the surface for such boring and idiotic interrogations. He would sulk, and probably grow a moustache. Up to now Alice had always refused to let him grow one because it made his chin look so weak and undershot. He would stop at nothing now.

He looked forward to a mutual retreat and regrouping; something like a month's holiday. But an unrepenting and violent Alice appeared suddenly at the hotel, thirsting for drama.

It took all his forbearance to avoid a serious engagement during the first quarter of an hour. Alice piled reproaches upon him for being a bad husband, for taking all the travellers' cheques with him, and for being too cowardly even to reproach her for what she had done.

To her distracted mind it seemed unbelievable that John should be standing there in front of her exhibiting the merest pique and disapproval; in her own eyes the crime had been enlarging itself until it seemed now to be worth a more distinct response. But no. There he stood, in the middle of this drama, refusing to be drawn in beyond the gentlemanly limits laid down in Kipling's "If". That he should be able to sit in front of a pile of saucers, dressed in his pork pie hat, blue diceboard tie, canary-coloured cardigan and grey slacks, seemed to be almost irreverent. She noticed that he even fingered an incipient moustache once or twice in a furtive manner.

They continued to sleep in the same bed, though here again

John's caution prevented her from enjoying the scenes of which she felt so much need. He did not even try to make love to her. She had planned a dramatic scene about that. "Don't touch me," she had decided to say in a strangled voice, "can't you see what I've been through?"

Worse, however, was in store for them. Alice discovered that she *was* going to have a baby after all. There was every indication that it would be Coréze's. The thought gave them both a fright. Even John sat up a bit. As for her, she was filled with violent self-loathing for the trick which her body had played upon her. Meanwhile, John conquered his aristocratic disgust sufficiently to carry his inexperience into the consulting-rooms of shabby gynaecologists in the Boulevard Raspail. An operation was arranged and a very cowed Alice thought desperately that poison was really better than dishonour—but submitted herself to science in the person of Dr. Magnoun, a jolly little twig of a Frenchman with an Academy rosette in his button-hole and moustache-ends waxed into a guardee stiffness. "Vous connaissez, Madame," he said with a certain roguishness, placing her ankles in the canvas hooks hanging from the ceiling and pulling until she was practically standing on her head. "Vous connaissez l'épigramme du grand génie Pascal qui dit: 'Le coeur a des raisons que la raison ne connait pas'?"

Alice returned to a little studio overlooking Parc Montsouris which John had taken. She felt old and worn, and full of a sense of dismal insufficiency. Her anger was changed to gratitude for John's patience and kindness. He looked after her with complete devotion and did not utter a single reproach. If he had she might have rallied more quickly. As it was she spent over a month in bed. This incident effectively disrupted their lives. Their circle of Paris friends seemed to be no longer as "amusing" and as "vital" as heretofore. Alice gave up painting entirely and could not raise enough interest to visit picture galleries to criticize the work of her contemporaries. As for John, the very concerts at the Salle Pleyel became something between a mockery and a bore—so deep a gulf, it seemed, stretched between life and art.

It was at this time, when the frustrating sense of unresolved conflict was making him unhappy, that he ran into Campion again. The latter was making a name for himself. He lived in a little studio behind Alésia and was painting with his customary facility.

Campion at this time was already an expatriate of several years' standing who had found that the life of Paris, which in those days seemed miraculously to exist only for and through the artist, was more congenial to his temper than the fogs and rigours of London. Baird was having a cognac at the Dome when he saw the small self-possessed figure approach from among the tables with the curious swiftness and stealth that always reminded him of a cat. He had seen Campion about quite often in Paris, had visited his exhibitions, and had even bought one of his nudes for Alice. They had never spoken to one another and he was surprised now to see that Campion was smiling in recognition. Baird wondered whether he was perhaps out to cadge a meal as he watched the small figure in the soiled blue shirt and grey trousers. He half-rose to greet him.

Campion was a little drunk and his eyes sparkled. As it was he had just come from a party and was looking for a victim upon whom to fasten and pour out all the dammed-up feelings of persecution and envy which the society of English people seemed to foster in him. "Baird," he said, with a smile, "a very long time since we met."

They sat down and ordered drinks, and Baird found not only that Campion remembered him perfectly, but he had even read two small articles he had written in which his work was mentioned favourably. It was not this, however, that was his business, for Campion almost immediately plunged into a description of his party to ease those pent-up feelings within him. Baird at once recognized behind the acid and brilliant sketches he drew of other people the familiar motive: the sense of social inferiority which had made so many artists difficult companions for him. He remembered one horrible occasion when D. H. Lawrence, upset by some imagined slight, refused to talk to him except in an outlandish Derbyshire dialect—which was intended to emphasize his peasant upbringing. Something of the same discomfort possessed him now as he heard Campion talk, and reflected that he had been born probably in Camberwell, and had left a Secondary school at sixteen. His accent sounded suspiciously correct. It was probably the result of studying the B.B.C. announcers.

Campion had been patronized by a gentleman and he was reacting to it now. His description of Lady Sholter barking like a shotgun and dropping her monocle to shake hands with him, was a masterpiece of ferocious miming. "The English, my God, the English," he said, pleased to have found an audience that did not contest his opinions. "The granite-bound idiocy and moral superiority. The planetary atmosphere of self-satisfaction each of them carries around, to look at himself through. It is staggering." He moved his toes in his sandals as he talked with exquisite pleasure. He was enjoying himself. "The sense of ritual they had evolved to cover their disastrous negation—their impotence."

Baird listened carefully and politely, observing his man with interest. Campion's small round face gleamed golden in the light of the street-lamps. His white, well-kept hands moved as he talked in a series of small graphic gestures as if they were drawing very lightly in the air the scenes he was describing.

Campion was doubly annoyed, because, in going to this party, he had broken a self-imposed rule. He had thought perhaps that this time it might be different—but no. Ferocious, and full of a suffocating sense of self-limitation, he had left it after a quarter of an hour. "To be patronized, to be permitted entry because of my talent rather than because of myself—that's what angers me."

Baird asked why he had gone. Campion gave a mirthless bark of a laugh. "I was told by old Mrs. Dubois that Lady Sholter was anxious to meet me, not only because she thought I was a significant artist, but because she wanted to commission someone to design her a studio for her castle. Idiot that I am, I went partly out of flattery and partly because I cannot afford to turn down two hundred pounds at my time of life." He drank deeply and ordered another drink. "Not a bit of it," he said. "She took one look at my clothes and said: 'Oh, but there's some mistake. You can't be Archie Worm's friend can you? Were you at Eton with Archie?' Madame Dubois whispered 'Lord Worms' in my ear in an ecstatic voice. Was I at Eton with him? Well, my dear Baird, it turned out that I had been mistaken for Campion the *couturier*."

Baird protested that this might have happened to anyone, but Campion would not hear of it. Only the English, it seemed, could be boorish or ignorant. "It's because they despise art in England," said Campion. "The artist is expected to be a sort of potboy or bagman." He laughed again. "Architectural drawings for Lady Sholter! English architecture, like the English character, is founded on the Draught. You should have seen them. What a fool I am!"

Baird was getting a little tired. "Schwabe says that the Englishman deserves neither his literature nor his penis—caring so little for either," he said in a half-hearted attempt to be jocular. Campion was staring at him with his peculiar wide-eyed stare which seemed to combine impudence and candour in equal parts. "As a victim of an English upbringing I suppose I ought to defend myself," said Baird. Campion was no longer listening. He scratched his foot through the web of his sandal. "A world of druids and bores," he said softly. The greater part of his rage had evaporated and he was once more becoming the pleasant and equable companion he normally was.

The two men talked in a desultory fashion, and Baird confessed that he wanted to get away for a complete rest. "And how are your wife's paintings?" asked Campion, who had once seen Alice and thought her beautiful. Baird made some evasive remark and they parted.

He wound his way home slowly to find that Alice was already in bed, reading. "I've decided to go away for a bit," he said, surprising himself, for he did not know that he had come to any decision. "I need a rest."

She did not even look up from her book.

She had been cultivating a stoical and speechless reserve of late. "Very well," she said in a tone which was tinged ever so slightly with anxiety. It was the first time in their lives that he had shown any initiative.

That was how Baird began his travels, drifting south into Italy and Greece, gradually emptying his ambitions one by one into the slow wake of a life which, curiously enough, seemed only now to be beginning. A year in Athens, a winter in Syria, confirmed the first fugitive feelings of happiness at being alone. When he got a letter from Alice asking for a divorce it was with a curious indifference that he read it, sitting in an olive-grove in Poros. A casual friend from Paris whom he encountered in Beirut told him that Alice was going to marry Campion—or said she was. Old Madame Dubois, whose trail he crossed as she was on her way to winter in Egypt, told him that Campion would never marry anyone and asked politely whether he was happy. Sitting on the terrace of the Café Moka, he admitted that he was very happy. "You have become a Mediterranean man, eh?" said the old lady, with her distinguished face concentrated upon his like a burning-glass in the shadow of that absurd straw hat. "It happens to people sometimes, you know." Baird tried to tell her something of his recent journeys, but found them completely lacking in the kind of detail which could make small-talk. No, he had not looked up the Adlers in Jerusalem, nor the Habib family in Beirut. He had, in fact, done none of the things he had been advised to do. He had presented not a single letter of introduction. He had been drifting vaguely about, he told her, becoming a sub-tropical man by degrees. The old lady sucked her iced coffee through a straw, watching his face closely all the time. There was just a tinge of mockery in her eyes. "You've got broader and older-looking," she said at last, removing the small creamy moustache she had allowed to form upon her upper lip with a lace handkerchief. "No doubt you are beginning to enjoy love-making too, without all your silly Anglo-Saxon sentiment?" He had indeed become broader and older-looking; it was partly due to the moustache. But he searched for some way to make the change more concrete so that it could be expressed in words. What could one say? The fundamental factor could, it seemed, only be expressed in negatives, like the first principle of the Hindu religions. "Nothing means very much any more," he said, and added anxiously, lest the phrase should bear a false interpretation. "I mean by that I am quite happy and full of life; but I don't try to feel through books any more. I can't." She smiled with her beautiful young-girl face, and laid a small tender hand on his wrist. "The world is so large," she said, "and a lifetime so short, and people so lovable and cruel and exciting."

It was indeed large, he thought, letting his mind slip back across the kaleidoscope of the last few years, from the courtyard of the fortune-teller in Fez to the day spent under the fig-tree in Poros: from a face reflected in a Damascus water-jar to a café in Homs.

"I think that it is only in the south that they warm themselves at life instead of transforming it into bad literature," said the old lady. Baird lit a cigarette.

He said: "I've begun a novel inside. It should take five years to experience and a year to write. It will be my only justification for taking such a long holiday from myself." He was surprised to see from this that he did consider himself (his English self) as someone quite separate, and his present life not simply an extension of the past—that peach-fed existence of parties and pretensions.

Madame Dubois settled her hands more deeply in her gloves.

"Let me tell you why I come to Egypt every year," she said, with the faintest suspicion of archness. "Fifteen years ago, in spring (she said the word with that little upcast inflexion of pleasure, as Parisians do) I fell in love. I was already married. I was in the temple at Baalbec and I met a young Greek officer. He was also married. We determined that though experience was to be respected—and ours was that spontaneous unfolding inevitable sequence of meetings which one covers with the inadequate word I have just used for the experience of love; while *that* had to be respected, the common forms of life too had their due. He had two children. I had a husband so gracious and human that I could not bear to hurt him. I come to Egypt every year, leaving George to his banking, and relive the experience which a year's domestic propinquity would kill but which had not died throughout these years. He has a little studio in the Arab quarter. We meet in secret. Each year it gets better. Oh my friend, all this was fifteen years ago, and here I am, an old lady. But this secret friendship, so superficial that a week of marriage would kill it, is one of the lovely things of my life."

She excused herself for a moment and crossed the café to the counter to buy some cakes. She had left her book and handbag on the table. Somewhere a radio played the piercing quarter-tones of some Arabic dance. Baird picked up the book and idly turned the pages. It was a little anthology of aphorisms. He noticed that she had placed an exclamation mark beside one of the aphorisms. "*L'amour maternel est le seul bonheur qui dépasse ce qu'on en espérait,*" he read. Madame Dubois, of course, had only that adopted daughter who was always away in Montreux at a Convent. The pencil-mark had scored into the soft white paper. "*L'amour maternel!*" Well, there remained mountain-ranges to be crossed for all of us; paradoxically enough, travel was only a sort of metaphorical journey—an outward symbol of an inward march upon reality.

Madame Dubois returned with a packet of crystallized fruit and some cream cakes of deleterious hue. "We have feasts," she said. "*Orgies* of iced cakes and Russian tea in the little studio. And I tell him once more the plot of the novel which I shall never write; and he brings me the presents he has had six months to choose." Blessed are the happy!

The war was approaching, he reflected, as he rode eastward across the deadly green Egyptian delta to Alexandria. There was perhaps only a year of this life to spend before the barriers came down. He stood up and examined his face in the pocket mirror of the carriage, steadying himself against the swaying of the train by placing his braced legs far apart. The face that stared back at him was certainly the face of a person. It was good, very good, to feel at last a responsibility for his own mind and body: to be rich with increase.

Madame Dubois had said, on that last evening: "I think, you know, that you have discovered the south, and you know that the only life for you is one of curiosity—sexual curiosity and metaphysical speculation."

In Haifa he was pounced upon, as he was having his shoes cleaned, by Miss Dombey, of all people. Rufous-red, burnt to brickdust by the sun and her perpetual pent-up rage against people for having dark skins, Miss Dombey was travelling for a missionary society. "Fancy seeing you here," she said. "I heard you were drifting round the Mediterranean."

"Drifting," thought Baird. It could not have been better put; in Miss Dombey's mouth the word carried a suppressed pejorative inflexion. Drifting was something that "remittance men" did. It was, however, impossible to escape from her. They had a cup of tea, and between them reconstructed the fragments of that old overcast life when Miss Dombey cycled to Thorsham every Saturday to change her books at the library and take Bible class for the vicar. The rain, the steaming fields. He heard fairly regularly from his father. Outside in the dusky street a thin rain began to fall, as if to heighten the verisimilitude of the atmosphere created by the tea-cups and the scrannel-harsh voice of Miss Dombey. She was fuller of freckles than a peacock's tail, he found himself thinking. Each freckle an eye, and every eye an inquisition. Now she wanted to talk about Alice. He changed the subject abruptly and told her about his little Moorish house in Fez, omitting any mention of the kohl-painted pair of dark eyes that watched the dusty road by the cypresses so anxiously for him. Miss Dombey had been sent east upon what she described as "the Lord's business." Leaving England had been a revelation. She had always heard of the "backward" races, she said, but had never realized how backward and *savage* they were. "The *filth*," she said challengingly, when he tried to defend Cairo and Jerusalem. Miss Dombey obliged with two examples of Egyptian life which were incontestably true to character. Walking down Kasr El Nil she had seen a little man in a black suit and hat approaching her. He had no nose, but in the space where the nose should have been was the cork of a bottle, across which lay the rim of his spectacles. On another occasion, travelling third the better to observe her quarry (the fellah), she had noticed that a strange smell of burning was emanating from the man seated next to her. He had a lighted cigarette in his hand which had burnt down to the flesh of the finger. He felt nothing. She realized that the smell was that of burnt flesh.

The man was a *leper!* She recounted these ancedotes with triumphant gestures and Baird had to admit that his Middle East was dirty; but how varied, and how delightful. "It's the same everywhere," said Miss Dombey, "*same* people saying the *same* things." That also was true. Everywhere there was the conventional Latin situation—hopeless broken-down provincial societies talking Lycée French and making Cirque Medrano love. But everywhere, too, the seduction of blue water and islands, and the occasional slant-eyed dark person who demanded only a fugitive devotion of the body, being unable to touch the heart or perhaps not even desiring it. How could one make this clear to Miss Dombey? He could imagine the expression on her face if he should say that he had become a sub-tropical man. "I must go," he said, "the taxi for Beirut is leaving in a few minutes." He shook her warmly by the hand and left her standing there in her torn mackintosh, with her uncombed, untidy red hair shaking in the wind from the open door.

He had spent several months in the Lebanon among the little Druse villages, and was travelling towards Gaza once more in a crowded second-class compartment, when he heard that war had been declared. A couple of Egyptians in their red tarbushes were eagerly reading an Arabic paper; opposite him an old Hebrew and his son were arguing in French about the possibilities of fighting spreading to the Middle East. As the train started rolling slowly away from the flower-scented groves of cultivation towards the twilit desert that stretched between them and Egypt, the old man was repeating: "A war is nothing at all." He was, like all Orientals, equipped with a massive rosary which he drew backwards and forwards through his fingers as he talked, touching the larger amber stones voluptuously. Baird could see the venal old face with its dark eye-pouches quickened by the thought of war and its profits; the movement of men and armies, the millions of tons

of provisions—concrete, steel, tobacco, and medical stores—
which would be spewed out and wasted in every theatre. "It is
nothing," he repeated; how many wars, expulsions, evacu-
ations had he seen that he could think of war in Europe with
nothing more than the restless cupidity of his race? He was
urging his son to join the army at the first opportunity. "Syria
will be a bastion," he repeated. But it was obvious from his
face that he was thinking how much a son in uniform could
help him to get contracts for fruit or wool or firewood. Their
argument became quite heated. "But the war will never come
here," said the younger man and his father's face fell, while the
face of one of the Egyptians in uniform brightened considerably.

Baird wrapped himself in his coat and tried to sleep. It
seemed to him that he had never been so well-equipped for
death. He confronted the idea with an utter calm. He was not
to know, however, how much worse than simple death a war
could be, with its power to deaden and whip the sensibility
into emptiness; he was not to foresee the dreadful post-war
world which became a frantic hunt, not for values, but
for the elementary feelings upon which any sense of community is founded. No. That remained to be revealed apo-
calyptically by Hogarth in the little smoke-filled room in
Harley Street.

At the time when Graecen was offering his diffident services
to his old regiment and writing a poem for *The Times* which
echoed all the proper sentiments: at a time when Fearmax
decided to enter a "retreat of atonement" and Mr. Truman
became a machine-gunner; Baird, with no specific aim or
determination found that three languages and a public school
translated him comfortably into the uniform of a second lieu-
tenant. The deathly staleness of Cairo and its climate were soon
enough exchanged. He was happy. The terrible feeling of
moral insensibility—the *Gleichgultigkeit* that Böcklin afterwards

spoke of on the Cretan mountains, before he killed him—that was an unforeseen enemy lying in futurity.

He saw a short fierce action in Libya, and the retreat across Crete; phenomena more exhilarating than frightening to a temperament as equably based in common-sense. But the first signs of discontent were already there. It was becoming difficult to stand the restricted, stupefying, idiotic system of Army life, which excluded every privacy and every comfort. Seeking for something with more freedom, he happened upon an embryonic department of counter-espionage in need of linguists.

Axelos, in the course of an exhausting interview, examined his claim to a knowledge of Greek, German and French, with penetration and care. He looked more like a Turkish brigand than a British colonel as he sat behind the shaded light, with his large hands spread before him on the green baize table. He was to found the little section in whose service Baird was so singularly successful. Axelos's small eye, deep-set and angry like the rhinoceros, could, he found, be persuaded to shine with laughter. Once he actually saw him open his mouth and expel a little soundless air in laughter. But, in general, it was a consistent picture he took away with him, of a large man with a vulture's profile and perfect teeth, seated over a table that was too small for him, on a chair without space enough between its legs to accommodate his fat and hairy calves. He was cynical about everything from the British character, which he found fatuous and boring, to the policy of the Foreign Office, which he considered frivolous and unimaginative.

It was due to Axelos, however, that Baird found himself grappling with a blowing parachute on a windy hillside in Crete early in 1942—struggling with the rearing and plunging silk like a man trying to put out a fire. The night before he left he had run into Campion of all people; a small stern-looking Campion dressed in a major's uniform which came through the barbed-wire enclosure at G.H.Q. with an almost affected military stiffness. "Baird," cried Campion with delight, catching his arm. "At last someone I can talk to." They made their way down to a Syrian restaurant in the centre of Cairo. There appeared to be a great deal Campion wished to get off his chest, and for some reason or other, he seemed to consider Baird a suitable recipient for his confidence. "Now it's going hell's bells," he said as they attacked their quails and rice. "A million imbeciles blowing each other's arms and legs off with incredible gallantry, and decorating each other with whatever members they have left. The pot hunting, the *laissez faire*, the idiocy." He was speechless with rage and disgust. "What on earth have you or I to do with a war?" It was a question Baird had never asked himself. Campion pressed him. "You, for example? It's the death of everything we believe in. Even the excuse that Hitler is at our throats can't blind us to the fact that we have quite a number of our own Hitlers, and our own organized Fascio," Baird sighed.

"Wait a minute," he said, wallowing in the wake of Campion's divagations. "How is it that you are a major?" Campion's snort of laughter could be heard over the whole room. "My dear Baird," he said reprovingly, as if his companion was demanding the answer to a question he should know only too well. "My dear fellow, when war broke out I made the supreme sacrifice. I joined the Ministry of Political War. Later on I found that if my choice was to lie between having my brains blown out, and having them permanently awash with the dirty bilge of political work, I would rather choose the former." He drank some more wine. "I tell you quite firmly that I do not intend to get killed in this nonsensical business. It is to this end that I have succeeded in getting myself this handsome job on the War Graves Commission. It is the only really academic job left in this world today. We are still investigating the sites of graves left over from the last war. The work is so slow and the pay so high that we do not expect

to finish our researches into this war before Armistice Day,
1999. Of course, once or twice I have been in a tight spot. We
were almost captured in that Libyan show owing to curiosity
about seventeen heroes who got themselves buried on a dune
near Siwa during 1917. All the fun of the fair, Baird."

Baird looked at him narrowly and wondered why it was that
he must be permanently in revolt. He missed one of the
common pleasures of community—that of participation.
"Well," he said slowly, "I suppose you would defend yourself
by saying that you were a coward but not a complete imbecile.
But apart from the moral justification for the war—and partial
as it is—I think it justified within the narrow frame of
reference. People will be happier if we win—in the long run.
Apart from that, perhaps the difference between you and other
people is that you have a sensibility to look after and work to
do with it, while a great number of us are still looking for
ourselves, and some of us might even find ourselves in this
war, through it. . . ." He broke off in some confusion, for
Campion's cynical impertinent eyes were upon him. "So
you've sold out," he said. "The English artist, with the load of
sentiment, as ever. . . ." For a moment he seemed to be looking
for a phrase. "You ought to do well," he said. "They are
looking for war-poets to help me to justify their messy little
rodent-conception of life. The how-bravely-we-are-suffering-
school. What a shameful disgusting business. One can only
hope the whole lot of them meet in the obituary columns of
The Times Literary Supplement."

"Well," said Baird, angered by this sally, "that is neither
here nor there. I dare say most people's behaviour is pretty
questionable even in peace-time. The test is whether you are
happy." Campion folded his arms. "Ah, yes," he said in a
small voice, "Ah, yes. And I have never been happy, I don't
think. Not once in my life. Or perhaps only when I was a
child."

It was odd the next morning to find oneself struggling on the wet grass of a Cretan hillside with a parachute harness. Baird thought of Campion often during the first few days of his mission in Crete. He had forgotten to ask him about Alice; but perhaps it was just as well.

Baird found himself sharing the command of a small group of guerillas with one other young officer and the Abbot John, that venerable old figure, whose resistance to the Germans during their occupation of Crete was widely written-up in the Press of two continents. The Abbot John was an imposing figure, with his massive patriarchal head and its tufted eyebrows, curly beard and ear-rings. Having renounced brigandage in 1923 and retired to the Monastery of St. Luke, he found a sudden invasion of the island not entirely uninteresting. It enabled him to revert to something of his old life. Things had been very quiet of late, and he welcomed a diversion from the relentless quest for holiness. Like all Greeks, he was without difficulty able to combine the mystic and the man of action. In his Byzantine belt, with its square iron studs, he carried not only several hand-grenades and a pistol, but also a tiny prayerbook attached to the buckle by a chain. He was at first so gruff as to be almost rude, and Baird was beginning to repent of his decision to accept the Cretan assignment, when a small incident suddenly made them firm friends. The Abbot John had a tame raven, an amusing and impertinent old bird called "Koax". It was the life and soul of the headquarters in which the Abbot lived when the weather was too bad or the omens unpropitious for a sortie into German-held territory; "Koax" hopped about all day in the large caves which marked the entrance of the labyrinth, making itself as much of a privileged nuisance as any court jester. It could swear mildly in Greek, and was now learning to do the same in English. It was always picking up scraps and hopping off into the shadows with them, and even managed to build itself a ramshackle nest high up in the roof above the natural vent which served them as a smoke-stack. "Koax", however, suddenly became extremely ill, due no doubt to something it had eaten in a greedy moment, and was only nursed back to life by the united devotion of the company; but to Baird fell the happy thought, when the bird seemed about to die, to feed it on brandy in a teaspoon. After one dose "Koax" rallied, and after a couple of days was back in his old form. This made the Abbot a firm friend. "Say 'thank you'," he would tell the bird as it flew up on to his shoulder, "Say 'thank you' to the officer," And "Koax" would give a little shriek and clap his wings.

The little group of saboteurs lived for almost two years in a comradeship and humour that was never tested. Baird learned the Cretan dances, and studied the particularities of the Cretan wines. His particular task was to build a small guerilla army, and to this end he devoted all his energies, backed by the hard-swearing Abbot. They operated from the mouth of the labyrinth, above the village of Cefalû, where later Axelos was to make his discoveries, and where the darkness was to close down on Fearmax, Campion and poor Miss Dombey. Despite its uglier moments, the life was at first merely tiring in the physical sense, in every other way there was the exhilaration to be enjoyed of freedom (the solitude of these immense white mountains in winter and autumn) and remoteness of control over his own actions. War, in terms of ambush and bluff, was something new and it taught him concentration and spareness without touching the springs of a nature already formed in an unreflective soldierly automatism. It was only after a considerable length of time that the strain began to tell. "I'm fed up," he told the old man one day, "my ten days in Cairo did me no good at all. I'm going to find another job. I'm getting numb." The Abbot John regarded him keenly from under his bushy eyebrows. He nodded. "I know how you feel. It is always the same. After a long time one gets sick of the killing.

One feels nothing—neither hate nor pity. It's like the soul getting pins and needles."

It was indeed something like the failure of experience itself to register; he killed now with a numbness and abstraction that passed for strength of mind; but it was as if he were acting in his sleep. As if he were a somnambulist leading his small parties out to ambush patrols or to examine installations. Now it was out of all this that Böcklin's death arose; and yet at first it was simply a term in a crowded life based on animal values—fear, cunning, lice, damp blankets, snow.

Böcklin was the remaining survivor of a German mission visiting the island, which had strayed into an ambush laid for them by the Abbot. He was a rather self-conscious, almost effeminate figure, and he showed a quixotic expectancy of death when he was captured that made the Abbot, who was usually merciless to Germans, stay his hand. His English was almost perfect, and Baird discovered that he had been educated partly in England and partly in France. A Bavarian, his gentleness of manner and politeness completely won over the old man. "Since we did not kill him at the first rush," said the Abbot looking slowly round the little group of huddled figures which had fallen among the stacked leaves round the olive-boles, "we cannot kill him now, eh?" It was not a decision to be approved easily. If he should escape. . . .

It was, however, becoming increasingly difficult to remind the Abbot that he came under the orders of H.Q. Cairo, and that military decisions affecting the whole guerilla group should come from the British officers present. The Abbot had never been to Cairo. He thought it was somewhere near Singapore. While he liked the British and accepted their help, he showed no desire to be ordered about in his own country. Baird opened his mouth to protest against Böcklin being alive when he saw that he had fallen in with the baggage donkeys, his young slight figure shivering in the thin field-grey uniform.

They began the long trek back to the mouth of the labyrinth.

During the brief fortnight that Böcklin was with them, he proved to be a quiet and good-natured addition to the band. He took his turn at the cooking and sweeping, ran errands, played with "Koax", and became very friendly with the dour Cretan mountaineers; indeed they liked him so much that once they even set him on guard with a loaded rifle while they slept. Baird, returning to the network of caves, saw the shadow of an armed German on guard and very nearly shot him. Böcklin handed over his rifle and retired to his corner without a word. The next day he said: "Captain, do not scold the guard. They accepted me as one of them, and by the laws of hospitality I was bound not to escape or to harm them."

On another occasion he brought them food to a little observation post overlooking the plain from which Baird was watching the movements of a German patrol through glasses. "Who sent you up here?" he cried irritably, realizing that a prisoner should not be allowed to know too much. "The Abbot," said Böcklin. Baird gave a sigh and turned back to watch the group of small grey-blue figures crossing the plain in open order. The mad Greeks, with their irrepressible friendliness and *naïveté*, would be the death of them all. They liked Böcklin and immediately accepted him as one of them. Well, come to think of it, why not?

He looked at the keen features and yellow hair of the German, who was sitting behind a bush, arms clasped round his knees. "Böcklin," he said, "what did you do before you joined up?" Böcklin hung his head for a moment and looked confused. "I was going to be a priest, Captain," he said with a clumsy attempt to bring his heels smartly together in the manner of the approved salute accorded to officers by the common soldier. Baird said nothing for a long time. The patrol in the valley moved slowly across the sodden field combing the copses. They had obviously been sent out after the Abbot. "Did you", he said, lighting a cigarette, "believe in this war?" Böcklin, who had relapsed into reverie once more, went rigid at the knees and produced the faint simulacrum of a salute. "I did not believe either in the peace or the war, Captain," he said. His face flushed again. He was obviously afraid of appearing impertinent. Baird grunted. "I suppose the German people will be as pleased when it's over as we will," he said, and, to his surprise, Böcklin shook his head slowly. "You are still fresh," he said, "you can enjoy. We have had years now, and there is only—I do not know how to say it in English." Baird turned to him and said in German: "Say it in German." It was then that he heard from Böcklin's lips the word which was afterwards to sum up, far more accurately than any other in French or English, his feeling for the world —*Gleichgultigkeit*.

The next day the Abbot received a present of a whole lamb, and, despite Baird's protests, the mountaineers set to work to spit it and set it to turn on the huge fire which blazed in the fireplace. "German patrols?" said the Abbot loftily. It would take more than that to keep him from having some real meat to eat for a change. It was perhaps the smoke that gave them away.

At dawn a German patrol opened fire on the guard who was manning the light machine-gun on the outer rock-face. Wakened by the sharp scream of lead thrown off the rock-face and the hoarse winnowing noise of tommy-guns, the whole party awoke and found that their secret headquarters—not to mention the whole plan of operations—was in danger.

The only hope was to retreat further into the labyrinth along the main tunnel, which was known to two of the men who were shepherds. In a small rock chamber, too, was housed the transmitting set which kept Cairo informed of their activities. Böcklin could not go with them. In the confusion and the shouting Baird made his decision.

Böcklin must have followed his reasoning perfectly, for he sat at the entrance of one of the caves, trying to register a pathetic indifference, his thin hands in trouser-pockets. Baird came up to him at a run. In his hand he held a heavy captured Luger. Pressing the muzzle to the head of the boy he fired. The report was deafening in that confined space. The body, knocked from the old ammunition box on which it had been sitting, was thrown against the side of the rock, and fell back artfully like a character in a play, upon its back. His thick blond hair hid the wound. As Baird looked down at him he heard him draw one long and perfectly calm breath.

Now the hunt was up, and the whole party raced into the labyrinth, the Abbot holding a large leg of lamb in his left hand as he uttered terrible threats against the "cuckold bastards" who had interrupted their sleep. He was also laughing, for excitement always made him a little hysterical.

Later in the day the enemy patrol withdrew and they were able to return to their headquarters. Nothing had been touched and it seemed as if by some chance the enemy had missed the narrow entrance to the grotto. Böcklin's body lay where it had fallen and they set about burying it in a shallow grave under the single cypress tree. The Abbot was angry that the German had had to be killed, but he said nothing. Two days later a signal recalled Baird to Cairo to prepare for another theatre of war, and the whole incident passed from his mind. He was glad to leave Crete. He had become stale.

The war unrolled itself gradually; an infinity of boredom settled down over him which even the goads of action could not make him forget. He became more than tired now. He was losing his nerve. He felt around him the gathering unrest of armies which had realized at last that this war was only to be a foundation-stone for a yet bigger and more boring war—the atomic war. Peace came so late as to be an anti-climax. Baird found himself once more at home in the dirty constricted industrial suburb that England had become. His father was very old and very worn. He was glad to see him again, but their long estrangement had widened their common interests. They had nothing to say to each other.

It was during the ice-bound January that followed the year of the peace that Baird began to dream of Böcklin. He saw him one night holding a lighted match to his cigarette. He saw himself place the revolver to his temple and press the trigger. For a time it took quite an effort of memory to disinter Böcklin from among his other memories of dead friends and enemies. Then he remembered. After that he dreamed of him frequently. Sometimes he had just fired the shot and Böcklin was falling away from him towards the rock—almost as if he had taken flight. At others he simply saw the white face detached from its surroundings and, as he watched, the nostrils slowly brim with blood from the shattered brain-case, and noiselessly spill over into the surrounding darkness. He awoke always in great anguish of mind and could not go to sleep again. As a conscious recollection it meant nothing to him—he had seen plenty of uglier scenes. Why, then, should his memory select this particular scene with which to trouble his sleep?

This is why he found himself one day in Hogarth's consulting-room, facing not only the problem of Böcklin's dream, but also the other—the pre-occupation which seemed somehow bound up with it—his *Gleichgultigkeit*: that feeling of dreadful moral insensibility and detachment which is the peculiar legacy of wars. It seemed then bizarre to imagine that psycho-analysis should have anything to say to him, but he liked Hogarth, with his massive Baconian cranium and his blunt hands. And he felt that at least the insomnia might have a mechanical reason.

In those days Hogarth was not, as he is now, the chopping-block for débutantes with palace nerves; he was not, as he is today, consulted upon the sexual maladjustments of earls and financiers. His reputation, which was still growing, rested upon a lengthy hospital practice and two volumes on the nature of the subconscious which the *Medical Year* had characterized as "too daring by far in their sweeping assumptions". Their author's appearance belied any suggestion of daring, however; if his mind was a reflection of his physiognomy, then it must have been a blunt and heavy weapon— by no means a scalpel.

Hogarth was immense and of heavy build, with the clumsiness of a water-buffalo in movement. His thick brown hair, chopped off short and clipped round the ears, fell upon a low white forehead which topped off the coarse blunt nose and immature chin of a Neronian bust. One of his eyes was blue; the other was flecked with a honey-coloured spot towards the outer part of the iris. His hands, too, were of different sizes— an acromegalic feature which one did not easily notice since he kept them for preference buried in his trouser-pockets. His clothes were as baggy as a Dutchman and smelt strongly of tobacco. As he rose to shake hands Baird saw that his ears, which were prominent and covered with a fine blond fur, were set away from his head, giving him a curious and slightly comical expression. His voice too added in some measure to this impression, for it was displeasing, and had odd variations in it. If he tried to raise it too suddenly it broke disconcertingly.

At that time Hogarth's theatre of operations was a small shabby room at the corner of Harley Street and Marylebone Road. He had, however, a private door which opened on to mews, and he also shared part of the building with other medical men. He travelled up every day from his suburb with a paper parcel containing his lunch and a green canister full of cold tea.

From the moment Baird met him he realized that his habits and pretensions had come under a disturbing and steady scrutiny. He attempted a politeness, but he saw that Hogarth did not answer his smile; and indeed cut him short with a brusque question: "Why did you come to me?" It was not calculated to put him at his ease; nor were the other questions that Hogarth asked in his strangely varying voice, but he passed from annoyance to relief when he realized that his defences were being tested at all the obvious points. More than that. He was really being observed for the first time as a sort of specimen. Hogarth's eyes were resting on his fingers. Following the direction of his gaze Baird found himself for the first time regarding his own hands as if they belonged to another man. What could one make of them? Were they the hands of an artist, a writer, a criminal?

He noticed a great bull-nosed pipe which lay fully-charged on the desk before the analyst. On the bookshelf in the corner, upon a jumble of medical papers, he saw a soft green Tyrolean hat with a bright cock-pheasant's feather in it tucked into the cord. "I notice", said Hogarth idly, "that on your tunic there is a little green piece where you obviously have worn some medals—a faded spot there." He delighted in the unconscious intention. "Did you leave them off before coming to see me?" It had been the merest whim that morning to put on his clean tunic; he had forgotten the campaign medals and the M.C. Hogarth put back his head and said rather sententiously: "In my job whims like that might count for a lot. Tell me why you did it."

As Baird began to talk in his deep and rather musical voice the elder man assembled himself to listen. As always, he was calling up all his long clinical experience and trying to marry it to that part of his mind which in his books he calls the "Inself". He was busy attempting to record the outlines of this newcomer's personality, recording the physique, the texture and colour of the skin; the determined short upper lip and the large forehead. His opening questions were really the merest gambits. It was necessary to see whether Baird could talk, could think about himself and objectify the thought in words. At the same time, the frailer side of his own mind was wearily thinking how little, at the most, one can know about another human being. Hogarth was full of that sickness which the faintest success breeds in a man of sensibility. He allowed the voice, with its pleasant modulations, to tell him more than the phrases it uttered. Its harshness was natural to it and not a reflection of an interior distress.

"Do you dream much?"

"I have a nightmare which keeps returning."

"Are you married?"

"Divorced."

"Regular army?"

"I've signed on for another three years."

Slowly through these opening statements he seemed to see the type and colour of Baird's anxiety opening like a paper flower in water. He slipped open the drawer of his desk and inserted a paw. He always kept a packet of boiled sweets to suck as he worked. He put one on his tongue with a quick gesture and settled himself further in his oak chair. It was hard and cruel work, he was reflecting, to bore down through the carapace of pride, self-esteem, apathy; dragging out the forgotten or the discarded from the rubbish-heap of another man's experience. Particularly so when what he had to give was not a mechanical cure—a particular focus of trauma or anxiety, a particular fact or incident—but a technique and a stance. And how did this come about? Not through any will of his own—it was as if he had turned down his conscious self to the smallest bud of flame. No. It all happened by a fluke— by an extra-sensory awareness which was being called up now from inside him ready to penetrate and seize. He felt, as he listened, quite light and empty, quite devoid of will or ambition or desire—or even interest in his patient.

Baird, it seemed, was well-read and familiar with the general theories of Freud and Adler. So much the worse. But, at any rate, he could express himself freely and without difficulty and he seemed honest enough. It was enough for the first "wax impression", as he called it. It only remained to see what reciprocal impression he had made on the younger man.

"Well, that'll be a guinea," said Hogarth with a sigh as the clock struck. "Now will you go away and think me over? If you decide that you want me to help you come back tomorrow at nine. Tonight I would like you to go out and get drunk, if possible. A hangover loosens up the mind no end, and makes you able to dissociate fluently. Will you do that? Good. If you don't want to go on with me telephone me before half past eight tomorrow."

The sunlight suddenly shone in at the murky window and turned the lobes of his ears to coral as he stood up awkwardly on one leg. He had already placed his pipe between his teeth and was fumbling for a box of matches. Baird had not yet told him about the Böcklin dream; well, it could wait until to-morrow. He felt a tinge of chagrin to be thus dismissed at the striking of a clock. "Well, Doctor Hogarth," he said. "Thank you very much." Hogarth folded his cheque up and put it in his pocket. He nodded and blew a couple of puffs on his pipe.

In the waiting-room Fearmax was waiting, walking up and down like a metronome with his hands behind his back. In his hand he held some folded papers. His hat and stick lay upon the sofa. He looked tired and ill. Baird went out into the rainy street wondering whether Hogarth could be of any use to him, and whether the Böcklin dream would return.

His analysis progressed more slowly even than his friend-ship—for Hogarth, that dealer in sensibility often found that his best way towards a cure was to turn a patient into a friend. Baird found him a fascinating character with his ponderous medical equipment backed up by an intuition which was com-pletely female and amoral. Between them they worked towards

Böcklin's ghost through the muddled debris of a life which Baird himself had never stopped to examine properly. Hogarth's analytical technique was an uncompromising one; it not only combed out the purely factual data of a life, but it made the liver of it realize his responsibilities in regard to it. "Why do you think you are here?" "What sort of purpose do you imagine you have in life?" "Do you feel that you have ever contributed towards the well-being of another person?" Such were some of the questions which managed to get sandwiched in between others as cogent. "Why did you forget your latch-key?" "What do you think of when you see a spilled ink-pot?" "Do you enjoy pain?"

Together they disinterred Böcklin from his unceremonious grave. They recovered, it seemed, every thought and action connected with the incident and with those hundred and one other incidents which appeared to be connected to it in his memory. They became great friends, and when the work became too painful to continue—when the big metal ash-trays were brimming with charred tobacco and cigarette-ends—they would put on their overcoats and walk for hours along the Embankment. Hogarth would explain his theories about the structure of the psyche and give him summaries of his own condition, which were not always comprehensible. And yet behind it all, Baird felt, there was design and purpose in what he said; he was a man trying to grapple with a philosophy not only of disease, but also of life.

"All right. You kill Böcklin. It is a senseless and beastly murder; but then you are pressed into the service of murder. In the abstract, murder is being committed in your name all over the world. But this actual act shakes you. Now though killing him may be the source of a moral guilt, I'd like to know whether it illustrates merely the guilt for that act, or a much more deep-seated guilt about your role in society. Böcklin may simply be an illustration. But in point of fact your life indicates another, and—may I say?—more fruitful disturbance. You were unhappy before the war too, you say. As a puritan living unpuritanly you would have been. You found an inability to enjoy because your education, with its gentlemanly prohibitions, had taught you merely how to endure. Sometimes—" here Hogarth affectionately put his arm round the shoulders of the younger man. "Sometimes, Baird, I think there is only politics left for you—the last refuge of the diseased ego. You notice how all the young men are burning to reform things? It's to escape the terrible nullity and emptiness and guilt of the last six years. They are now going to nationalize everything, including joy, sex and sleep. There will be enough for everyone now because the Government will control it. Those who can't sleep will be locked up."

They walked in silence for a quarter of a mile along the deserted Embankment, their footsteps sounding hollow in the crisp night air.

"And yet," pursued Hogarth, "I think I see also symptoms of a purely metaphysical disturbance going on too; you are not alone, you know, in anything except the fact that it has chosen a single incident from your own life to illustrate what is common to the whole of your generation. I tell you everywhere the young men are sleeping with the night-light burning. You ask me about Böcklin and I say this is less interesting than that other feeling which you have been telling me about—what the old Abbot called 'pins and needles of the soul' and Böcklin himself called '*Gleichgultigkeit*'. It seems to me that this sharpening of focus, this aridity of feeling, this sense of inner frustration, must be leading to a kind of inner growth at the end of which lies mystical experience. Now you are laughing at me again." He placed his pork-pie hat firmly on his head and walked a few steps in silence. "It seems to me that when you have exhausted *action* (which is always destructive) and people and the material things, there comes a great empty gap. That is what you have reached—the great hurdle which stands on this side of the real joyous life of the inside self. Then comes illumination—dear, oh dear. I know it sounds nonsense, but it's the poverty of language that is at fault. What do you think the medical term for William Blake would be? A euphoric? A hysterical pycnik? It's too absurd. The next few years will be a crisis not only for you but your generation too. You are approaching spiritual puberty—the world is. It is hard going I know—but there is always worse ahead, I have found. Yet there is a merciful law by which nothing heavier than you can bear is ever put upon you. Remember it! It is not the burden which causes you pain—the burden of excessive sensibility—but the degree of your refusal to accept responsibility for it. That sets up a stress and conflict. It sounds balls, doesn't it? Well, so does St. John of the Cross, I suppose."

They stopped at an early coffee-stall and ordered the plate of sausage and mash that Hogarth so loved to eat before he caught his last tram back to Balham. They smiled at each other over a cup of steaming coffee and wrangled good-naturedly about who should pay.

"Admit it," said Hogarth. "I'm talking about something that you don't understand at all. Gibberish, eh?"

Baird shook his head. "It sounds like sense—with a fourth dimension added to it. It reminds me a good deal of the Californian prophets, Huxley, Maugham, *et alia*."

"Ah," said Hogarth, "the propaganda squad."

"The sphere and navel group. New World Taoists."

"Well, you are not very far wrong; for although I think some of them have the answer, it often represents little more than a retrenchment upon an original pragmatism. Dealing in revelation, they obviously lack the true illumination. Why? Because if they had the secret they could perfectly carry on with the Christian corpus—you would not need these humpty-dumpty Eastern religions to fall back on, with their athleticism.

A mass attack on the Gita has the effect of merely getting sections of it printed in the *Reader's Digest*. To what end? It is mere non-creative theorizing. If we could get the West to study the Karma Sutra it would be more to the point. If we could unfreeze the Dutch canal of the average man's blood up here. . . . Hullo! My tram."

Hogarth was always in an ecstasy of apprehension lest he miss the last tram. "No it isn't," he said, turning back. "And while I'm on the subject of pins and needles I might ask you to tell me just what *you* want to do with your life."

Baird shrugged his shoulders. "I wanted to write once. I was born a yeoman, I think, and pressed too early into the science of arms. You are right about my being merely typical. The whole of my generation believes in nothing beyond the aimless death-activity. We were sold into slavery—action— while we were unformed. Now we don't belong anywhere, don't want to have homes and families and roots. We are a sort of Hitler Youth, used to armies, and battles and small adventures. I thought of enlisting in this civil war in China when my time is up. If it's still on, I mean."

"Nothing more appropriate," said Hogarth ironically. "You evade your own civil war in order to stick your nose into someone else's. Why don't you commit suicide and have done with it?"

"I have thought of that. More than you imagine."

"Here comes my tram," said Hogarth for the tenth time, and launched himself into space like a goose, his neck thrust forward. It was not. He returned rather crestfallen, adjusting his crooked hat brim and dusting ash off his lapels with both hands. "I have an idea," he said. "To what sort of merit on earth do you attach importance? Are you proud of your medals? Your prowess with women? Would you like to have children? Be a doctor and save people? At what point of your character do you flow out? No. Don't tell me," he added hurriedly, catching sight of his Balham tram at last, "I don't give a hang. I'm trying to get you to draw your own portrait."

He clutched the rail and boarded the groaning monster. Then, thinking of something more he wanted to say, he turned his huge body round and leaning out, shouted, "Or is it something beyond all these things?" His voice rose as the distance widened. The other passengers standing outside regarded him with concern. "Do you think it is somewhere in the region we call God? Ask yourself? Eh? Just ask yourself." He was borne gesticulating out of earshot. The look of concern on the faces of the other passengers changed to one of relief. They looked at one another knowingly. It was clear that he was a harmless religious maniac.

It was not unlike editing a very long and very dreary film, thought Baird walking homeward across London. Immense discursive spools of recollection run through at every sitting—the greater part of it irrelevant: mocking in its irrelevance. Still the experience had done him good; he had been able to expand to the full extent in his talk at least. And, as Hogarth said, the major function of analysis seemed to consist of re-living and re-digesting experience. He felt lighter, more buoyant in himself. Only the dream of Böcklin did not vanish.

One Wednesday, Hogarth, who was very interested in painting, took him to a gallery where, among other things, he saw several of Campion's great raving canvases, and one that he recognized as Alice's; Hogarth examined the former with great attention and reverence. "The only English painter," he said. Baird was quite charmed to see Hogarth's look of awe when he said that he knew Campion. "Another candidate for your clinic," he said. "No doubt," said Hogarth softly, "no doubt." He stood back and admired the powerful landscape which has since become famous—Campion's *Tree Near Arles*. "But so long as he can keep spitting it out in pictures he's all right," he added. He made no comment on Alice's picture.

Walking across Oxford Street Baird said: "All English women kiss with their mouths shut. Now if your psychological axiom is true . . ."

"What axiom?"

"The identification of the mouth with the more intimate organism—then you have a thesis. . . ."

"What thesis?"

"Well, it explains the abnormal sexual emphasis of the English male in his dress—old school tie, bowler-hats, large pipes—like yours, Hogarth, if I may say so—and amnion-like tobacco-pouches."

"Young man," said Hogarth, "it is extremely unkind of you to wing your analyst like that. According to the text-books I must represent God to you—I must be above criticism."

"Well, I feel neither here nor there as regards God. I let you represent my father, however. If he had given me half the advice you have I'd be a more thawed-out character. Anyway, Hogarth, you've made a mess of the analysis by letting me become your friend. I see you in a context now. As a father, for example, you are charming and touching."

Hogarth suddenly blushed scarlet. Baird was recalling that every Wednesday they had lunch together, after which Hogarth would allow him to keep him company to Balham where he lived with an only son and a middle-aged housekeeper. Together they lunched, and afterwards walked in the park each holding a small grubby hand. Hogarth was at his most endearing when he was with the child; all through the winter they would visit the shabby little park with its nude trees and crisp brown water—its three dejected ducks gabbling at their own reflections. Hogarth's son was nine and full of enthusiasm for the toy boat his father had made for him. It was a brave little cutter which bore the legend *Europa* upon its smart white breast. Hogarth himself was fascinated by the technique of sailing, and was hardly less eager than the boy to propose new ways of setting the sail, or a new run across the pond. Baird could see him now, down on one knee at the concrete margin, watching the little ship flutter and heel through the circles of still water under the willow-tree, or turn over on its side and run from one corner to the other of the pond without a fault.

"Father, it's not set properly."

"Yes it is: be patient."

In an ecstasy of apprehension they watch it come into the wind and hang trembling. Hogarth is making ludicrous gestures at the boat, as if trying to coax it towards them. His pipe goes so hard that the dottle gleams red. His trousers are baggy and dusty at the knee. From time to time his son slips an absent hand into his vast pockets in search of boiled sweet to suck. It is a moment of intense excitement, for the little craft has turned over on its side and threatens to sink. Hogarth and the boy squat down and begin to paddle the water with their hands in the hope of creating concentric ripples which will draw it within reach. Hogarth groans. Their attempts are useless it seems. The boy starts to take off his shoes, but his father, fearful of letting him get his feet wet, lumbers into the pond, shoes and all, and skids uncouthly out to where the boat lies, flapping hard. He comes ashore laughing and cursing at the same time. Mrs. Gregory is going to scold him again for his wet feet.

"That's the third salvage he's done this month," says the boy, shaking the water from the flapping canvas of the *Europa*.

Afterwards, walking home to tea, their noses and fingers burned blue with cold, the father and son wrangle interminably about the boat, the one protesting that the mast is too high and the sail area too large, the other shrilly maintaining that the *Europa* would be better for a little extra lead on her keel.

Hogarth lives in one of those common-place semi-detached villas. In the cosy little front parlour a big coal fire is blazing and Mrs. Gregory has laid out an excellent tea: muffins fume in butter on the fender. They get out of their wet things and draw up chairs: and the boy, fetching a sigh, says thankfully, "It's so wonderful. I'm glad I haven't got a mother, Dad." Hogarth looks at him indulgently. He is so secure and happy in a habit of male friendship, a male world with its triumphant relations to purpose and adventure. "Women always spoil things," he says. Presently Mrs. Gregory will come in with her silly talk about unwashed hands and wet socks. Hogarth smiles.

"What do *you* think, Baird?" he asks.

Hogarth's own wife, whose picture stands on the mantel-piece, was much younger than he when they married. Her face is smooth and round and innocent in a Germanic way: she was a student of Hogarth's.

Now he has taken up his spectacles and placed them upon his nose. A radiant contentment shines upon his face. His feet are clad in old battered carpet-slippers, one of which has a convenient hole in the sole; convenient because he enjoys holding to the fire his slippered foot, into which a toasting fork has been cunningly lodged.

At such moments Baird is filled with envy for the elder man as he watches him taking his ease, while on the carpet at their feet the boy strips the *Europa* and sets the canvas to dry.

On April Fool's Day Hogarth gave it up. "Baird," he said, "we've reached a point where we are over-elaborating the problem. We are indulging you and pandering to the bloody dream. I've got all the factual data I need; you've had the whole works. But somewhere I must have made a mess of it, or else you need to keep on dreaming the dream until something happens to you—I mean until you change inside. You know, the dream may be simply a sort of prompting to change inside;

it's possible that it might be necessary to you—until you change. It's no good following it down the time-track any farther. Anyway, our method is not inclusive enough. Come back in a thousand years when psychology has become an adult science. Meanwhile I'm going to suggest something."

Baird put out his cigarette and listened attentively.

"Can you get away abroad now?"

"I should think so. On sick leave. Why?"

"To Crete?"

Baird looked surprised and a trifle pained. "It is part of your system to propose long and expensive journeys to your poorer patients?" he said ironically. But Hogarth continued seriously.

"I'm suggesting something that would occur to any intelligent Hottentot. That you should return like a good murderer to the scene of your crime. Dig up Böcklin with your own hands once more. It's just an idea. I know it sounds shocking. But get him buried in a cemetery or something. Take a responsible line. It's worth it: you might come to terms with him—who knows? Besides I'm tired of indulging your maimed literary genius. Think it over."

Baird sat for a moment in silence. They looked at each other. "It's a curious thing," he said, "but I was offered a mission about a month ago to do precisely that. To go to Crete and try and find something out for the Intelligence people."

Hogarth spread his hands out. "Well, there you are. What more do you want? Accept, my dear fellow."

It was more easily said than done; the idea was rather a startling one, and Baird felt that he needed time to think it over. "And by the way," said Hogarth, as he was putting on his mackintosh, "let me know when you are off: and don't forget you are a tenner behind with your payments—the child is going to school soon, you know"

In the vestibule, Baird met Fearmax. He had called to leave a cheque for Hogarth. From time to time during the last few months when their paths had crossed they had been in the habit of exchanging civilities. Now Fearmax walked down to the corner of the street with Baird. He looked pale and tired. He walked with an eccentric springiness beside the young man, remarking that spring would soon be here, though it was plain to see that his mind was not on the weather. He said that he was going abroad for a short holiday—to Egypt he thought. He hoped the weather would not be too hot. Baird, who knew what Cairo could be like in June and July, said nothing. It was not the best time of the year to visit Egypt, and he wondered whether Hogarth knew of the journey. "Hogarth is a remarkable man," said Fearmax with vehemence, "a very remarkable man. He has been of considerable use to me—both as a friend and a doctor." Baird found it curious that Hogarth had never introduced them. "He has attended all my séances this year: I've been trying to put him in communication with his dead wife, you know." This was rather an interesting sidelight on Hogarth. Fearmax shook his head and sighed, watching the shining toecaps of his shoes as they performed their eccentric progress under him.

Baird suggested that the Lebanon or Greece would provide a cooler climate for a rest during the late spring and summer than Egypt, and Fearmax nodded very precisely. "I wish, however," he said, "to make one or two observations on the pyramids. And I imagined the sea-journey will be refreshing. I am going on . . . Let me see." He fumbled in his wallet and produced a green ticket for Baird's inspection. "A large comfortable summer-cruise boat, the *Europa*. It is only half-full I'm told."

It was this piece of information that decided Baird, for want of any other, to ask for a reservation on the *Europa* before he next visited Hogarth. The civil servant in the dingy office above the roar of Whitehall had been more than accommodating. There were certain independent inquiries that the

Foreign Office would like made in Crete. It appeared that a certain quantity of small arms had been shipped across from an organization in Palestine. It had been gathered and hidden in caves—possibly the labyrinth which had been mentioned recently in the Press as having been discovered by Axelos. The Foreign Office would like to know what it meant. It might mean a danger to the monarchy in Greece, which England had determined to maintain. Could Baird undertake such an inquiry and report back as soon as possible?

It sounded to Baird as if the old Abbot John had once more tired of his search for higher truth and was entering politics—for want of a war to interest him and exploit his talents as a man of action. It would not be so unpromising an adventure as he had at first thought. He would go and see; the investigation into the Böcklin business would fit into place neatly enough. He wondered, as he pressed Hogarth's bell, whether Axelos would remember him after all these years?

He found a note waiting for him. Hogarth was out, but the note suggested a rendezvous in a familiar pub later that evening. Baird spent the rest of his time packing and touring the bookshops for suitable reading material with which to while away the journey. He did not fancy that Fearmax's conversation would provide sufficient entertainment to justify setting forth bookless.

He was surprised to meet Graecen. He knew his work slightly, and did not like it; but the man was pleasant and friendly, and apparently an old friend of Hogarth. The analyst himself was delighted with the news that Baird was going; he had been kept in touch with developments by phone, and had heard all the details.

"Graecen will introduce you to Axelos," he said, "who will interest you a great deal. He's a real character from a film—a German film. No doubt you could stay at Cefalû."

Graecen was charitable enough to echo these sentiments.

The invitation he had received was explicit enough; and he liked the look of this young Army officer who seemed to be, for a change, moderately well-read and whose manners had not been abbreviated with his weaning. He was also secretly rather glad to have at least one acquaintance on the *Europa*. The sudden prospect of leaving England—almost in itself a death—perplexed and troubled him. London, which he loathed normally, seemed to him for the few days left, too enchanting a capital to lose. He walked across the Green Park, hat in hand, talking softly to himself, wondering what could be expected of a future which had been so clearly and abruptly circumscribed. It hurt him too that Hogarth's manner showed no special tenderness or consideration towards himself. Indeed, Hogarth protested firmly that he did not believe that his old friend was under sentence; when Graecen pressed him and gave him his proofs, Hogarth simply snorted and laughed. "Well, if it's death, Dickie," he said. "It's death. You may steal a march on us, but we'll catch you up in the end. See if we don't."

Another of Graecen's preoccupations had been with the question of the Cefalû statues. He had managed to get the chemical expert of the Museum to part with small quantities of his reagents without, he thought, arousing his suspicions as to the validity of Axelos's claims. The new nitrous oxide process promised to tell one, in the case of stone-cutting, not only the approximate age of the stone but also the nature of the instrument used to shape it. With these he hoped to keep a sharp check on his eccentric friend.

His mood, however, as they all drove down to Southampton in his big car, was one of sentimental taciturnity. He was leaving England—perhaps for ever. Baird sat in front with the driver, while in the back Hogarth and his son held an endless discussion as to the capabilities of the car. Graecen saw the hedgerows flowing by with a sharp and useless regret; every

turning of the great main road held memories for him—
memories of great country houses buried in trees: houses
where he had spent so much of his time idling, flirting, and
cultivating the fine five senses. There, beyond Winchester, was
Bolser, where he had had that miserable love affair with Anne
Granchester. What a bitch! How miserable he had been, and
how ineffectual. The road bent northward through an immense avenue of dusty oaks. Behind them, hidden from sight,
lay the old house. It belonged to the National Trust now. And
what had happened to Anne? She, by rights, should also
belong to the National Trust, he found himself thinking
vindictively. She had become in later years a sort of beauty
spot trampled flat by the feet of the worshippers; a sort of
Niagara Falls of a woman. Why had she never let him love her?
He grimaced and tucked his chin deeper in his coat collar. At
any rate she had been good for two not unsatisfactory sonnets.
What a life, he thought—or rather what a death. Leopardi
could not face it when it finally came. Could he? He held his
breath for a second and closed his eyes, imagining what it felt
like to surrender his identity. Nothing. He felt nothing, heard
nothing save the soft uniform ticking of his own heart.
Hogarth was speaking.

"You know, Dickie," he was saying. "It's very romantic of
you to go off like this into the blue—very romantic."

Graccen was flattered. It was really, when you considered it.
A poet *en route* for Elysium. It was curious that he had never
written a poem about death.

Baird leaned back from his seat beside the driver and
suggested lunch at a wayside inn. They all got out in the rain
and hurried indoors. It was still cold.

"Ah," said Hogarth. "How lucky you are to go south."

"Yes," said Baird, whose enthusiasm mounted at the
thought of the perennial blue skies and temperate winds of the
Mediterranean. It was as if a film had lain over everything—

the magic of Greece, Egypt, Syria. He felt the premonitory approach of the happiness he had known before the war.

They had an excellent meal before continuing their journey. Graecen, who had rather a tendency to be frugal when it came to ordering food, stood them a lavish lunch. His cigar-case was full too: so that they settled back in the car with the air of millionaires making a pilgrimage to Carlsbad.

"This chap Fearmax," said Baird suddenly. "What is he?"

Hogarth looked at him for a second, and quietly closed one eye. "I want Dickie to meet him," he said. "He is the founder of a psychic society—almost a religious brotherhood. Dickie, he will do your horoscope, read your palm, and terrify you."

Graecen looked rather alarmed. He was very superstitious. "I think you do him an injustice," said Baird, and Hogarth nodded. He said: "Fearmax is most interesting. He has hold of one end of the magic cord of knowledge. There's no doubt that he is a very curious fellow, and a suffering one. I hope the blue sky does him good too."

They cruised down to the dock, where the *Europa* lay at the great wharf, like a rich banker smoking a cigar. Hogarth's son was thrilled by her size and the opulence of her lines. It was too late for prolonged conversation, and when Hogarth and son stumbled ashore after an admiring inspection of Graecen's state-room, there was little to do but to wave to them, and watch them get into the big car. There was no sign of Fearmax. Baird noticed the couple he afterwards came to know as the Trumans standing at the rail waving shyly to an old lady who stood sniffing on the pier.

A thin spring rain was falling once more. The gleaming cobbles stretched away into the middle distance—a long aisle of masts and funnels. Graecen stood for a little while gazing over the side with a sudden sense of hopeless depression. The boat-train was in and a straggle of passengers advanced towards the gangway of the *Europa* followed by their baggage piled high on trucks.

"I expect we'll leave tonight," he said.

"Yes," said Baird, his heart suddenly leaping at the idea; he settled his neck back against the wet collar of his coat and repeated the words to himself slowly. They would cleave that blank curtain of spring mists, dense with wheeling sea-birds, and broach the gradual blue horizon in which Spain lay hidden, and the Majorcas. He wondered why Graecen should look so downcast.

"I suppose you feel sad, leaving England?" he said lightly; it was merely a conversational politeness. He was not really interested in anything but this feeling of joy which slowly grew inside him at the prospect of leaving it all behind.

"Yes and no," said Graecen guardedly. He was sad because there was no one who shared his confidence in the matter of his death-sentence. He felt all of a sudden damnably alone; he wondered whether there was a ship's doctor to whom he could speak openly—to create that sense of dependency without which his happiness could not outface the shadow which lay over him. Baird was pleasant enough—but too self-contained and uncommunicative. He went below to supervise his own unpacking.

It was now that Miss Dombey came down the deck at full tilt, being dragged along by her fox-terrier, which advanced in a series of half-strangled bounds towards the ship's cat. "John," she cried in piercing recognition, and would have been carried quite past him had not the lead conveniently caught itself in some obstruction. It was an unexpected displeasure. Miss Dombey was still the red-freckled parson's daughter he had known so long ago in the country; only she had become more strident, more dishevelled, less attentive to her dress as the urgency of her Mission had increased: the Second Coming, he remembered, had been predicted for the following year. Miss Dombey had been working frantically to advertise its approach in the hope of preparing as many souls as possible for the judgment they would have to face. Her voice sounded more harsh, more emphatic and crackling than ever. She talked like someone with a high temperature. She was going to Egypt to try and prepare the infidel for the expected event. Baird swallowed his displeasure and exchanged a quarter of an hour's small talk about the village. Miss Dombey had seen his father: she said so with the faintest reproach. He was looking much older and seemed to have fewer interests. Tobin was bedridden, and his wife had been gored by a bull. Miss Tewksbury, the postmistress, had been sentenced to six months for writing poison pen letters to the Vicar's wife: it was curious—she had always been so fond of the Vicar.

Baird excused himself and went below full of annoyance at the thought that he was going to have her for a travelling companion. Through an open door he caught sight of Fearmax wrestling with a cabin-trunk. So he had arrived after all. His own dispositions were easily made. He had taken the barest necessities for the journey. The two anthologies he put aside for the moment. His little India-paper copy of the *Phaedo* seemed to be the sort of thing one always took on journeys and never read. Lying in his bunk and idly turning the pages he fell asleep, and when he awoke there was that faint interior stir of excitement, that faint preoccupied stillness of a great ship heading out to sea, that told him they were off. It was true. A strip of dark sea curled between them and the bleak grey cliffs with their small fractured groups of houses shining dun and drab in the late evening light. The *Europa* moved without a tremor—as if she were moving down rails. A bell rang somewhere, and the fans in the corridors suddenly started to bore out their little furry cones of sound. Then they too fell silent; and from the very heart of his preoccupation he distinguished the small even pulse of the ship's engines driving them southward.

Baird entered the saloon in dread of Miss Dombey, for he saw that he would sooner or later have to introduce her to Graecen—the innocent Graecen who had done nothing to deserve such an imposition. To his surprise, however, they seemed to get on quite well together. It was perhaps because no sooner had he introduced Miss Dombey than he found she had introduced her own Mission. "Thousands are living in the shadow of death," she said juicily to Graecen. "And my job is to prepare them for the state of death, to wake them up, to shrive them, if necessary." This struck something of a chord in Graecen's heart. He had been pondering on his condition as he unpacked, and these forthright propositions seemed to him to refer almost directly to his own mental and spiritual state. Had he thought enough of death? Had he prepared himself? The idea had seemed repugnant to a poet, a hedonist. Miss Dombey's vehemence gave him a jolt. It was like meeting a prophet. She clawed her hair off her forehead and gave him a brief outline of what was going to happen when the Second Coming started to be fulfilled. Graecen listened to her with incredulity mixed with a certain not unpleasant fear; it reminded him of his childhood at Rickshaw Hall—the stories of hellfire and brimstone which his mother had told him and which he had believed. Miss Dombey was enchanted by so influential a convert. She pressed upon him no less than five separate tracts, which he promised to study at leisure. Baird looked on curiously at this little scene, wondering whether Graecen's obvious good nature made him indulgent; but, to his surprise, when Miss Dombey left them, he turned to him and said: "Baird, what an extraordinary woman. Thank you for introducing her." In some obscure way he felt glad to be in touch with someone actively concerned with death—even if it wasn't his particular death. The tracts, however, were awful.

He tried to read them but gave it up as hopeless. The prose, to begin with, was so bad; one could not be carried away by fairy tales of the Second Coming written in this Praed Street vein. Nevertheless, Graecen clung to Miss Dombey.

As for Fearmax, he was concerned with problems of a different order. He lay for hours in his cabin with his eyes fixed on the ceiling. His door was always open, so that whenever he passed Baird could look in and see him there, hands crossed on his breast, collar open, staring at the paintwork. He did not appear to any meals for the first twenty-four hours and Baird wondered idly if he were having a severe bout of sea-sickness; yet his door stood open, and whenever Baird passed it he saw him lying there. Led by the promptings no less of curiosity than of courtesy, he at last tapped at the door and put his head in, asking Fearmax in his pleasant way if he could be of any use to him. For a time he did not seem to hear—but at last, with an effort, he turned in the bunk and raised himself on one elbow.

"That's kind of you," he said hoarsely. "Very kind. No. I am just resting, that's all. I do not suffer from sea-sickness. But I hate journeys. Do come in."

The cabin was heavy with the smell of cigar-smoke. There were several large stoutly-bound books lying beside the bunk, a rosary, and a number of yellow envelopes full of papers. Fearmax looked pale and weary.

"I've never been out of England before," he said. "It's rather a big adventure for me—like the start of a new chapter; and I am trying to read the omens. They are very strange, very strange."

Between the wall and the bulkhead lay a bound set of Ephemerides, and a notebook covered with jottings. "Omens?" said Baird. ("Omens?" said Graecen later in a much higher key of superstition, of anxiety, when Fearmax made the same remark.)

"You probably don't believe in astrology?" said Fearmax. What was one to say? It was on the tip of Baird's tongue to reply, "Not since the atom bomb was discovered," but he checked himself. Fearmax went on in his hoarse voice.

"I didn't myself once, but even if it's an inexact science I've found that it could tell me things: potentialities of my own character, for example: forces inherent in the world around me. At any rate I worked out a progressed chart today in the train for the next few months. It shows some curious things. As far as I can see I am in danger of being lost in one of the tunnels of the Great Pyramid."

Baird stifled his amusement. There was something oddly impressive about Fearmax. He did not talk like a quack, but like a man who had been genuinely in search of something— some principle of truth or order in the world: and who had failed in his quest. With a bony finger the medium traced out the houses and planets on his chart, talking of conjunctions and trines. The influence of Saturn caused him considerable anxiety it appeared. He had no fear for the journey while he was at sea—the influences are favourable. But somewhere on land, in the company of others, there was to be an accident. The nature of that accident he could not guess as yet—nor whether it would be fatal. He simply knew it would assist him in his discovery of "The Absolute".

It was an odd word to hear at such a time and place, Baird thought. But then Fearmax, as Hogarth said, was an odd person. To be engaged in a search for The Absolute was, however, a fine medieval conception. He wondered what it could mean!

The Voyage Out

It was some few days before Fearmax emerged from his seclusion; indeed he was not the only one that sunlight persuaded to emerge from the privacy of his cabin. Yet Graecen found the sight of him a little distressing; his nervous habit of pacing the deck, as if he were on the look-out for expected catastrophe; his habit of sitting for long intervals with his head sunk on his breast, of making notes in a leather-bound notebook. His preoccupations seemed to match so little with those of the rest of them that even Miss Dombey was abashed in his presence. He confessed to a slight knowledge of palmistry, and once he took Graecen's hand, without a word, and studied its lines and curves with great attention. "You have a bad heart," he said, and Graecen felt the sudden grip of an icy hand upon his throat. Nothing more.

The Trumans, despite their unprepossessing appearance, turned out to be rather a find. They were not only amusing in their way, but self-sufficient and out to enjoy the journey. Truman, they discovered, played and sang comic songs at the piano in the saloon, and enjoyed nothing better than an audience. He had once been a member of a concert party, he said ("a real proper black coon") and his repertoire was inexhaustible. In particular Baird enjoyed a comic recitation entitled "A Martyr to Chastity", which he produced whenever Miss Dombey was around. The rawness of the jests usually made her run for cover. Indeed they found that the only way to shake off Miss Dombey was to be seen with the Trumans. She could not bear them. An attempt to interest Mr. Truman in the Second Coming had been a failure.

Fearmax, however, seemed already to have established some sort of link. No sooner did he appear on deck than Mrs. Truman nudged her husband with evident excitement. They converged upon him. Did he remember them? He did not. Once, long ago, he had got in touch with Mr. Truman's elder sister at Shrewsbury during a séance. The medium passed his hand over his forehead and muttered something about having met so many people; but he seemed flattered. Mrs. Truman had even read a book of his on the astral self.

On the whole the company was not uncongenial, thought Graecen as he lay in his bunk to take the afternoon nap prescribed for him by London's most fashionable doctors. He had been keeping a diary for the first time in his life and he was propped up by three pillows, his fountain-pen poised over the page on which he was to account for his actions of today. "Account for." There it was again. That hell-fire note, influenced by Miss Dombey's preaching no doubt. He ruffled the pages slowly, reading his own large feminine handwriting with slow pleasure.

"Little enough", he noticed on one page, "have I done to render, as it were, a tidy account of my stewardship on earth, before taking leave of it (the earth). A peculiar sense of emptiness fills me. What am I? What have I been? I can think of little on either score to interest a recording angel. I have been neither good nor bad. The few sins of my grosser nature (Anne, Mrs. Sanguinetti, etc.) would, I am sure, all but cancel out with those few virtues, a quiet life, acts of kindness to friends, etc. I cannot see myself being damned. . . ."

Dimly, above his head, he could hear the piano in the saloon being strummed in the brisk manner affected by Mr. Truman, while that ineffable voice, half-talking, half-singing, uttered the opening phrases of "A Martyr to Chastity":

I'm a martyr to Chastity
I'm a victim of laxity
Damned from the cradle I was.

Graecen read on thoughtfully. "I cannot see myself being damned, nor can I see myself being exalted in any way. What, then, is the spiritual fate of the very ordinary person after death?" What indeed? It seemed to him that in the last few weeks all those questions which have baffled the minds of men, had accumulated round him, importuning him for a solution; or, if not a solution, at least some ratification in his own mind as beliefs. The immortality of the soul? The nature of the Trinity? Was progress an illusion? He had simply nothing to say about any of these things. The diary went on: "In some ways I feel very immature, as I do not seem to have any decided opinions about the basic problems of the day. Or is there a discernible attitude to things visible in my poetry?" He shut his eyes and thought about his poetry; all that could be got out of it was a thin Khayamish hedonism, filtered through Georgian influences. "I suppose", the diary summed up, "that I am rather an unsatisfactory person really."

Graecen turned back further in the diary and glanced at the period of a week before his decision to resign and set out for Cefalû. Tea, dinner and lunch engagements followed hot upon each other's heels. There was almost no thought directed upon himself, upon his own inward workings: "Feel rather low," he saw in one place, "Heart not compensating again." Further down the page he came upon the note: "If Hogarth were not my oldest friend I wonder whether I could tolerate him for a second? Callous. Yet somehow warming."

He grimaced impatiently. This was hardly the kind of literary legacy one should leave behind. He had bought such an expensive diary too—twenty-one shillings. He pictured

himself writing madly as his life drew to an end; the mantic
phrases of some English Rimbaud written on the edge of the
abyss. But Rimbaud was only a child. This reminded him of
his age; it was some time now since he had worried about
getting old—all his energies had been spent in worrying about
keeping alive. Mrs. Sanguinetti had said that his hair was
getting thin at the back. Graecen stood up and tried to verify
this observation in the shaving mirror. It was an impossible
task, however, and he gave it up to return to his bunk. He
sighed and took up his pen again. He would try to write
something simple and honest; he would trust to time to make
it moving. A corner of his tongue showed between his lips as
he started.

"Today was the first lovely day. We are beating down the
coast of Spain." (As an afterthought he deleted the second
verb and replaced it with "sweeping up".) "Some vague
brown cliffs came out of the dawn-haze to greet us; a chapel, a
lighthouse; and one small brown man, with a string of onions
round his neck who waved a minute arm like an insect in
answer to our gestures. The air has suddenly turned warmer
and the weather much clearer though the sea is still rough.
This morning I noticed the girl I spoke of yesterday as seeming
to be ill; I saw her lying in the sun asleep, stretched out in a
deck-chair, her body swathed in a rug. The wind was moving
her thin fair hair on her forehead. As I passed I noticed that a
book lay open on her lap and with my usual bookish curiosity
I stooped down over her shoulder to see what it might be. By
the strangest of strange coincidences it was Greville's *Modern
Poets*, and it lay open at the poem of mine called 'The Winds of
Folly'. One may imagine my surprise, pride and pleasure. It is
so seldom an unknown writer has the fun of seeing someone
read his work. I intended on my second trip round the deck to
speak to her and find out what she thought of it and the other
poems in the book, but when I returned she had gone below.

Never mind. I shall reserve this little conversation for some more propitious moment."

Graecen lit a cigarette, closed his diary, and lay back more comfortably, smoothing the pillows. It was annoying to be ordered to rest every afternoon when you detested it; it was like the prohibition on smoking. The doctor must have known that he could not live without a cigarette. But then if one, why the other? If he disobeyed about smoking, why should he not drop the afternoon siesta? The weather was warm. He would prefer a stroll on deck. Why not? He got up and put on his coat again, and muttering an objurgation against medical men and their works.

On deck it was pleasant enough; the wind was kicking up a sparkling sea, while to the East loomed the capes and inlets of Spain. Graecen saw with pleasure that the girl in the deck-chair was lying asleep in the same place again today. On her lap, too, was the identical book. He approached as stealthily as a hunter to verify it. Yes, Greville's *Modern Poets*. He seated himself on a convenient davit-support and waited until she should wake, studying the soft dark plume of smoke flowing from the funnels and the deep white trench gashed by the progress of the *Europa* through the sea. He felt light of heart all of a sudden. Miss Dale (he had looked up her name on the passenger list) slept with no sign of motion. She hardly seemed to breathe. The wind troubled her soft hair in which shone threads of gold and points of light. She was pretty in a rather watered-down way; her pale skin and soft features seemed to suggest that she was a convalescent. Graecen watched her sleeping and began to spin idle stories in his mind about her.

She had just left Newnham perhaps, where she had been reading literature. She probably wrote poetry herself. Perhaps she had just done a thesis on him for her D.Litt. She would be amazed to look up and see Graecen bending over her; a poet whose work she so much admired. They would be spark to flint. On Majorca they would go for long walks together in that perfect scenery, and she would ask him to help her with a book on Keats she was going to write. They would not be able to part from each other. He would tell her that he was . . . (Her anguish at this Keatsian repetition of things gave him great pleasure to imagine). Quixotically, madly, they would marry in Naples and visit Keats' grave together. Then . . . Then . . . It all became a little misty. The great liner had moved off a couple of points. A bell rang. The patch of sun in which they were was overloomed by the great hind funnel; in the shadow it was rather chilly. Graecen was roused from this pleasurable maze of conjecture by the fact that the girl started to cry in her sleep. Tears welled out from the closed lashes and her mouth puckered at the corners. From time to time she gave a small gasp of pain. Of what could she be dreaming? Terrified that he might shame her if he stayed, he tiptoed away and went down the companionway into the saloon, where the Truman couple were playing vingt-et-un with Baird, while Fearmax sat calmly by them and watched. That night Graecen added, in his diary, an account of Miss Dale's behaviour of the afternoon. He felt interested and sympathetic.

In the end, however, it turned out rather differently. It was Baird who introduced them; and Miss Dale had never been nearer to Newnham than Golder's Green. Graecen was saddened to hear the flattened accent of London's poorer suburbs ring in her voice. She was, it is true, a convalescent; but that is the nearest she got to a resemblance with the girl of his imagination.

Virginia Dale was a shorthand typist at the Ministry of Labour. She lived with her aunt at Golder's Green in a semi-detached house. The doctor had ordered her abroad because she showed signs of being tubercular. "A victim of the unconscious intention," said Campion later, when he heard a recital of her woes. Perhaps this was true. At any rate, it was when Bob, her fiancé, died in an air accident in Greece that Virginia Dale began to lose a hold on the life in which he was to play the part of a deliverer. She could not contemplate going on living with her aunt. She became very ill.

So much was easily told, but what interested Graecen was this: what should such a girl be doing with Greville's *Modern Poets*, in which his work was well represented? He could not approach the subject for a couple of days until he managed to see her alone. Then at last, one afternoon, he saw her lying alone in the deck-chair aft, and brought up the subject.

"The other day", he said, "you were lying there with a book of poems." (Miss Dale blushed scarlet, as if he had said something indecent.) Graecen went on: "You had it open at a poem which I myself wrote. I was so curious to know whether you read poetry for pleasure, or what you were doing with the book." Miss Dale licked her lips and smiled.

"I'm trying to get my school cert.," she said, "in order to get into the post office. You see, in my present work there's no old-age scheme, no pensions, nothing. In the post office, when you get to a certain age, you get a pension." She said it with considerable middle-class pride. "I have no money of my own, you see."

"But, good gracious," said Graecen, both annoyed that he should be taught for the Oxford Locals, and flattered that he should be taught at all. "Good gracious me." He often used expressions he had heard his mother use when he was a child. "So they are learning my verse in order to get jobs in the post office," he told himself angrily. Miss Dale was looking confused.

"I should jolly well hope that a girl like you will get herself sensibly married instead of bothering about the post office," said Graecen gallantly. To his annoyance, this seemed to dispose her to start crying again. He hated tearful women. She

recovered her composure, however, with some effort. Whenever people spoke of marriage it made her remember Bob,
after whose death she felt that her good looks, as well as
whatever little courage she possessed, had gone for ever. As a
matter of fact she remembered reading and re-reading
Graecen's poem with an increasing sense of confusion and
annoyance. Perhaps since he had written it. . . .

"I suppose", she said, "you wouldn't care to help me a bit
with my Litt. paper? I find the poems in that book so difficult."

Was there ever an author who was not flattered by a request
for an explanation? Perhaps. But Graecen was not he. He
enjoyed himself a great deal in reading "The Winds of Folly"
to Miss Dale in his best radio voice. He enjoyed even more
dismantling it for her, showing the syntactical subtleties that
held it together, the interior rhyme, the metrical felicities—in
fact everything that made it one of the duller anthology pieces
of our time. He was flattered at so attentive and modest a
listener, and took Virginia Dale in hand. He not only explained
his own work, but he explained also the work of his contemporaries—some of which he did not understand himself. "It
will not be my fault", he thought, "if the damned girl does not
get a credit in English composition."

They passed the coarse brown rock of Gibraltar and
entered the Mediterranean.

The weather became milder, the air softer. The days of
blueness began.

At Marseilles Campion came aboard with his rucksack and
easel; his arrival was a not unwelcome surprise to Baird, who
noticed that he had aged. "Fancy seeing you," said Campion
coming upon him as he was on his way down to the cabin he
had wangled with the help of a shipping agent.

"You are the last person I expected to see," said Baird, and
accompanied him down to his cabin to help him unpack. "I

wangled it," said Campion crisply, unfastening his rucksack and pulling out a lot of dirty clothes, a tube of toothpaste, and a toothbrush. He proceeded to clean his teeth and explain in little asides how he had managed to get aboard the *Europa* without troubling the purser or registering in the ordinary way. "I'm only going to Crete," he said. "By the way, Baird, it will amuse you to know that I am still attached to the War Graves people. Not content with keeping me busy during the war and preventing me having my head blown off, they are keeping me busy in peace. I've got to paint a row of graves somewhere in Crete where half a score of idiots were interred after a gallant if unwise operation. Farcical, isn't it? But I'm painting like a fiend now. If only I didn't feel so much at the end of everything." He sat down on the edge of the bunk and lit a cigarette. Then he took off his beret and absently combed his hair. "It's like getting farther and farther away from the human race—getting lost. Queer feeling." Baird was interested. Campion whistled a couple of bars of a popular song and looked across at the stack of canvases on stretchers that lay in the corner of the cabin. "It's a dull world to live in," he said at last, as if the impetus to frankness had been succeeded by a reticence more worthy of his listener. "What have you been up to?" he said, peering at Baird's medals. "Campaign medals I see. And the M.C. Well, my dear fellow, I have some campaign medals too. I wore them on the seat of my trousers last Armistice Day and coughed slightly at the Cenotaph during the silence."

One's dislike for Campion was always halted, reflected Baird, by the memory of those innocent powerful paintings. Perhaps an artist was not made to be liked, but to be put up with. Or was it possible to be a great spirit on one plane, and to be at odds with the whole canon of accepted human belief, on another? Or rather, perhaps, was not the work part of the life—a sort of propaganda for it in which one could see the

miserable limitations of the human mind? He did not like
Campion. Did Campion like himself?

"I'm on the edge of something good," Campion was saying.
"Something bigger than I've done to date. And it always
makes one feel ill at ease and anxious. I've felt awful about this
trip—a premonition that something would happen."

He got up abruptly and took his sketch block and a thick
copying pencil. "Let's go up," he said. "I've never seen the
town from the sea."

Graecen was filled with vague alarm at being introduced to
Campion. The little man looked so cold and intense, and was
so articulate; he radiated a kind of power which put one on the
alert. His very glance was critical and divining. One did not
feel quite safe. It was as if the small figure had condensed and
crystallized its essential experiences of men, enabling it to
bring summary judgments to bear upon them. He was mollified, however, by Campion's description of old Conklin as a
moron. The article on *Syrinx* still rankled. "You probably
know the man," said Campion. "I don't but I used to keep a
file of his criticisms—some of the things in it were just unbelievable. I remember once, for example, he began an article
'If Dostoievski had lived today he would be classed as un-
British as well as unstable. The persistent vein of cruelty in his
work makes one fear that he was the kind of man who would
shoot at a fox.' " Graecen laughed politely. He was glad that
Campion found Conklin so third-rate as a critic. He was
flattered when he found that Campion was doing a sketch of
him as he sat reading. The nervous small fingers moved in
spidery fashion over the paper, deft and yet cautious. The eyes
had puckered into slits. Graecen, whose taste in painting and
sculpture was far more dependable than his taste in books or
people, knew and admired Campion's work. He, too, found
himself wondering why so violently unorthodox a man should
produce painting whose innocence and serene power seemed

to be the antithesis of his troubled, obscure and rebellious nature.

That night Campion went to bed early, after taking three aspirins. It was always the same. He was upset at leaving Francesca behind. And yet he made a point of breaking off his relations with the woman of the moment with wounding suddenness. Hardly had the telegram arrived from London when he felt as if a cloud which had been obscuring his vision for weeks was removed. He must leave at once. Marseilles had become stale. He must walk out of the old life once again into the new. There were problems to be resolved. Crete would make an admirable theatre of operations. This decision was so easily, so suddenly made that he wondered why it was necessary for the telegram to come at all. Could he not have thought of it himself? No, life itself was binding: to have a woman or a studio was binding: it needed a jolt from outside sometimes. How should he tell Francesca, who had been his mistress for a year now? In order to assist his own decision to become determination, he walked across the cobbles and tramlines of the Rue Pigalle to where the shipping agent had his offices. The *Europa* would be in that night. It was really a holiday-cruise liner, but it was half empty; for a small consideration he could have a cabin. . . .

Francesca was busy in the kitchen among a litter of pans. He caught sight of her long coltish figure and beautiful legs as he shut the door and threw his beret on the table. She had, he guessed, spent the morning mending his clothes, about which he had made a row yesterday, and in trying to make him the little sesame cakes he had demanded. He sat down, a small and grim figure, at the table and studied the newspaper, reading with great deliberation the account of a murder. It was as if he had no other object in life than to sit there, his lips moving, as he spelt out the unfamiliar French words and let their meaning soak into his brain. "C'est toi, Campyon?" she called musically from the kitchen. He grunted. No one was ever allowed to call him anything but Campion. He laid down the paper and stared with a grave deliberate abstraction at the painting on the wall. It was one of the Arles paintings that Francesca had liked and had insisted on keeping. A peasant seated at the door of a cabin. A tree. It was a complete statement made with the utmost economy, the utmost concentration. What could Francesca like in it? He half-closed his eyes, the better to test the blue of the wall against the shell-pink, almost nacreous tone of the woman's dress. Still sitting thus, he cleared his throat, and said in a definite clear voice. "Francesca, je pars ce soir pour l'Angleterre." She came in to him, all concern, with a dish in her hands. He continued to look at the painting, focusing all his interest on it. She put down the dish and said: "Mais, Campyon." He felt the faintest stirrings of compassion, mixed with an overwhelming disgust. Why the devil did one need women; or needing them, why the devil did one create dependencies that one could not satisfy? "I have to go," he heard himself saying stonily. "Help me pack." She moved across and taking his face between her hands she turned it towards her, fixing her great troubled eyes upon his two stony blue eyes. "Is it true?" she asked. You could never be sure. Campion was always pretending to leave her for ever whenever the evening meal was late. "My mother is dead," said Campion—a remark which he felt was almost irresistibly funny; yet his voice preserved its leaden calmness. "I must leave tonight." For a long moment they stared at one another. Then she bent down and kissed him on the mouth, carefully wiping away the lipstick mark with the corner of her apron. "It is not true," she said slowly and sadly. "It is not true. You are leaving me."

It seemed to him that all his life he had been enacting and re-enacting this scene, in dozens of different languages. Francesca was a charming and a beautiful creature, but she was no easier to shake off than had been the girl in Syria, or the girl in Paris. Or was she? Francesca sat down opposite him and put her chin on her elbows. He turned his gaze back to the painting and began to study it with complete absorption. They sat for a long time thus. Then she burst into tears, which she quickly stifled in the folds of her apron. Campion winced. Now it was coming.

"Why?" she said.

"My mother is dead," he said, suppressing a temptation to giggle.

"Your mother died years ago. You said so."

"I lied."

"Is it because the food was late?"

"No."

"Because I did not mend your sandals?"

"No."

"Is it because you are tired of me?"

"It is because my mother died," said Campion with a freezing dignity. He took out the War Office telegram and laid it on the table. The pose of her head with its long throat was beautiful as she bent down to study it. Francesca was incapable of reading English, so there was no fear that she would realize what was in the telegram. He fell to studying her pose with the same concentration as he had studied the picture on the wall. His eye indulged itself with the sweet firm line of the chin and the broad mouth. She had been a wonderful bedfellow. And an excellent girl to have about the house. Why did he not take her with him? It was not because he was tired of Francesca as a person. It was because he was tired of all women—fed up with the whole race of women he told himself. As for Francesca, if he had met her as he was getting off the boat the other end he would in all probability start all over again with her. She was a fine creature. But he just could not be bothered. As he sat on the uncomfortable wicker chair he felt his freedom oozing away second by second. Why could not women realize that all he wanted of them was their friendship—and their cooking? It was reasonable enough. They considered that by making love with you they had the right to tie you down to a small orbit of domestic life. Campion longed suddenly to become a domestic man—a husband, a father, a churchwarden. Anything to break the monotony of this life of change. But not here; not now; not with Francesca.

He got up suddenly and began to pack while she sat with her face red from the heat of the kitchen stove, crying very softly and repeating to herself in a small voice, "J'comprends pas pourquoi, J'comprends pas pourquoi."

"Oh, shut up," said Campion in his own mind, as he packed his few belongings. His mind was already busy with the thought of escape, escape across the sea to Crete. He had never been to Crete. He stifled a temptation to whistle. Francesca was not making as much of a scene as he had imagined she would; if his attention wandered she might get really angry. Hence it was wiser not to whistle or sing until he was in the street. And yet, how lovely she was; what a beautiful animal with her tawny skin and brown eyes.

When everything was ready, his easel folded, his rucksack full to bursting point, he went in and stood facing her across the table.

"Francesca," he said. "Darling."

She continued her little muffled sobbing. She sat there with a look of preoccupied pain on her features, turned towards the wall. It was as if the hurt that found expression in this muffled whimpering belonged to her alone—had no reference to the Campion that faced her. Pain created its own privacy in her mind, so that she was like a person with a deep toothache, focused on it with such concentration that she could hardly raise her head to answer questions. He laid his small cold hands upon the back of her neck, and softly rubbed the nape, where her dark hair ran down into a little V-shaped peak. This is what one got, he was thinking, for indulging the lust of hand and eye—not to mention the lusts of the mind and body. He wound up his wrist-watch, making little soothing sounds as he did so. "Don't cry, then," he said over and over again. "I shall come back next month. You know I shall come back."

Francesca paid no attention whatsoever to him. She remained sitting on the chair, rocking slightly and whimpering like a spoiled child over a broken toy. Campion took up his beret and dusted it, tightened the thong of his sandal, and hoisted his rucksack on to the table. As he was getting his arms through the straps a sudden gust of compunction passed over him. It was cruel enough to leave her there alone like this; he had, after all, taken her from her family, made her pregnant, detached her from her ordinary life. Her family would never take her back. And she had been a fine mate for him—not like one of those English girls whose reactions to sex were, medically speaking, ear, nose and throat only. Francesca was a nymph compared to so many other women he had loved. He really ought to consider her. But already an obstinate part of his mind had begun insisting that the *Europa* would dock in half an hour, and his agent friend had warned him not to be late. He stood at last, pack on back, bundles in hand, and looked at the girl, who had not moved from the chair though her tears seemed to have abated. She sat with her back to him, hands in her lap, her shoulders round with dejection. What should he say? Campion cleared his throat and then decided that there was nothing very illuminating to be said. He had promised to come back. It was wonderful how women could tell at a glance when one was lying or not. In his pocket there was some loose money—about a thousand francs: quite a lot, in fact. He put it on the table saying: "There, I have left some money to carry on with till I get back. I shall telegraph you from London, Francesca." The girl said nothing. She did not move. She seemed to be in a trance. He moved the door with his hand in order that its creaking should wake her, but it did not. "Good-bye then," he said, with such accents of relief that he was ashamed of the sound of his own voice. "Good-bye." He was down the long staircase in a flash and to the corner of the street. Going down the cobbled side-streets in the direction of the port he began to whistle, filled with an exaggerated sense of freedom and independence. His eyes drank in the streets, their colour and shape, as if they were the eyes of someone newly born. Under his breath he sang:

> *Aux bidets noirs*
> *Gros comme des poires*
> *Du Languedoc, du Languedoc*
> *Les couillons d'un cocu cocu cocu*
> *Tirra lirra lirra bim bim bim . . .*

The Medium

"**M**r. Fearmax?"

Fearmax detached himself from those absorbing preoccupations which kept him for the greater part of the day lying down in his bunk, and turned slowly to find that Campion had entered the cabin. "Yes," he said.

"I learned your name from Baird. I wonder if you can be the same Fearmax who used to give séances in the Euston Road before the war?"

Fearmax fixed a confused eye upon his visitor. Campion went on, with the utmost politeness. "Not that I ever came to any of them, but I saw them advertised in the weeklies; and some time afterwards I read a series of articles in a paper called *The Occult* which seemed to me to be quite extraordinary."

Fearmax made a gesture of the hand and Campion obediently sat down. "Are you the same?" he said.

Fearmax made an attempt to sit up, but his lassitude was too great. He turned, therefore, on his side and rested his head upon one elbow. His voice was hoarse. "I am *the* Olaf Fearmax," he said slowly. "No doubt you've read about my exposure as a common fraud. I wrote those articles and I gave séances in the Euston Road."

Campion said crisply, "My name is Campion. I am a painter. I carried those articles about with me for years. The idea of reality you put forward in them was something for which I owe you a great debt."

Fearmax frowned and then smiled; a polar smile of indifference and apathy. "I'm glad," he said. Campion lit a cigarette. "At the time I read them", he said, "I was coming out of what you call the First Astral State and entering the second. I felt that I knew so clearly what you were talking about, that I wanted to meet you. I wrote you a letter."

Fearmax knitted his brows once more. "One gets so many letters," he said, "I'm sorry if I didn't answer it."

Campion brushed the idea aside summarily. His face had become animated and his eyes sparkled: "The theory of the life-death polarity is something which I've actually proved for myself—in my own life. You remember? That when the death-principle asserts itself in our lives reality itself gets turned inside out, so that instead of being detached from it—watching it happen as an extraneous thing—one begins to manufacture it, like a silkworm manufactures its own cocoon?"

Fearmax sat up and yawned. "I was much younger then," he said. "I thought I was being original. I had not read the Chinese then, or even the medieval people of the Caballa. Did you say you were a painter?"

"Yes," said Campion. "I am putting everything I've got into painting—and yet it is the least part of me." He put his hands upon his knees carefully, cautiously, almost as if to balance himself as he talked of these vertiginous things. "I've followed out the cycle you mentioned," he said, "but I'm beginning to wonder whether your theory covered the whole of experience—or only a part. When one begins, you say, reality is everything that is outside; when the principle of death germinates, first as a conscious idea, then as a fugitive subconscious premonition, finally as something beyond these: when that happens the fundamental *nature of reality* is changed. The individual gets fixed in his destiny and irresistibly begins to manufacture his own personal myth, his reality. Around himself there gradually accumulates a kind of mythological ectoplasm—it informs his acts and his words. The cocoon forms in which his—for want of a better word—immortal self is enshrined. Meanwhile his stance *vis-à-vis* life and society becomes as irrevocably fixed as an atrophied bone. What he does he is *forced* to do by the very nature of his mythopaeic role; like Luther saying, 'Here I stand. *I can do no other.*' " As he said the words Campion threw his arms wide and an expression of pain seemed to settle on his features. Fearmax felt suddenly ten years younger. His eyes cleared and a smile settled upon that harsh mouth, in those eyes in their charred orbits. "How well," he said, "how very well you put it."

Campion went on like a river in spate almost unconscious that he had an audience. "Then it is that you begin to loosen the ties of duty and obligation. If you have been a husband or a lover or a banker you renounce the role in order to withdraw more fully on to the stage of your own personal myth. You condense and refine. And when people you knew come up and take your hand, recalling incidents of ten years back, you wonder if they realize that they are talking to a corpse."

He licked his lips and stubbed out his cigarette on the floor. "Or else", says Fearmax, "you accept dutifully, joyfully, the demands made upon you by obligation, secure that your world is your own even if it is bounded by a nutshell, circumscribed by monogamy or the calendar. Joyfully, Mr. Campion, joyfully. But what has all this to do with painting, may I ask?"

"Exactly," said Campion. "It has nothing to do with it— and everything. Painting by the power of the hand and eye is one thing. Painting with the lust of the soul is quite another. I am spinning a myth about myself in a series of canvases. It is so lucid and clear that it scares me. I am not troubled now by what I might be unable to say. I am troubled by what I shall, unknown to myself, reveal. And yet the process is irresistible. I am forced to separate from people and conditions because, like a leper, I am afraid of infecting them with my own contrived disease."

He got up and walked up and down, striking his knee with a rolled-up newspaper from time to time. Fearmax watched him curiously. It reminded him of his own years of anguish and questioning in Exeter before he found what he thought would become his true métier. There was something very appealing about Campion's fierce and uncompromising forthrightness.

"Sit down," he said slowly. "And if it doesn't bore you I will tell you about my own life. You can compare the experience, not the events, with your own. Perhaps we shall each see more clearly."

Fearmax was a remarkable type of the provincial derailed by wide reading. An orphan, he had spent all the long years of a friendless youth working as a bookseller's assistant in Exeter. His childhood, which was spent behind the rusting iron gates and faded shrubbery of a provincial orphanage, had been remarkable for nothing except a tendency to fits which were diagnosed as epileptic. He was a sickly child, and at the age of thirteen his wards were happy to be rid of him; the special food and treatment recommended for him by a humane district doctor was something that did not come into the terms of reference under which the institution worked. He suffered, indeed, not from any marked cruelty on the part of the guardians as from the neglect inseparable from the routine of all institutions. He never smiled during his childhood; the fact was borne upon him one day when he caught sight of his face in the long mirror of a Hastings hotel, after one of his early triumphs as a medium. He saw his face—parched and pale from those years of concentrated reading—twisted into a wolfish grin. It was a smile—a simulacrum of happiness—that he saw trying to break through the armature of lean skin and bone which was his face.

At thirteen the bookseller's shop seemed an exciting place. The only book he had seen was the institution Bible, which was kept chained to a wooden eagle in the chapel, and out of which the Rev. Dohgerty read the children pejorative and declamatory extracts on Sunday. His voice raged like a toothache across the visions of John or the fearful lists of prohibitions shored up in Leviticus. They did not understand, but they trembled.

The bookshop was different. There were books full of drawings and engravings, books on history and science, on topography; there were children's books and novels in bright wrappers. The bookseller was a kindly fattish man who disguised a sense of failure and depression, in a false Pickwickian benevolence and loquacity. He was kind to the boy, found him lodgings, trained him in the trade, and occasionally saw to it that he had somewhere to go on holidays and at Christmas. Fearmax was in heaven. Though he was so poor that his wages only just covered his board and lodging, the freedom of this new life stimulated him. He had no friends, but he had the streets of the town to explore, and as many books as he wished to read at his elbow. For five years he was contented with life; but by the time he had turned eighteen the restlessness of a delayed adolescence began to take possession of him. Was he to spend the whole of his life as a bookseller's assistant in a provincial town? And yet he had no hopes, no plans, no shadow of a programme for a new life to replace this one which offered, it is true, few material difficulties. To a great degree it was the reading that had been responsible for this; his mind had begun to lead him down strange by-paths of literature, strange back-alleys of thought and speculation; tiring quickly of novels and romances, he had begun to feed upon the out-of-the-way, the speculative, the occult. Indeed, by the time he was twenty-one his reading was immense though sporadic. He had created around himself a jungle of ill-cultivated plants—philosophies, with their weird blooms and stunted systems, like Christian Science or Theosophy. It was a disinterested hunger for some illuminating text which would explain not only the mystery of the world around him, but also his existence in it. What was he doing on earth? Since he had no friends to ask these questions of, there remained only the dusty attics of the shop. Surely there among the thousand books there might be some product of illumination and reason mixed which would put him into focus with himself. It was at this time that he began to be conscious that he was lonely. All these years he had not recognized the numb anaesthetic feeling that filled so much of his life with an unexpressed—indeed an inarticulate—anguish. He walked about most of the night through the rainy streets of the town wrapped in his old policeman's cape and hood, absently trying empty cigarette-machines in shop-doors, or studying his own features reflected in the windows of shops. So great was the singleness of mind that moved him, that he never thought of wanting either money or a woman. His book-filled dusty lodging differed from his book-filled dusty office only in that it contained a hip-bath, a chamber-pot and an iron bedstead. Rising at five, he would sluice his lean body with the icy water from the jug, and be already taking down the shutters of the shop by seven o'clock, winter and summer. In his work he was punctual, diligent and uncommunicative. But every spare moment of his time was spent at the little desk under the grimy window, reading. He travelled into Tibet with Huc and Gabet; he tried to solve the puzzle of the Inca stone alphabet with Fédor; Froebenius excited him by his records of customs and parables; the raw images of Nostradamus assuaged and tantalized him with their beauties and half-concealed promises; the *incunabula*, the prophetic books, the books of ritual—everything promised, and everything disappointed. He sat absolutely motionless on his three-legged stool, his rounded shoulders letting his head rest upon the thin shank of an arm in its frayed cuffs, and read until he was dizzy. "Why", said the bookseller one day, "are you reading so much? You don't seem to enjoy it. It's like you are studying for an exam. Books are for pleasure, you know." The remark struck him. A pleasure! Did he get any pleasure, in the strict meaning of the term, from them? Did he, if it came to that, understand exactly what the word meant? What was pleasure? He read like a hungry animal. By his thirtieth year he seemed to have become a charnel house of blasted hopes and other men's writings. What was he searching for? Neither pleasure nor instruction or even illumination seemed to be at the back of this hunger—but something that should combine, should synthesize all three; neither truth nor beauty, but a Something which would offer him a foothold. Something which would bridge the gap between the universe of light and matter, and the small circumscribed universe of the world he lived in—two book-filled rooms linked by streets ghostly with rain and mist.

It was at this time that the old Methodist preacher took to calling at the shop for books. Fearmax would hear the stairs creak under his heavy frame, and the rap of his wooden leg on the linoleum of the top landing. He would put his book away and wait for the door to open and admit the portly, silver-haired figure. Snowden was a strange choleric old man, but an excellent buyer. He would stand leaning on his stick and look across at Fearmax in silence for a moment, while he took out his silver snuff-box and grabbed up a pinch in his knotted rheumatism-twisted finger and thumb. "I want *everything* on the following subjects," he would announce, consulting a list taken from his waistcoat-pocket. He seemed to have plenty of money, and was able to buy himself complete sets of the books he wanted, without any hesitation. He too, seemed filled with a wayward discontent that impressed Fearmax as bearing a likeness to his own. "Young man," he said once, "you no doubt think me mad. I am not buying books for a library. I read them. Yes, even the 'Golden Bough' and suchlike dullness. Reading is like a worm in the marrow." He came a few steps nearer, peering at the younger man through his light blue, innocent old eyes. "A worm in the marrow," he repeated in a whisper. Fearmax put a chair for him, and taking his list from his hand, ran up a ladder and started to hunt. As usual there were out-of-the-way things. Budge's "Egyptian Book of the Dead", Evans-Wentz, Férier's pamphlet on the Hero Cult, Pamfrey on Prayer, Donne's Sermons. The old man in the chair suddenly began to talk. "You will be thinking", he said, "that it's my faith I've lost, hunting in all these books. Yes, and you won't be wrong. After fifty years in the Ministry too, and me surely near the edge of the grave." Fearmax turned round on his ladder and gazed at him with his mouth open. Snowden seemed half-asleep. His hair twinkled in silver points as the faint rays of spring sunlight touched it. He smiled.

"Here we are, in our old age, suddenly woken up with the feeling that there is something wrong. Suddenly it seems as if a whole tract of knowledge had been withheld from me; knowledge of the ordinary secular affairs of men. After all, what am I? What have I been preaching all these years? I am a doctor of souls, am I not? And therefore a specialist in sin? And do I know what sin is? Have I explored it? Have I entered into the real world at any point and transformed it, so that what I have is my own by right of experience, and not an algebraic incantation taught me when I was a child? These are the questions you'll come to one day—I hope before you reach my age." He stood up and tapped his way to the foot of the ladder. "Have you ever seen a Minister of God who discovered one day that prayer is useless?" he asked in a surprisingly gentle and naïve voice. "Look upon him. Useless. Useless." Fearmax came gently down his ladder with the books under his arm. He was too astonished to speak.

Snowden took them from him and examined the titles slowly and with care. Then he tapped his way downstairs again to pay for them, without saying good-bye. Some weeks later his death was announced in the paper. The obituary notice told Fearmax only that his wife had died the year before, and that he had been living in retirement in a country cottage outside the town.

It was at this period too that his own life took a turn for the better. During a sleepless summer night, when he was thirty-eight, his hand took up a pencil and began to write, he knew not what, in the margin of a book. In the morning he suddenly felt as he awoke that he had been granted, after all these years of searching, an outlet, a gift, a skill of his own.

The phenomenon of automatic writing he had read about; and had not believed in it, except as a form of wilful auto-intoxication. Yet he saw, with numb apprehension one night, that his hand, without dictation, was writing upon the flyleaf and margins of Isaac's *Bookseller* a series of disconnected words and phrases. He had been particularly tired that day, having made a bus journey to the country to buy up a collection of books belonging to a deceased lawyer. The next day and the next there was no sign on the part of his hand to perform anything beyond its normally dictated functions. But he put a writing-pad and pencil beside his bed, and on the third day found the phenomenon repeated. He began to write fluently and copiously in the notebook; and what he wrote made sense. It was a long, rather disjointed message from a woman to her husband. He puzzled over it all that day. It was not written in his own handwriting, yet in a hand that was quite consistent and well-formed.

Fearmax experimented for several weeks before submitting his work to a neighbouring bookseller, who was a medium, together with a request for his advice. He was encouraged to renew his experiments and he did so gladly, with the wonderful feeling of someone who has found his true place in life. The fruit of these months is to be found in that little pamphlet now a bibliographical rarity, "New Essays by Goldsmith". His heart had become lighter, his intelligence more alert. He began to attend the local psychic society which met every month, and whose members busied themselves with automatic writing, planchette-messages, and séances given by visiting mediums; it was during one of the latter performances that Fearmax surprised his hosts by falling into a deep sleep, preceded by a sort of seizure, in the course of which he found himself transmitting feverishly for a spirit guide called "French Marie". Yes, her name should be familiar. It was she, the reader will remember, who predicted not only the date of Edward's Abdication, but also the exact date and cause of the outbreak of war, among other things.

Her first message was of no particular importance save that it gave Fearmax exactly the focus he needed for all his nervous energy. His mind began to play upon these studies like a burning-glass. He found that concentration and solitude had given a remarkable command over himself, so that it was not long before he could induce the trance at will, and establish contact with the disembodied voice whose messages were to become of such interest to the public at large.

It was not long before his growing fame made it possible for him to free himself from the irksome hold of the bookshop. He travelled across England, giving lectures and séances by invitation in many towns. Wherever he went "French Marie" obediently followed, and as obediently answered his questions, however trivial. There was only one unaccountable failure and that was at Hastings. "French Marie" refused to appear, but sent instead an unsatisfactory deputy called "Raja Patma", who informed him that "French Marie" could not stand the town ever since she spent her earthly honeymoon there. Fearmax, however, had developed into an impressive lecturer. He had studiously modelled his accent on that of the B.B.C. announcers, he had bought himself a velvet cape with a scarlet neck-cord, he had combed his already greying hair back across his head. His confidence in himself (a commodity the absence of which he had been unaware of) grew with every success. His energies were drained off once and for all from the stagnant reaches of aimless reading and speculation. To do him full justice it must be added that he felt for the first time that he had discovered the meaning of the lifelong tendency towards epilepsy. Surely it must have been the magnetic flow of this remarkable gift speaking to him across the dam of books he had erected to hem it in? His health improved with his self-assurance.

"Mr. Olaf Fearmax, the Exeter Medium." The Press backed him up, printing almost every one of "French Marie's" prophecies concerning Derby Winners, Conflagrations, Stock Exchange Slumps. Fearmax was tested by the Royal Society for Occult Studies and emerged unscathed despite his nervousness about the appearance of "French Marie". But the spirit guide was in first-class form. "French Marie" not only transmitted messages from Edward Gibbon and Ramon Novarro to such of their descendants as might still be living; she also left the "materializations" of her plump hands with unerring accuracy in bubbles of liquid paraffin.

Walking across London afterwards, towards the Gray's Inn Road where he lived (he had recently leased a small flat of his own there) Fearmax felt that all his ambitions had been realized. There was nothing more to strive for—except perhaps to preserve his nervous equilibrium under the strain of repeated séances. But he had a mission.

It was some time before the implications of that work began to hold any meaning for him; it came gradually at first—the dawning realization that "French Marie" and the terms under which she chose to present herself to the world, constituted a commentary on the nature of reality itself. What *was* a materialization? If there were flesh enough for her to be able to imprint it in paraffin, how was it that the hand he so often felt upon his shoulder should not possess bone and muscle enough to be touched, to be held? How was it that she could sometimes appear in the dim red light of the séance room—a stout, good-looking youngish woman, dressed in flowing evening dresses, and with her hands gathered in front of her, below the heart, after the manner of opera singers? How was it? Why could she not step down one day out of her dimension, rich in the knowledge of both worlds, and be his partner in this? He smiled dryly as he turned from the thought of other urgent considerations. There was his American tour. Would "French Marie" cross the Atlantic for the benefit of the citizens of Chicago and Detroit? Or perhaps, like some French wines, she "did not travel"? Sitting late over a glass of hot milk an idea came to him.

The next day he was to conduct some private experiments on behalf of a young doctor, Edward Grew, who was very much interested in the physiological and psychological changes which came about during trance conditions. He would ask "French Marie" to send him her black kitten—the kitten without which, it seemed, she could hardly get through the great cycle of development in the spirit world. Fearmax was not surprised to feel the warm furry body of a kitten on his knee as he spoke the next day, but he was surprised when, according to plan, Grew broke his trance and showed him what was to all intents and purposes a *real* black kitten. The sweat started out among the sparse grey hairs on his scalp. Something had gone wrong, though whether his evil intention or "French Marie's" carelessness was to blame, they did not know. For several days after that Fearmax was bothered by a phenomenon he had hitherto not experienced; it was a noise, as of a window flying open above his head, and a voice starting to speak before being choked into a whisper; no actual word was articulated, but the sound that came from an invisible throat was obviously made of air propelled through a larynx. This happened several times, often in public places.

Nobody but himself seemed to hear it. And during this time it seemed quite impossible to get in touch with the spirit-guide. Meanwhile the "materialized" kitten was carried off to the laboratory of Grew, who examined it and professed it to be a real live kitten. What could all this mean?

The following Sunday "French Marie" re-established contact and appeared to be in a great state of emotion. Her kitten, she said, had "slipped". She could not live without it. She must have it back. She was incoherent with grief. That night Grew and Fearmax chloroformed the kitten and buried it in the garden, and for some time things went on as before. "French Marie" not only crossed the Atlantic, she "sent" the audiences which awaited her the other side.

But this was not to last for ever. After several lucrative years of practice Fearmax noticed that his spirit-guide began to be less dependable. Several times she failed him altogether and he found himself floundering in a shoal of inferior transmitters. He also became anxious about her, for a certain valedictory note appeared in her messages. "It won't be long," she said once: and "I shall be gone when you get here": and "can't talk much longer." It was alarming, for "French Marie" was very much more than a source of income; she had become as familiar as a wife or a child. He tuned in (if one may use the language of radio) to her transmissions with the certainty of a listener to a familiar station. He crossed the shoals and eddies of inferior voices clamouring for his attention, as an express train crosses points, to reach her. What would he do without her?

He broke down twice at Maidstone, once at Leeds, and once in London. Then one day "French Marie" said a tearful and final good-bye and went out like a light. It was during a private séance given for some close friends, and the medium threw himself on his knees, clasping his hands together and called out to her in great anguish not to leave him. She was the first woman to whom he had ever made a declaration of love, and it remained unanswered. He was bitterly humiliated; and found that not only had the spirit vanished, but also the faculty for inducing the seizure which preceded the trance. His gift, it seemed, had gone.

He retired to the house of an admirer in Cornwall, to rest and re-equip himself for further experiment. He felt the loss of "French Marie" almost as much as if she had been a mistress of his; so deeply, in fact, that when one day he opened a newspaper and found that a fellow-medium called Carpenter claimed to have transmitted messages from a "French Marie", he found himself seized by a paroxysm of jealousy so bitter that he could not speak. He was like a wild man. His friends feared for his reason. He walked about on the Cornish cliffs in the thunderstorms of winter, dragging behind him the sodden folds of his enchanter's cloak, talking to himself. What was to be done?

He sought Carpenter out in the East End. The latter was a tall, spindly old man with a bald head, an expression of extreme benevolence, an unctuous delivery, and a bad police-court record. He had been imprisoned three times for fraud. He closed one eye hard, as if he were taking aim down the barrel of a gun, and stared at Fearmax unwinkingly out of the other. What did he want with his questions about "French Marie"? After some reassurance he produced his records of a séance in which "French Marie" had appeared with messages. Fearmax read the shorthand notes with the jealousy growing in him; it was like recognizing a familiar prose style. "French Marie's" signature was written all over the communication. He went home in a trance—not a professional trance, but a brown study, wondering what it could all mean. A week later Carpenter was killed in a motor accident.

Fearmax combed the psychic Press for any other references to "French Marie", but it seemed that but for this faithless transfer of her affections, she had really been carried on to a new cycle of development. There was a spirit-guide called "Bonny Mary" among the repertoire of an Edinburgh medium called Alastair, but she was an irregular and inferior transmitter; no shorthand notes of séances were kept by Alastair, but a scrapbook indicated that her appearance had been contemporaneous with that of "French Marie". The subject lapsed, and Fearmax was free to continue his life of concentrated meditation. He suffered a good deal from insomnia, and once he heard the disturbing noise of the invisible window flying open above his head. But no voice followed—not even the ghost of a voice that he had identified with "French Marie". He felt, however, as if it had been a last desperate attempt to get in touch with him before her astral self was propelled beyond all reach upon the giant stairway of development. What was going to happen to him?

The following summer he had another of the seizures which preceded the trance-condition. But it came of its own accord, was not self-induced, and gave him little promise for the future. The spirit-guides he encountered, too, were of the most ordinary kind—inaccurate, fretful, or simply illiterate. It was humiliating for a medium of his standing to find himself in such an impasse; but Fearmax spent these months reading and writing, opening up correspondences with experts in the various fields, and contributing to the psychic Press on the general implications which lay behind a study of the occult. Some of these productions were far and away above the ordinary ill-digested theories and contentions of the medium class. His immense reading had given him powers of comparison and a range of self-expression denied to his brothers in the craft. It was now that he published the short series of articles which had struck Campion so forcibly. His essay on Lully, and his monograph on the theory of Healing as described in Paracelsus, are, of course, fairly well known to readers interested in the problems they outline. Indeed, Fearmax was well on the way to becoming a natural philosopher of sorts; yet the question of a profession was beginning to irk him. He had become affluent during his term of practice. He was living on capital.

How Hogarth's name cropped up, it is not very clear. It was probably Grew who suggested one day that he try a consulting analyst. At any rate, he found himself in the little room where Baird had found so much to think about and so much to say; Fearmax had not the faintest idea what was expected of him. "I am a medium who has lost his gift," he said simply to Hogarth, almost as if he expected the doctor to produce a packet of pills which would set the matter right. Hogarth, who knew something of automatic writing and kindred subjects, soon had him on to familiar ground. What ensued was more a dialectical battle than an analysis. For once he had found someone as widely read as himself; their conversations developed in volume and content until they sounded (played back on Hogarth's dictaphone) like the thunderous off-stage exchanges of Nietzsches. Hogarth always recorded his cases on wax, whenever his interest in the case showed him good cause. Fearmax was not sorry to be so honoured. The conversations with Hogarth were a milestone in his life. He learned valuable things. Probably the most valuable of them all was Hogarth's theory of nervous stress, and his precepts about activity as a form of automatic repose—"sweeping assumptions", "vague generalizations", said the Sunday papers of the time. It was Hogarth who taught him to face the thought that he might never be a medium again. There was only one secret he kept—or tried to keep. Here again, of course, he might have known that Hogarth would take the trouble to keep a check on him. Shortly after the death of Carpenter and the examination of the messages transmitted through the egregious Alastair, Fearmax had succumbed to the temptation of fraud. Never having been one, and being interested in the polemics surrounding the whole question of mediumship as a fraudulent profession, he undertook what he described to himself privately as an experiment. He agreed to give a séance, together with three other mediums, to the general public. Looking back on it, in the light of Hogarth's logic, it seemed to him that perhaps it had been something like an act of desperation. Who knows? His true gift might have awakened. He might not have needed recourse to rubber gloves, moving tables, gramophone records and the like. His choice of Edinburgh, too, was unlucky, for the police had been conducting investigations into the private life of a medium called Pons, who was also to give a demonstration of his powers that evening. The whole incident was very sad. Police were present, an infra-red camera recorded Fearmax's sleights-of-hand with blasting fidelity. He found himself in the dock with the other mediums, charged under the Witchcraft Act of 1735. Only his previous record enabled him to escape a prison sentence by the payment of a large fine. . . . Hogarth threw the copy of *Psychic News* containing a record of the case across the table at him one day. Why, he asked, with asperity, had Fearmax never mentioned this discreditable episode? Why indeed?

But if Hogarth prepared Fearmax to renounce his gift with a good grace, he also showed great curiosity as to the nature of the trance-condition, and even encouraged the medium to give two or three séances for friends, despite the uncertainty of reception. Hogarth listened solemnly to the ridiculous gibberish of inferior spirits, and asked very firmly for some contact to be made with his wife—without effect. Fearmax had sunk, it seemed, to the rank of third-class medium; he could not induce the preliminary seizure at will; his spirit-guides were either tongue-tied or frivolous; he could not guarantee a séance at all, in fact. It was, professionally speaking, no use at all.

"French Marie"—the only woman he had ever really loved —had gone, and with her his esteem among the general. There remained only the whole unbeaten jungle of the occult for a province of study.

During the war Fearmax had gone into a strict retreat of atonement for the sin of war, together with a few friends. They had spent their time in Cornwall obstructing the war-effort, answering foolish questions at C.O. Boards, and working vaguely on the land to the intense annoyance of their employers. During this time he founded the group which afterwards came to be known as the Astrophysical Believers. There is not room to go into the philosophy propounded by its founder, but the society flourished and had continued to grow. It had lecture rooms in the Euston Road, and a small publishing house of its own, through which the official propaganda of the body was conducted. It was to this society that Fearmax turned during the period of his analysis by Hogarth, devoting nearly all his spare time to elaborating his Swedenborgian system, and clearing up the obscurer points in a series of extremely well-written pamphlets. It was something to do. The system demanded an immense amount of elaboration: it professed to bring the whole body of occult thought (even branches like palmistry, alchemy, and astrology) into line with the latest metaphysical ideas of the age. Its existence served as a perpetual irritant to Professor Joad. It was attacked by Ouspensky, Hotchkiss, Eustace Pfoff, and Joseph G. Sthyker, the exponent of Dynamic Massage, as well as the Rudolf Steiner Society. It prospered so greatly that even the Baconian Society attacked it. Fearmax felt that he was making up for lost ground. Perhaps he was to be a new Blavatsky or Krishnamurti.

"As one crank to another," said Hogarth one day, "why don't you go abroad and give the whole thing a rest?"

The idea was echoed by the inner circle of the Believers.

The one outstanding metaphysical account that remained to be settled was with the Society of the Great Pyramid. Their publications were beginning to disturb the Believers with their implications. Someone should visit the Pyramids, make independent observations, and fit them into the general scheme.

"Whether you believe the world is an egg or an onion," said Hogarth, "it doesn't matter. The point is that you are run down, and you will suddenly start going off your rocker unless you take a rest."

Fearmax had aged a great deal. "Hogarth," he said, "if I don't return . . ." Hogarth snorted. "No. I'm serious," said Fearmax, "quite serious. I've seen something here." He held out his wrinkled palm. Hogarth looked at it through the huge magnifying glass. "It's probably a love affair. You'll probably meet 'French Marie' on the boat-train and elope with her."

Fearmax winced and put his hand back in his pocket. He did not refer to the subject again, but at the end of the week he informed Hogarth that he planned to leave towards the end of the month. Hogarth congratulated him. To tell the truth he was getting rather bored with Fearmax. He had been a most useful case to treat because of his professional pursuits. Fearmax would, in the long run, have to work out his own destiny.

Campion listened with intense concentration to this recital of Fearmax's life. His eyes never moved from the face of the elder man, and he never attempted to smile at any of the half-humorous asides of the medium. He seemed to find the story quite absorbing. It seemed in some way to bear comparison with his own experience, but he did not say how, or to what degree. He simply smoked in silence and, when Fearmax had finished, stayed gazing at the floor in an abstracted sort of way.

Fearmax felt tired and yet proud of himself, to be able to drag out these torn susceptibilities and old memories so fluently before a stranger—a non-professional stranger, that is.

It was something that Hogarth had made possible—an estimate of his life and work in objective terms. He was filled with gratitude suddenly for the absent Hogarth, who had so patiently endured his growing pains, his faults, his lapses.

"And you expect to get some further bearing on reality from the Great Pyramid?" said Campion with the faintest note of cynicism.

"Let me put it this way," said Fearmax. "To endeavour to reduce the universe to a system is one thing. To maintain that system as anything but a personal view is another. If I seem touchy or slightly ashamed of some of the things I say it is not because I don't believe in them. They are valid for me; but I have the horrifying knowledge that several hundred men and women have become my disciples, and accept my view of the world as right for them, without bothering to think for themselves along original lines. In the final analysis the Great Pyramid will give me only what I set out to find in it. It is unlikely that it will conflict with the general theories I have erected into a philosophy; if it did, I should probably neglect those elements quite unconsciously, and find myself selecting others. But it's the disciples that bother me. Tell me, as a painter, have you ever influenced enough people to find a school growing up devoted to your *manner*?"

"Yes," said Campion.

"It is horrible, is it not?"

"Yes."

"A total disregard for the experience, the struggle, the what-not, that lies behind every new step in technique, of expression. Well, what ails me is that my own original man, the suffering part, is prevented from growing by the dead weight of discipleship."

"Why don't you shake it off? Renounce it?"

"Why don't I? I ask myself. I don't."

"There are things one can't." Campion was thinking now

of Francesca. She would be looking out of the window and weeping. If he could eliminate women from his scheme of things how smooth everything would be. Fearmax was saying softly, "I'm not sure that the weakness, the corruption of one's doctrine, if you like, isn't necessary. After all, what one discovers one must unload—the imperative is inflexible."

Yes, there was the rub. "Here I stand. I can do no other." Campion lit another cigarette and, taking leave of Fearmax, sauntered on deck. A fierce competition in deck quoits was going on. Mrs. Truman was winning. In the lee of a ventilator Graecen was doing his bit towards the post office career of Miss Dale.

"It's more than just melody," he was saying. "It's form too. Now, you just compare this one with John Gilpin."

Baird was lying flat on his back with a pipe between his teeth. He was asleep.

"Come on, Mother," said Campion to Mrs. Truman. "Time to do your pitcher." He had immediately struck a chord of sympathy with the Trumans, immediately adopted something of Truman's own benevolent attitude towards her. He saw her almost as soon as he boarded the *Europa*, a fine-looking woman with a grave and noble head in repose. He had noticed her standing at the rail—her hair lifted from the side of her head by the wind to disclose small well-shaped ears, a cigarette in her mouth. Later at dinner their eyes had met in one of those unspeaking, spontaneous recognitions upon which the inner erotic world of each of us is built. Elsie Truman was beautiful. Later he had joined the little circle of pontoon-players and had met her husband. Truman was warm and friendly. They found Campion capital company, and when the sea became calm, he dragged his little folding easel and paints on deck, and promised to paint her portrait.

"Wait," said Mrs. Truman. "I ought to do my 'air."

"Do your 'air nothing," said Campion. "Come and sit down

here." At the stern of the ship was a great locker brimming with coils of rope. It was comfortable enough, and dazzling light was broken by the awning into patches of lemon-yellow, green, mauve. Campion looked at her as she moved about with a detached, yet rather greedy eye. It was a magnificent head. He could have broken it off and walked away with it under his arm. He took her chin and tilted it until the firm line of flesh from the high cheekbones was thrown in shadow. "Now," he said with stern compressed lips. "Stay like that."

"Mind you make it like me," said Mrs. Truman. "You're not one of them modern painters are you?" Campion grunted. He was squeezing paint on to his palette and setting up his stretched canvas.

"And make me young," said Mrs. Truman.

"You're young enough," he said, still busy, his mind working on ways and means. It was like watching a dentist sterilize his equipment. "A Hecuba," he said, and at last stood up. He was looking at her now as if she were a lump of inanimate matter; it was a glance in which was mixed some of his mind's delight in the smooth lines of the chin and mouth.

"So you want a likeness?" he said grimly, in a faraway voice. "I wonder if you've ever seen yourself?"

Mrs. Truman was startled out of her self-possession. She blushed. "The face of a great courtesan," said Campion, more to himself than to anyone else. He had put a brush between his teeth now and was drawing in soft pencil on the canvas.

"I suppose you know all about them," said Mrs. Truman, uncomfortably aware that under the badinage there might lie observations of some interest. Campion seemed to be breaking up her face into small fragments. It was no longer a synthesis —an entity called Mrs. Truman—which faced him, but a series of plastic forms and planes. It was a disturbing scrutiny. She became aware that her nose was unpowdered ("Stop

squinting," said Campion peremptorily), and that the spot on
her lip looked awful.

"A courtesan," repeated Campion. "Now if you'd lived in
the south there might have been scope for your talents."

Mrs. Truman moistened her lips and said nothing. Campion
mixed smears of paint on to his palette, lit a cigarette, leaving
it balanced upon a stanchion and said: "I had a girl who
looked like you when I was an undergraduate. She was jolly
and rough—like a blast of hot air from a tube-station. But she
couldn't make love."

"Must have come from Scotland," she said.

"She came from Leeds."

"It's a libel," said Mrs. Truman, scratching one ankle with
the sole of her shoe.

"It wasn't till I met a Rumanian girl in Paris that I discovered the fact," admitted Campion. He was talking in order
to see the fugitive expressions of interest and amusement flit
across his sitter's face. "Her name was Lola."

"Exotic," suggested Mrs. Truman.

"She was an awful slut really. She lay in bed all day eating
chocolates with soft centres and reading novels; but she
hummed like a top in the evening."

"So Leeds girls don't hum, eh?" said Mrs. Truman, with
good-natured amusement. "Better ask my husband. He knows
Leeds."

"You're moving," said Campion with a sigh, waking up
from his trance and staring at her bad-temperedly. She
apologized and made an attempt to freeze back into her
original pose. Campion moved her head back, holding it by
the nose. "There," he said.

"I hope", said Mrs. Truman, "that you don't make me look
like Lola. My husband is old-fashioned, you know."

"Don't you want a likeness?" said Campion ironically. But
now he had sunk back into his concentration. He had begun

to build up the portrait in a series of blocks of colour. His small fingers gripped the tall brushes tightly, with a nervous energy, as if he were afraid of dropping them. They reminded Mrs. Truman of the claws of a bird. From time to time he whistled to himself softly, or paused to drag at his cigarette.

After half an hour he allowed her a rest, and they sat together smoking and looking at the vague series of blobs on the canvas. "It looks like a street scene in Barcelona," she said. "Here's the fire brigade, and there's the main street."

"That, my good woman, is your nose emerging."

"Bright brown?"

"A scorbutic tendency which is due to being unable to sit still without fidgeting for a second."

"Well, I never," said Mrs. Truman. She retired for a minute to powder it.

When she emerged on deck again Campion had started in on the painting without her. She threw away her cigarette and sat down again in the required pose. "Tell me," she said, "how do artists happen?" It was a question that had occurred to her as she examined her face in the smoky little mirror of the cabin.

Campion was as far away as ever now. "Do you really want to know? Or are you wasting my time?"

She pursed her lips and shook her head. Campion painted on in silence for a moment. "It's easy," he said at last. "When they're babies you drop them on their heads or neglect them, so they are driven to try and recapture something; so they learn a skill; then those as are bad artists are content to go on copying Nature, while those as are good—something funny happens to them."

"What?" she said. Under his lightness she felt as if there were something else, something profound perhaps.

"They begin to make love to the object."

"How?"

"In paint. This face of yours is so lovely. I am in a sort of inner sense making love to it with every brush-stroke. You can't have a purer love than that can you? Which probably explains why I am so unprincipled in my private life. But this is far deeper than just sleeping with you."

Mrs. Truman blushed crimson. Campion went on painting, apparently unaware that he had said anything to disturb her. His hands moved quickly, mixing the paint, and applying light dabs of it to the rough hollow canvas. Indeed, she suddenly had a suffocating feeling of self-consciousness, as if indeed each brush-stroke were a soft kiss, an endearment. After the session was over she went down to her cabin once more and stared at her own features in the glass. She could dimly locate its familiar qualities—good-humour, honesty, ingenuity. Was beauty among those qualities, and, if so, in what did it lie?

Her husband, who was lying in his bunk with a newspaper, turned a quizzical eye upon her. "I see," he said, "getting vain, eh? You'll be heading for Hollywood next."

Mrs. Truman sat down beside him and asked in her most serious tone: "Would you say I was beautiful? I mean *beautiful*—the word."

Her husband went on with his reading, absently patting her shoulder. "Yes," he said vaguely. "Of course." Mrs. Truman got up with dignity. "You don't have to tell me lies, you don't," she said, and went on deck. Campion and Graecen were smoking over the painting. "Of course," Campion was saying, "if you get the massive butt of the nose, the sort of way the root thickens into the frontal bone, the whole face falls into shape."

She turned away disappointedly and strolled forward to her favourite place on A deck. They spoke as if her face were something quite separate from herself, something that was completely detached; not as if it were a personal instrument on which she registered her moods and graces. Elsie Truman looked out over the calm sea, to where the snow-capped mountains of the Peloponnesus glowed in the azure sky. Flying fish exploded in flashing beads of light at the passage of the *Europa* through the still sea; farther away a dolphin jumped into the air and disappeared again, leaving a black blot like an ink-stain. Tonight they would make the Piraeus. Tomorrow Crete.

They had yet to hear of the labyrinth.

The Labyrinth

The visit to Athens, so proudly announced on the agenda of the company, was a hollow boast. There really was not time to include Greece proper in the tour; and yet the advertising department thought that the existence of the name, both on the charts and in the text, was a well-justified inclusion. Thus it was that the *Europa* sailed round the Peloponnesus to the Piraeus, arriving there at dusk, and setting sail once more in the small hours for Crete. By straining both logic and every nerve the passengers might visit the Acropolis, but few bothered.

The halt at Piraeus, however, served one useful purpose. It enabled one of the Jannadis brothers to board the *Europa* with a notice for the green baize board in the dining saloon.

"The Labyrinth of Crete," read Graecen with curiosity that night as he came down to dinner. "Famous from ancient times, the discoveries of a famous archaeologist have once more been made available to the general public, thanks to the enterprise of Jannadis Brothers of Athens. From the quay passengers will please to proceed in cars arranged by Jannadis Cretan office to the labyrinth in charge of a qualified guide. Whole journey costing 780 drachmas. Please place your name underneath if you wish."

The Jannadis Brothers had received a large part of their business education in America. Farther down in a heavy display type were the words "TERRIFIC . LEGENDARY . HEART-THROBBING . ASTOUNDING . WHOOPEEE".

"That rather sums it up," said Baird, who was looking over his shoulder. "Shall we go?"

Graecen thought for a moment. It would certainly carry them as far as Cefalù, their destination. It would also give him a chance to see the city of the rock before he called on its discoverer. The idea was perhaps a good one. "Perhaps", said Baird, "Axelos would like to show us his discovery himself. It might be a *gaffe* to see it without him."

Graecen pursed his lips and shook his head. He did not think so at all. Taking out his fountain-pen he wrote his name neatly at the head of the list. "Shall I put yours?" he asked. Baird thanked him. "And mine, please," said Campion, who was craning over Baird's shoulder. "Golly," he added, catching sight of the display type.

Few of the other passengers showed much interest, except the Trumans, who spent an earnest five minutes calculating the cost at the rate of exchange and wondering whether the expenditure would be justified. Finally, they added their names to the list. Fearmax pondered the question gravely over dinner, and only added his name after the purser had made a short announcement to the effect that he would like the list closed by ten o'clock that night as the Captain would have to send a signal on to Crete stating the number of prospective excursionists and asking that cars be engaged.

Miss Dale and Miss Dombey brought up the rear; the one because she had a vague feeling that the visit might help her with her examination, the latter because she was an inveterate sightseer, and because humanitarian motives demanded that Spot, her dog, should have a run on dry land after so many days at sea. Several other names were also added to the list, but were afterwards erased as further inquiry showed that the trip was to take nearly the whole day. The name of Colonel Sinclair was actually on the list, but its owner was too prostrated by sea-sickness to avail himself of the opportunity offered by the Jannadis Brothers. He lay in his bunk groaning for Cheltenham. Later, of course, he claimed that a premonition had prevented him from going rather than sea-sickness. Indeed, his local paper on his return published this myth under the heading of *Colonel's Premonition*.

It had blown up rough again in the Cretan channel and several people, including Miss Dombey, suffered from sea-sickness—not because the *Europa* rolled. Rather it was because the ship moved so steadily, without a tremor, through a raging sea, with whitecaps piled up round her like the froth on a *café viennois*. By dawn, however, the squall had blown itself out and the great ship nosed cautiously into the magnificent bay of Suda (Canea harbour was too small) and anchored opposite the twisted wreck of the old warship *York*, which lay, a rusting relic of the Cretan campaign, belly-down in the shallows.

Baird had been up at dawn to watch the sunrise breaking over the familiar Grecian landscape. He was troubled by an obscure excitement whose source he was not able to trace. The sun rose slowly from among the snow-capped peaks of the White Mountains. It was bitterly cold, and he had found himself a vantage point on the boat-deck which kept off the light but piercing wind. From here, looking down into the harbour, he could see the great ship's reflection rustling under her, motionless save for the thick black plume of smoke from the white stacks. He stared out eagerly across the island, taking in every detail, surprised to find how intimately he remembered it all.

A foreground of olive trees and turned red earth: a few box-like houses: an oil refinery: a dusty road winding into the middle distance—in his imagination peopled by dusty columns of New Zealanders and British, plodding away towards Sphakia. He could have walked inland with his eyes shut.

As he was standing thus a car came over the brow of the hill and took the curling road, fringed with pines, which led to the jetty. It stopped at the water's edge and a man got out. Was it perhaps Axelos who had come to meet Graecen? He saw al-

most immediately that it was someone much smaller than
Axelos. A fisherman in a blue jersey, standing at his oars, conveyed the newcomer slowly across the intervening distance,
until his boat rested in the shadow of the *Europa*. The man
seemed to be English, from the cut of his clothes. It was probably the Consul, though why he should come aboard at this
hour was more than Baird could fathom. "Prosechete, kirie,"
he heard the boatman say. It was the first Greek he had heard
spoken for some time; it filled him with a kind of nostalgic
pain. He scanned the face of the boatman eagerly to see if it
was anyone he knew. (One always does this in Greece.)
Octopus, pinnae and red mullet lay in a basket at the bottom
of the boat. He had obviously been out all night fishing.

The British Consul (for it was he) came aboard in his time.
He was tired and peevish, and walked like a person of some
consequence to the bridge, where he asked smartly for the
officer of the watch. "I understand that you have passengers
wishing to visit the labyrinth. I have come to inform you that
the trip is simply not safe."

He was conducted below to see the Captain, to whom he
explained his business more clearly, slightly mollified by the
excellent coffee and biscuit of the ship.

"There's a travel agency run by two young Greeks," he
said. "They advertise tours of the labyrinth. Now, my advice
is to dissuade passengers from running the risk. The labyrinth simply isn't safe. I don't want to have British subjects
lost in the island, it upsets the Embassy; I've no doubt your
company would also not like to risk the lives of its passengers."

The Captain listened to him carefully and decided that his
manner was too peremptory for a mere vice-Consul. The company, he pointed out, was exempt from any responsibility in
the matter. The Jannadis Agency had merely canvassed visitors to the labyrinth. It was not up to him to stop people

enjoying themselves. At any rate, he would post a notice on the board, explaining that the place was considered dangerous by the Consul, and advising passengers not to risk it. "Let me see," he said, "I think we've only a few this time."

Over breakfast the six of them read the Captain's notice with interest not unmixed with excitement. They felt rather bold to be visiting a place considered unsafe by the Consul. Even Miss Dombey, who was not feeling very well, felt that it was up to her to show that she was no coward. "You're intrepid, that's what you are," said Campion to her in his stage-cockney accent, buttering himself a side of toast. "What happens if the Second Coming comes while you're inside? You might miss the whole thing." Latterly, Miss Dombey had found that the best way of dealing with Campion was to ignore him. She had not spoken a word to him since the day he had said: "Miss Dombey, if Spot uses my easel for a lamp-post once more I'll cut his legs off and throw him in the sea." It had been simply outrageous; even Graecen was shocked by his rudeness. Now she simply ignored him. It did not seem to bother Campion, however, who always had something either offensive or comical to say to her when they met.

Truman met Graecen dragging his grip along to the stair-case, and gave him a hand. "Thanks," panted Graecen. He was very puffed and sat down upon it to exchange a cigarette. "Coming to the labyrinth?" he said. Truman nodded. "I see you are leaving us for good," he said, with genuine regret. The voyage had been a pleasant one so far. "Not all of us," said Graecen. "Baird and Campion and I, are going to stay with a friend of mine. But we're coming up to see the labyrinth with you first."

The Truman couple slipped ashore rather earlier than the others. They had observed Miss Dombey taking the dog ashore in the pinnace—and had decided to have a look round on their own. They went for a walk in the meadow hand in hand, exchanging private jokes and banter. "My," she said, "it is a lovely place. You'd never think it was an island, would you?" Truman swung himself into an olive tree by his wrists, and hung for a second before dropping back to earth. "I feel fine," he said. "And you look fine."

She wore a bright dappled frock of some light summer material, a wide-brimmed straw hat, and shoes with heavy rope soles such as one buys in Spain—*espadrilles*. She had brought a rucksack and an overcoat, in case the journey proved cold. "I feel fine," she said, smiling her friendly, innocent smile.

They could hear the shrill barking of Miss Dombey and her dog over the next hillock. Avoiding her they walked along the flat shore by the jetty. The keen air, the blue sky, the meadows sloping away to the foothills splashed with fruit trees—it was overpowering. "Why don't we just pick a place like this? Stay here for ever and ever?" She was thinking of Campion sitting under an olive tree, drinking a glass of wine and painting with his small hands. Her husband sniffed. "Don't mind if I do," he said. "If you learn the language and do the housekeeping." They passed several low cottages, whence elderly, wrinkled faces peered out at them. Voices greeted them politely, for Greece is the country where the stranger is honoured like a god, and where hospitality is a domestic art. "I wish I knew how to say good day," she said as they passed. Farther on they came upon rows of coloured fishing-boats drawn up upon a brown seaweed-covered beach. Tattered fishermen sat cross-legged in a wilderness of nets, darning and sifting them. A small boy offered flowers with the compliments of his uncle. Truman took them in his clumsy British way, blushing as he did so; he felt effeminate in his stupid northern way to be holding a bunch of tinted anemones. "Come on," he said gruffly, handing them to his wife. "What price Whitby?" said his wife irrelevantly, wondering whether they could go for a row in a boat. They gave the urchin a packet of sweets from the ship's canteen.

Under an olive tree she put down the rucksack to search for a handkerchief. Not finding one she blew her nose in a letter, catching her husband's disapproving eye as she did so. "I knew it," he said. "No hanky." It was one of her most irritating traits. Later, of course, she would demand the nice clean one that protruded from the breast pocket of his smart summer suit. Women were like that.

They sat under an olive tree together arm in arm, and lapsed into silence. Bees hummed. In the middle distance a caravan of hill-ponies moved across towards the wood bearing sacks of charcoal on their backs, driven by men in blue trousers, jack-boots and tasselled caps. Behind them the mountains glowed grey below the snowline, and deep green where the rich foot-hills sent their orchards straggling up them.

Elsie Truman suddenly felt full of the silence. It had been running noiselessly in her mind like an open tap, and now there came an overflowing, a pause. She sighed, and looked at her face in the pocket mirror she had brought. "Look over there," said Truman, lazily chewing a grass stalk, and trying to remember the name of a single ancient Greek god or goddess. "It's old Baird."

Baird sat under a tree upon a cane chair, deep in conversation with one of the chauffeurs. Over the brow of the hill there appeared a dilapidated taxi with a functionary of some kind seated behind the wheel. Baird at last had seen someone who recognized him. He was asking news of his guerilla comrades; it was all at once as if time had been telescoped all together, as if he had only been away a few moments. He felt close to Böcklin, closer than he had ever felt before; and close to the obscure dream that had troubled him for so long. He put his questions eagerly, asking where this one lived now, and whether that one's wound had healed. There were few of the original band left on the island. The Abbot John, however, was thought to be still up at the monastery. Baird could hardly wait for the party to arrive, so close did he seem to the heart of the mystery. It was as if some deeply-troubling enigma were going to be elucidated.

From the sides of the *Europa* a white dot broke away and fussed towards the shore. It was the pinnace bearing Fearmax, Campion, Miss Dale and Graecen—the last having said good-bye to everyone including the Captain with an elaborate over-politeness. As he turned back to his companion, Baird's eye caught sight of the Truman couple, sitting under a tree. He waved to them, and they got to their feet. Miss Dombey was advancing across the middle landscape with strident barks of encouragement to Spot. The dog was a lymphatic animal, neither grateful for a chance to decorate genuine trees instead of stanchions, nor particularly enthusiastic about Crete. It cantered tepidly along by the side of its mistress, who, between barks, exclaimed breathlessly, "Have a good run. There's a good Spot. Chase him, boy. Chase him. Woof, woof, woof, woof." She came up considerably puffed and accepted Baird's chair with faint thanks. "How the English love their four-footed pets," said Campion admiringly, as the rest of the party gathered round.

On the knoll, under the olive tree from which hung the inn-sign reading "Kapheneion", the taxis were drawn up. For some reason there were six of them, and on Graecen's recommendation they decided that three would be ample, both for the luggage and for the eight of them. This having been determined upon after considerable debate with the drivers, the guide emerged from the depths of the wineshop cellar, wiping a pair of long mournful moustaches on the backs of both hands. "Please to attend to me one minute," he said hoarsely. He wore a battered German field-marshal's hat upon his head, around which the Jannadis Brothers had placed a band upon which the company's name was inscribed. The hinder end of a British battledress was surmounted by a blue woollen pullover, on the front of which was written "Beach Guard", and on the back "Property of UNRRA Canteen. Not to be taken away." He had evidently something impressive to say, but his English was halt, deaf and blind. He was grateful, therefore, when Baird came to his rescue and offered to translate. He caught both his hands in his and began a long conversation, which sounded to the rest—as all Greek conversations do—like a violent quarrel. Baird was interested.

The rest of the party stood in a semicircle watching. Finally Baird turned to them with twinkling eyes and an incredulous smile on his face. "Something new to me," he said, obviously doubtful whether an explanation of his conversation with the guide would justify translation. "He says that there is an animal of some kind in the labyrinth. No one has ever seen it. But they hear it roar—we shall probably hear it too."

"A minotaur," said Graecen excitedly.

"Extraordinary," said Fearmax, drawing closer to catch what Baird had to say. "What do they call it?"

"The man calls it '*τό Θηρξον*'," said Baird. "It means 'monster' or 'beast'. It's probably a bear."

He did not add to the translation. The guide had told him that once a shepherd, badly mauled, had been found at the mouth of the labyrinth. He had entered the main cave in pursuit of a sheep, and had encountered some animal in the darkness. He had not been able to give any clear account of it.

They had all managed to bring torches with them, however, so he felt that the party was sufficiently well-equipped to start moving. "A minotaur," said Graecen, sniffing the cold air from the mountains. "If we could take it back to the British Museum how pleased they would be."

"Well, after all these warnings we may expect either to be eaten alive or buried by a fall of rock. Does anyone feel his courage fail? If so, let him speak now or forever hold his peace." Campion climbed into the nearest taxi as he spoke, with all his possessions. The rest of them followed.

The Cefalù Road

The idea at the back of Graecen's mind was a comparatively simple one; he wanted a chance to see the city in the rock, to get to work with his little bottle of acid, before he visited Axelos. He sat, with Baird, in the back seat of the foremost taxi, and meditated as he saw the pink sun-burned neck of Miss Dale, who had sat beside the driver. Her blonde hair had been gathered into a coloured handkerchief to keep it from the dust, and the bright cloth threw into relief her sad cheek-bones, and the small childish mouth when she turned to exclaim at the scenery or ask a question. Graecen had noticed an increase of his sentimental weakness for blonde women; she had been, indeed, a charming if uncultured companion. And so grateful for his help with her literature paper. They had spent whole afternoons sitting side by side and working; Virginia had loved being read to, and he had loved the sound of his own voice. And now somehow, directly his feet had touched the land again, his old preoccupation with the doctor's diagnosis had come over him. Life was so beautiful in the sun—how could one forfeit it all of a sudden, like a shutter closing? The girl turned back and gave him a little smile, wrinkling up her nose. She had seen some peasants in bright costumes. "Are you all right, Richard?" she said. She used his name with a delightful timidity. Yes, he was all right. But for how long? That was the question.

It seemed to him, too, that Virginia herself was perhaps a little sentimentally inclined towards him. "So after tomorrow," she had said, "I shan't see you any more?" It seemed to him that her lip trembled ever so slightly; and he blushed to the

roots of his—well, not exactly his hair—to the little bald spot
on his crown. Now, sitting in the jolting car, he felt suddenly
overwhelmed by the depression of his thoughts, and a haunting longing for someone in whom he could confide. Suddenly
he was reminded of those illnesses when he was a boy—how
he had enjoyed them. The luxury of those long bouts of
measles and mumps. He cast a glance sideways at Baird, half
afraid that his thoughts might be told from his expression; but
Baird was hunched in his corner, his eyes fixed on the crags
ahead of them, thinking—who knows what?—thoughts of his
past life.

Graecen returned with pleasure to his own preoccupation
with death. He closed his eyes and saw the great white house,
set back among the flowering oleanders and the supple green
myrtles of Cefalû. The large quiet rooms with their balconies.
The chaffer of the fishermen at the mole beyond the clump of
cypresses. Did he dare to tell Axelos? And then again, the
prospect of keeping his secret filled him with an aching sense
of emptiness and gloom. He needed comfort, he needed to be
secured against the approaching darkness. What a fool he was,
he said to himself, not to have married; to have sacrificed
everything for selfish comforts of bachelorhood. Virginia was
smiling at him again. At the ball she had danced beautifully—
her body had seemed to him so resilient, so warm, so passive;
inviting almost. He had felt that subtle correspondence of
limbs as he held her lightly against his own body. What had
she been thinking? Now, mixed with the desire to re-create the
image of his mother through somebody else, there came also
the feeling that his life had been worthless, had been untouched at any point except by indifference or gluttony or
power. He felt a sudden urge to dedicate himself to something
or somebody—to fulfil in patient, indulgent service all that he
felt remained in him, seed without flower. Why should he not
marry Virginia?

The thought brought him up with a jerk. The suggestion was completely unexpected. Virginia, the pallid little cockney waif—why should he not marry her? Devote himself to her; try and give her life a little meaning, a little form, from his own experience? Share some of his gifts with her? Above all, confide in her, look after her, until such a time as . . . But he averted his mind from that suddenly closing shutter which was to come down over this sunny world, and concentrated his gaze upon the childish contours of that face in front, whose excitement was manifest in every feature. Poor child, he said to himself, over and over again, thinking of her cockney accent. He had come to enjoy it almost. He had found her errors and defects almost an added charm. Why should he not marry Virginia?

But the whole thing was preposterous. Graecen was one of those hopelessly self-divided people who are so often made the victims of their own whims. Idly he would get an idea, as idly play with it; and then, all of a sudden, find himself dragged protesting towards it. He recognized this as one of those momentous ideas which would, if he did not act, enslave him utterly.

Damn the girl, she was smiling at him again. Apologetically he leaned forward and patted her arm. Virginia's face melted sympathetically into a kind of smiling sadness. Graecen began calling himself names, but underneath he heard the systematic echo of the idea vibrating in the hollows of his consciousness. Why should he not marry Virginia? "Don't be a fool," he said aloud.

"Eh?" said Baird, coming out of his reverie.

"Sorry," said Graecen with confusion. "I was thinking of something. I was miles away."

Baird looked tired all of a sudden, and excited. His hand shook as he lit a cigarette. "I think", he said, "I'll not come directly to the labyrinth with you. I've got some other business to do first." His effort to make it sound a business transaction was a palpable failure. He averted his eyes and added: "I know where the house is. If you'd be good enough to send on my bag, Graecen, I'll come in to dinner." He caught sight of the perplexity on his companion's face and said: "Oh, it's nothing serious. Perhaps I'll be able to explain a little later."

Graecen primmed his lips and nodded. Baird had already hinted at an official mission. No doubt this had something to do with it.

Canea had gone spinning away southwards with its orange trees and powdery houses of red and white. Painted into the hard blue frame of the horizon lay the unruffled cobalt of the sea, yellow and green where it touched the coastline. The three taxis rumbled across the verdant valleys, trailing behind them a great cloud of soft dust. The queer noise of their klaxons woke the uplands towards which they headed, and curious ink-spot jays dropped down from the trees to watch their progress.

Never had Elsie Truman dreamed of such scenery; flawless in their purity the valleys were picked out in rectangles and squares of colour by the sunlight. It was better, she told her husband, than the best Technicolor film. Riding down the winding roads she pressed his hand under the decent privacy of the rug, and handed him boiled sweets to suck.

Miss Dombey sat beside them, finding the dust very trying. She repeated the charge several times, as if to express her disapproval of a world in which one had to make long journeys in deep dust—and in such company. The implication was not lost on Mrs. Truman. She smiled as she saw Miss Dombey wind her face in a veil and lie back against the moth-eaten hood of the car, closing her eyes. The dog lay quietly at their feet.

Something of her irritation must have been communicated to the guide, who sat in front beside the driver. He removed his arm from its position round the neck of the latter and leaned back to ask a question. His conversation was rendered unintelligible by the wind, however, and he was forced to shout until Miss Dombey winced with pain. Was she ill, he asked? No? He gave an imitation of Miss Dombey in a veil, which the Trumans found delightfully comic. When they smiled at him he roared with laughter. If she was not ill, then why?—and he made the gesture of wrapping himself in a veil once more. Miss Dombey was so revolted by his performance that she told him to shut up and turn round. The guide's hurt feelings were only partly assuaged by Mrs Truman's offer of an acid-drop. He sucked it for a moment with a sad and pouting air of wounded *amour-propre*. Then, to return the courtesy, he removed his hat, and taking a cigarette-end from inside it, solemnly pressed it upon Mr. Truman who found himself forced to accept the object with thanks. Miss Dombey's lips were compressed into a thimble-top of disapproval. Truman muttered angrily to his wife: "There you go again. Can't let people be." And she laughed until she nearly swallowed her sweet, then coughed until he had to thump her on the back.

In the taxi behind them Campion and Fearmax sat deep in conversation, while all around them were packed the trunks, suitcases and packs of those who were to stay the night at Cefalû. "But of course," Campion was saying emphatically, "the artist's job is to present concrete findings about the un-known inside himself and other people. How else can you justify art? The paintings of a man like Picasso are just as much discovery as the atom bomb. That is why one gets filled with such a hideous sense of uselessness in realizing that the next war is inevitable, inevitable." He banged his hand on his knee. Fearmax buried his jowls deeper in his coat. "Most likely," he said.

"Inevitable," said Campion vehemently. "You don't even have to read the texts of the peace-pacts to see that, or read about the new bomb they call 'Fragmentation X' to see that the whole silly farce is going to begin over again. The nation will be led automatically to victory this time with all the flags out. No sacrifice too great. Buy to save to spend to lend to end to buy to slave to rend. Eliot will be banished to Iceland: mystics have green dossiers now: they are known as PCS—'possibly controversial subjects'. Industry will be geared to war-pitch in a matter of hours. The Pope won't know whether to intervene and offer the peace which passeth all misunderstanding or not . . . we should really get Graecen to set it to music:

> *'Tis the voice of the idealist*
> *I hear him declare*
> *Though you hide at the North Pole*
> *They'll follow you there*
> *With honour and unction*
> *Debentures and bonds!*
> *Till they close the green dossier*
> *And drag all the ponds.''*

Fearmax smiled dryly. "I have so much to do," he said. "So much to do."

Campion lit a new cigarette from the stub of the old. "And I", he said, "am just on the edge of becoming a real artist, a suffering member of the world: just able to contribute what is positive in me after a lifetime of revolt and wasted energy. It is not important. If there were no alternative to the present state of things I could accept it. But there is. The equipment is lying like an unpressed switch in the heart of every man. Damn, bugger, blast the world."

Even as he said it he thought that it was not true—it was rather a dramatic approximation of truth which he wished to become. Actually what was he. He saw Fearmax's eyes on him, measured the glance of those experienced eyes and turned his own head away. And now suddenly he thought of Francesca with a pang; Francesca, so beautiful a companion and friend. He had left her as one leaves a bundle of laundry. Did the interests of the search justify, on the ordinary scale of loyalties and decencies, so sudden and pointless a betrayal? He heard himself once more saying: "My mother is dead," with that flat unemotional tone of voice.

"It seems to me", said Fearmax, "that you affirm far too much. You are right, of course, that we all work through the various states of being, our negatives, our husks, which we discard. But can we, at any given point, know that we've arrived at the end of the quest? Surely the self-consciousness of the illumination you talk about does not tell us we have reached the—what shall I say?—'The Absolute,' 'God,' 'Tao'. It is, on the contrary, that growing awareness which disposes of the act of searching. I think the man you want to be would have a humbler attitude, a non-affirming attitude, a passivity towards the whole process—even if he were sitting on an atom-bomb. The sage has nothing to tell us, you know. It is by his silence alone that we deduce the fact of his existence."

The cars had blundered over the dusty part of the road, and now their tyres crunched on the pot-holed surfaces of the mountain roads. They had mounted the first three gradients which led slowly along the first escarpments of the White Mountains. The road wound in and out of several frowning ravines, where white torrents broke from the parapets of rock, and the air was full of the cries of swifts. It had become purer and more limpid, and the atmosphere colder. They were glad of their coats. Behind them the ancient Cretan sea had petrified into an unearthly blueness.

"Soon we'll be reaching Namia," said Baird, stirring from his silence to examine the time. "I'll drop off there and take the short cut across the range. You wouldn't think you were so near to Cefalû—it's just beyond the crag there, only lower down almost on the sea. You can just see the tip of the crag from here."

Two hours had gone by before the little convoy rumbled up on to the cypress-edged plateau where the village of Namia turned its whitewashed box-like houses to the sunlight. Cefalû lay about a quarter of an hour's drive due west along the road. It was at Namia, however, that the guide insisted on having a drink to brace himself for the trip round the labyrinth. Baird took the opportunity to dismount, as did the others. They stood for a while watching the eagles turning slowly below them, and the chequer-board of plain stretching away to the sea with the damp black patches of shadow from clouds racing across it.

"Well," said Baird, whose heart was beating uncomfortably at the prospect of returning to the cave-mouth where Böcklin lay buried, "this is where I say good-bye to some of you. I shall see you again, Campion, tonight. Good-bye, Fearmax, Miss Dombey . . . ," he made the round of the company, shaking hands, having hoisted his rucksack on his back. They were almost embarrassed, for somehow up here in this country of cloud-swept peaks, this panorama of stage-mountains, the quality of parting seemed to have taken on a new meaning. An unexpected regret stirred in them as they said good-bye. As for Virginia, he was surprised at the warmth of her handclasp, the tenderness of her glance; and then his native intuition told him that she had transferred to him her feelings about Graecen, and that in her imagination it was to Graecen that she was saying good-bye. "Why the knapsack?" said Campion suddenly. "Leave it and we'll bring it along to Cefalû." Baird muttered something about having to take his lunch with him. In point of fact his knapsack housed the old army entrenching tool which he had (to Hogarth's mused interest) carried about with him for so long, unwilling to throw it away.

"Until later, then," he said, and started off down the mule-track which led across the ravine. They stood silently in a semicircle and watched him go before getting back into the cars.

"Well," said Campion, "what about the labyrinth?" The guide was run to earth in the cellar of a tavern, discoursing amiably over his third cognac. He managed to get the drivers together and start the procession going. Their dispositions had altered slightly after the halt and Campion now found himself with the Trumans instead of with Fearmax. A coolness had sprung up between himself and Mrs. Truman over the painting which he had tossed overboard in a fit of temper. She had been in a rather capricious mood that day, and had been addressing remarks to her husband through the open porthole of the saloon. For some reason this had irritated Campion.

"All right," he'd said suddenly, with a savagery that had frightened her, "talk your bloody head off and move about. I'm a painter, you know, not a camera with a high-speed lens." And with a sudden gesture he had flicked the painting overboard. It lay for a moment on the creamy wrack of the *Europa*, Mrs. Truman's face floating steadily away from them. She gave a cry and ran to the rail. "What a shame, Campion," she said. "What a shame," and to her surprise he was smiling, his rage all consumed at her genuine anger and dismay. Without a word he gathered up his materials and went down to his cabin, where he sat for a while in a chair, smoking. Then, taking up his notebook, he started to copy the head once more in charcoal. The painting had been a rotten one anyhow; he had been glad of the excuse to destroy it, and at the same time to make her uncomfortable. She had not forgiven him, however, and repulsed all his efforts at badinage with a cool civility. Campion was interesting, she told herself, but he was not going to run roughshod over her. She had hoped to take the painting back home with her; she had suddenly seen, in a sudden moment of revelation, what he had meant by calling her beautiful; it was herself, her real self that he was trying to capture, and nobody had ever paid any attention to Elsie Truman's true self, save this eccentric and violent little man in the soiled beret. It was as if there had been something valuable to be learned from the painting: as if the act of destruction were a wanton and wasteful refusal to let her learn about herself.

The cars rumbled down the hill towards the village of Cefalû and the labyrinth.

The City in the Rock

They had at last arrived at the foot of the fantastic cone of conglomerate, to the sides of which clung the small group of brightly-coloured buildings which composed the village of Cefalû. The road ran out upon a causeway, and turned abruptly up a tree-lined gradient which brought them at last to the village itself, lying up against the mountain, one house overlooking the roof of the next, like the habitation of trolls or dolls. The cone sloped away downward with vertiginous directness into the blue sea, its sides dappled with coverts of green scrub, and broken by seams of red and grey rock. From above they could look down upon the bright roof of Cefalû, the house, in its quiet garden, and upon the little yellow rowing boats tethered to the moat beyond the garden.

All was still in the village as the convoy rattled through and took the stony path which led for another fifty yards to where the three dwarf cypresses marked the entrance to the labyrinth. The church bell chimed brokenly. A workman in blue trousers sat before a small glass of ouzo outside the door of the tavern. To him were confided the possessions of those who were to stay with Axelos.

"Well," said Graecen, "now for the big adventure." He was loading his box-lunch into the pockets of his overcoat and testing the battery of his torch. Firbank's little bottle of chemicals lay snugly in his waistcoat pocket. The new process, he had explained, was smelly but infallible; Graecen had only to paint a rock-cutting with it to be able to tell whether the tools used in the cutting were of iron or not. Then there was the tiny blue lens through which he should see whether the grain showed its fine shades of black. . . . He hoped Axelos was not up in the Cefalû this morning.

The others had bundled out of the cars and were busy putting on coats at the suggestion by Fearmax that the corridors of the labyrinth might be extremely chilly. The guide himself had put on a tattered overcoat, and had produced a hurricane lantern which he now proceeded to light.

"I haven't any light," said Campion, and a chorus of voices answered him saying that their combined torches would be light enough to see by; the guide smiled amiably as he got to his feet. "Now," he said, with the air of one about to conduct a delicate experiment, "forward please to follow."

At first they hesitated, so narrow and uninviting was the entrance—a single corridor of orange-red rock which took a steep turn after five paces and passed out of sight. "It is little bigger than an Egyptian rock-tomb," said Graecen fretfully, as he turned up the collar of his coat and felt for his torch. The guide turned back and beckoned. "Plenty light inside," he shouted encouragingly and disappeared. They followed him one by one. "Not too fast," said Campion, as they entered the stone cave and heard the church bell of Cefalû become suddenly very distant, and then at last smother out in the subterranean roar and splash of a spring hammering on rock.

They were standing in another corridor, but longer than the first, and ending in a narrow causeway over a spring. "Dear me," said Graecen. It was impossible that so small a spring should produce this thunderous echo; his own voice as he spoke sounded distorted and magnified out of all recognition Campion was pushing the others from behind. "Forward," said the guide, swinging his lantern and advancing, while Virginia Dale timidly held on to the corner of his overcoat. They shuffled in single file along the stony path, ducked through another corridor, and crossed the middle-sized antechamber.

Mrs. Truman had taken her husband's arm. She gave it

excited little tugs, not to signal anything in particular, but simply to register her pleasure and excitement. "What a place," said Truman, turning his torch-beam this way and that. Fearmax was peering about him with his eyes screwed up, and with an uneasy expression upon his face.

"Sounds like a river somewhere," said Virginia Dale, and the guide who had been lacing up his shoes gave her a glance of approbation and repeated his cry of "Forward". He started to walk into the darkness beyond the dazzle of torch-light, swinging before him the little yellow puddle of light cast by the hurricane lamp. They followed him slowly, picking their way through the dimness over mounds of rubble and huge boulders which seemed, in the gloom, to bear the trace of human working. The fragile beam of Truman's torch seemed quite inadequate to pierce the almost solid blackness of the place; it showed merely a number of ledges covered thickly with the droppings of bats, while, when he turned it upward towards the roof, it simply thinned away and evaporated, rendering nothing. "This way to the two and sixes," said his wife behind him in the shadow and gave a little tug at the tail of his coat.

Fearmax was busily examining a heap of stone and rubble from some ancient landslide. Campion stood by him striking matches and peering. Between them they lifted one or two of the stones and turned them over. "No, I don't think they are worked," Campion was saying when the other interrupted him with a cry: "Look out!" A large scorpion stared unwinking into the beam of torchlight, its tail set as if by a spring, to strike. Fearmax laughed ruefully and they made their way farther along in pursuit of the others. "Lucky I didn't sit on it," said Campion.

After negotiating the two small chambers, the whole party passed in single file down a rock-gallery which opened off from between them. "I think we've gone far enough," said

Virginia Dale. "Don't you? It's so eerie." Despite the coldness of the air Graecen was sweating. He turned off his torch and mopped his forehead. The poor girl was afraid. He didn't blame her. Truman, however, whistled a few bars of "The Merry Widow Waltz", and in the darkness—the cold eddyless air of the cavern—it had a consoling human ring.

The gallery led them down at an ever-steepening angle until they stood before another natural door in the rock. The ladies found their feet beginning to hurt in their high-heeled shoes; all except for Mrs. Truman, whose rope soles were ideal for these harsh variations of surface and direction. Once assembled, the guide counted them as if they had been chickens. "Now please together," he said earnestly, "and careful too." Elsie Truman gave an excited tug at her husband's arm and he replied by pinching her arm reassuringly; in the little booth of light from the torches he saw her face with its young, friendly lines turned towards the short tunnel which was to lead them yet farther into the labyrinth.

"Another cave," said Graecen.

"Underground river," said the guide with a ridiculously proprietary air. It was obvious from his manner that the Jannadis Brothers were responsible for all these wonders. He placed the tail of his coat once more in Virginia's reluctant hand, and ordered them all to follow suit. Lantern in hand, he led his shuffling crocodile through the tunnel and into a cavern with a discernible flue in which filtered the vague semblance of light from the outside world; the reflections were strong enough for them to mark the track of the stream which passed through the farther end of the cavern with the noise of a miniature electric train. It flowed, greenish black, without a ripple except where it once more disappeared by vaulting clear through a piece of natural fan-vaulting. Truman knelt down beside it but his torch could not pierce the dark water. This time the interest and excitement of the party was not quite so loudly expressed. A silence had fallen on them; a sense of fatigue and suffocation at being so long out of the air. Yet when Graecen looked at his watch he found that they had spent barely half an hour in the labyrinth. And the air they breathed was cold and pure.

"Can we cross it?" said Mrs. Truman.

"Yes, please," said the guide with alacrity, leading them to an overhanging bluff from which they could see a line of stepping-stones dotting the shining surface of the water. Despite its speed Fearmax noticed that the water did not break upon these stones but flowed round them, black and even as silk. He dabbled his fingers in the stream and withdrew them almost at once, exclaiming against the coolness of it. "What is odd," he said to Campion, "is the rubbing noise; because the bed is scooped clean out of rock, and yet one seems to hear gravel being churned down it or something." They stared down for a moment on to that placid surface, while the guide demonstrated how easy a crossing was for the benefit of Mr. Truman, whose native caution had suggested that the stepping-stones might sink. The guide, however, walked with an exaggerated sure-footedness, and appeared to satisfy the rest of them that the journey involved no great hazard. Virginia Dale, after a number of false starts and hesitations, obeyed Graecen's promptings and crossed, holding tight to his hand. They followed, one by one.

It was when Fearmax was mid-way across that they heard it for the first time: a long-drawn muffled roar which rose above the noise of the stream and echoed through the wilderness of galleries which surrounded them. The guide waved his lantern excitedly and laughed. "Good heavens," said Fearmax, standing on the last stone, "what on earth was that?" They stood still, listening to the sound as it slowly died away in the distance.

"It was not a roar," said Graecen, "was it?" Mrs Truman

was reminded of the upstairs' lodgers moving furniture about during a spring clean. Sound became so mangled and magnified in those corridors that it might be anything, thought Fearmax, with a superstitious dread.

"The minotaur," said Campion to no one in particular.

"A very queer sound though," said Fearmax, "very queer." The sound had tailed away into a series of dim tremulous reverberations which knocked and banged their way into the distance. It was like the banging noise of an engine, knocking one truck against another, into infinity. In each new cavern the echo was further distorted and further magnified as it was passed on. What could it be?

They stood still for a moment to listen, forming a clear tableau in the light, and reflected upside down in the black waters of the stream, Fearmax and Campion sharing the last two stepping-stones; Virginia's hand clasped in Graecen's; the Truman couple sitting idly on a rock, side by side.

"I bet if you rolled a cannon-ball down these corridors you'd get exactly the same sound effect," said Fearmax at last. Campion made an irritable gesture to silence him. "Listen," he said. They listened fervently until Mrs. Truman felt a desire to giggle—the same desire she always had during the two minutes' silence on Armistice Day. Fearmax looked so comical with his jowl stuck out, and Campion standing on one leg. . . . Graecen pressed Virginia's arm softly, comfortingly, and cursed himself as he felt her own warm answering pressure. Under his breath he whispered every opprobrious epithet he could lay his mind to. It was becoming a conspiracy—his own weakness allied with circumstances—to entrap him. He was sliding invisibly downhill in ever-increasing speeds of idiotic quixotry until . . . until . . .

They stood listening to rubbing of water at their feet, the noise of a concrete-mixer, and the harsh spotted sound of water leaking into a cistern somewhere.

The guide, for some reason best known to himself, was silent. His face looked grave and preoccupied. He was picking his teeth with a match-stick. He did not venture to comment on the sound or try to explain it. When at last he caught Mrs. Truman's eye he merely raised his eyebrows, threw up his hands and crossed himself. Campion began to wonder whether they should go on. "Let's go back," he said, "I've had enough of this place. And when do we get to the antiquities anyway?" When indeed.

At last they felt able to relax the torment of listening for the sound. It had not repeated itself, that anguished and reverberating trump. Fearmax shook himself. "It might have been anything," he said. "Rocks dropping into a cavern full of water. I've heard the same sort of noise in the workings of a disused mine." As a matter of fact he had never been anywhere near a disused mine, but he felt a vague desire to raise morale by producing a mundane explanation of the sound.

They gathered themselves together and were about to debate whether they should proceed or not when the guide, who had been sitting apart resting, rose and clapped his hands for silence. "Forward," he called again and set off towards yet another tunnel. Virginia showed some disinclination to follow, but Fearmax called out: "Oh, come along there. It can't be much farther." It was not.

Ducking at last through a sort of postern, they followed the guide into what at first seemed to them to be a Gothic cathedral. It was very nearly as large—a tremendous and grandiose cavern, through the roof of which shone the pure rays of the sun, falling like a spotlight through the dense atmosphere and the dust. Peering up, they saw once more a piece of the sky, a sight which banished their depression instantly.

"Now for the sights," said Graecen, glad that the publicity of light made any further advances to Virginia impossible. "What is that? I think I see the cella."

As they advanced through the white circle of light blazing upon the stone floor they heard once more the roar of the minotaur—but this time more remote, less unearthly. They stopped to listen to it as it banged its way into silence, however. "Seems farther away," said Fearmax with evident relief. The guide took absolutely no notice of the sound but led the way across the great nave, his footsteps echoing like those of a verger in the crypt of St. Paul's. High above, in the indistinguishable blue of buttress shapes, they heard the flap and chitter of bats.

Sure enough in one corner Graecen traced out a cella, and there at last, undercut into the rock, lay the chambers Axelos had described. Each was about the size of a chapel, and had four or five tunnels leading off it into the labyrinth. The first two were empty; in the third was a massively-carved plinth, fallen on its side and much rubbed. The fourth, then, must contain the bas-relief and the statues. Graecen was so excited that he completely forgot Virginia. This latter chapel also admitted light through a chink in the roof.

The guide was demonstrating the phenomenon of the echo. He threw his head back and shouted. It was as if a hand had suddenly begun to smack down over a laughing mouth; the echo was tossed backwards and forwards from the coigns and nooks in the great curved roof until it died slowly into a whisper, almost a tone above its original. Silence fell. Beyond the swirling shaft of pollen-like light, down which (as in Bible illustrations) the Holy Ghost might be expected to descend, lay the serene unclouded blue eye of the sky. They all tested the echo to their hearts' content. Graecen heard them as he was searching for his little chemical bottle. Their talk and laughter provided him with just the cover he needed for his experiment. He stepped forward into the little chapel and found his attention arrested by the perfect detachment and purity of the statues, by the coarse yet sensitive stone-cutting of the bas-relief. No, his experience had not been at fault. These were certainly not fakes: they were too weathered and lichened by damp: too self-consciously primitive and innocent to deceive. Typology was satisfied no less than experience. He stood with his mouth open and let his eyes delight in the ponderous archaic forms, their grace as they stood, big with the weight of their material stone: and yet somehow aerial like boulders learning to fly. One was a winged man, his arms raised, his belly depressed in the effort of flight. One was a boy. Campion was standing beside him smoking furiously and walking from point to point to vary the view; or reaching down to see at close quarters how the cutting had been achieved. "What do you think?" said Graecen. It came upon him suddenly that it would be an insult to mess about with chemicals here, in such a place. After all, if one was not sure the onus was on oneself. He was an expert and he was prepared to stake his whole experience upon the issue. "What do I think?" said Campion absently. "It's grand work, isn't it?" Graecen's fingers pressed the rubber stopper of the bottle that Firbank had given him. Damn old Firbank with his beastly chemical tests. He turned aside and walked out into the main cavern once more. The place was honeycombed with tunnels. He once more began to trace out the cella and examine the workmanship. Where now was the inscription?

The rest of the party were standing in the side-chapel examining the statues when Graecen found them. Inscriptions? The guide would show him immediately. There was a united groan when it was found that these would involve the negotiation of a further tunnel. The guide spread his hands resignedly. What could he do?

It was a very narrow tunnel, whose walls were of a soft shaley conglomerate. Graecen realized how easily it crumbled when he put out a hand to steady himself. It did not seem safe at all. However, they managed to enter the small cave in

which there stood a battered inscription in marble. Graecen
saw with a thrill that it was part hieroglyph and part character.
The air was so close, however, in the confined space that they
could not stay long.

It was on the return journey that it happened; they had
entered one of the larger of the side-chapels and were about to
enter a tunnel in single file when with the noise of wet linen
flapping on a line a large partridge got up from a dark corner
and sailed through the roof like a comet. At once the guide
began to show interest; there was possibly a nest. If so it was
skilfully hidden, for though they combed the ledges in the
direction from which it had come they could see no trace of a
nest. Not content with this exploration, the guide hoisted himself upon a boulder and began to climb the wall. It was particularly silly and dangerous, as Campion had pointed out in
acid tones, since if he broke his leg they would never find their
way out. To Fearmax's remonstration the guide, however, only
turned a grinning face and waved one hand, imploring patience
and confidence in his powers. He disappeared across one of
the ledges and returned into the light to show them his find—
eggs; as he did so the projecting rock on which he was standing began to move.

Graecen, who was standing farther back just inside the entrance of the greater cavern saw the whole thing happen like a
slow-motion film of some great disaster; for a moment the
guide stood, his hands raised in a desperate effort to get his
balance. The huge stone, dislodged, appeared to move with
the slowness of a safe door; the ring of lights below opened
like a flower as the panic-stricken shout went up. "Look out!"
He heard Miss Dombey's voice above all the rest, and caught a
sudden flash of Fearmax's face in a beam of torch-light. The
concussion, too, seemed drawn out into slow-motion sound.
It was tremendous. Stone on stone, it rang out like a terrific
hammer-blow on the stagnant air. From the side of the cavern

issued a hail of complementary boulders and a great stream of mud and debris. The echo seemed to split his ear-drums. In the space of a few seconds he found himself lying on his back upon a moving tide of mud and stones which had completely blocked up the entrance to the cavern and cut him off from the rest of the party. The noise was still going on, though whether it was merely the echo or its original he could not tell. Somewhere in the very core of the noise he thought he heard, for a second, human voices shouting, but he could not be sure. Now from all quarters of the labyrinth there came noises of boulders falling, walls peeling and caving in, sympathetic disturbances set in motion by this great fall, whose vibration still crammed the air with eddies of sound. Graecen found he had cut his wrist; a stone had hit him on the back of the head; apart from this he was all right—but for how long? Small stones were falling from the roof of the cavern. What had happened to the others? In that confined space they had been trapped and beaten to death or suffocated. Or perhaps through those side-corridors. . . .

The guide had not escaped. His body lay under a great stone in ten feet of debris; but the others had had time to dodge out of the way of the oncoming avalanche into the safety (or what seemed then to be the safety) of the undercut entrances of tunnels. Up these vents they were propelled by the air squeezed out of the cavern, jammed like cartridges in the muzzle of a gun. The Truman couple found themselves gasping in a narrow tunnel with a hail of sticks and stones pressing upon them; Fearmax found himself lying on the ground while Miss Dombey moaned and wrung her hands over him. The ends of his trousers were soaked. He was lying in a large stagnant puddle while the noise reverberated behind them. He had received a blow on the shoulders which had knocked all the wind out of his body. He moaned and sat up, feeling for his torch. Meanwhile Campion struggled up what seemed an endless flight of stairs, half supporting the figure of Virginia, who had fainted. The full proportions of the disaster had not had time to weigh on them; they were still full of the surprise and horror of the incident, and had none of them dared to think that they had suddenly been buried alive, lost, entombed in the labyrinth which they had set off to explore that morning.

Meanwhile Graecen was standing, not more than twenty feet away from the burrows where they crawled, turning over the cold coins in his pocket and mumbling incoherent blasphemies in a hysterical voice. To him at least the full magnitude of the tragedy was apparent, since he alone seemed to have any chance of finding his way out. Now as he sat on a rock and rubbed his face clean with his handkerchief his mind, never very mercuric, seemed to be working at lightning speed trying to memorize the twists and turns of the paths by which they had come. It was hopeless. Somewhere they had forded a river, a long time ago. He looked at his watch and found that it had stopped. What was to be done? Graecen felt the blood freeze in his veins as he got slowly to his feet and walked round the cavern examining the numerous tunnels which offered themselves to his frightened eyes like so many gaping mouths eager to swallow him.

He chose the most familiar and set off down it memorizing every detail as he did so. A phrase of Hogarth's came unexpectedly into his mind and comforted him. "After all, Dickie," Hogarth had said, "if you think of death as a continuation of a process that has been going on for a considerable time it is not so serious a business as it really seems."

Was it not? Dying in bed was one thing; dying while your mother stood by you to smooth the pillows and hold your hand. But to die, slowly suffocating in this dense black pit—that was quite another. And what of the others? He stopped suddenly. He should have shouted, should have tried to reach them. Yet this had been so obviously an impossibility. He raised his head and shouted their names, scared at the sound of the echo that he raised. Then he listened dully to the icy silence that descended over the network of chambers and tunnels. His own footsteps sounded tiny and remote, like the scratching of a mole a thousand miles under the world. Once indeed he thought he heard the thin wailing of a voice which might have belonged to Miss Dombey, but when he stopped to listen only silence seeped coldly out of the labyrinth.

It was like a nightmare—one of those nightmares in which one feels trapped: but it ended suddenly when he happened upon a narrow strip of daylight, and found that he had blundered out on to the back of Cefalû, in full sight of the house he had come to die in. Graecen was trembling all over at the narrowness of his escape. He sat on a rock drinking in mouthfuls of the blue air, tasting the scent of the thyme, watching the blue race of the sea beneath the house. Never had the world seemed so desirable a thing. Rising at last on unsteady legs he made his way towards the house.

Axelos was sitting in the middle of the lawn, in the shadow of a plane tree, counting out money on to the green baize top of a folding card-table. Before him stood his servants waiting to receive their wages. He looked up as Graecen lurched across the gravel to the lawn, his sense of urgency giving him a drunkard's stagger.

"Dickie," said Axelos, recognizing him and getting up. "How very nice."

Graecen stood foolishly agape, one hand pressed to his racing heart, trying to speak. His friend advanced slowly across the lawn, with his familiar waddle. He was wearing pyjamas with a green and blue striping and an old straw hat. A cigar smouldered slowly away under his nose.

"An accident," Graecen said at last, sinking into a chair. "They're all trapped in the labyrinth."

He gave as accurate an account of the accident as was possible under the circumstances. Axelos set out with two of the servants for the mouth of the labyrinth, leaving him there, seated in the low deck-chair, his head tilted back, his eyes closed. He was waiting for his heart to slow down—or stop altogether. The palpitations had made him feel cold and sick. As soon as his suitcase came down he would give himself an injection. Now he emptied his mind, drew his breath deeply and regularly, and watched the dappled shadow of the sunlight, playing through the plane tree, flicker upon his eyelids. Kestrels were skimming and alighting upon the great limestone cone of Cefalû. He could hear their thin cries suddenly cut off—as if by scissors—when they dived. From the direction of the house came voices arguing—a familiar sound; they were spreading the news of the accident. Graecen sighed and stirred. He had forgotten to tell them that Baird was safe. The only one besides himself. His thoughts turned once more to the little party smothered in rock and earth in that burst antrum of stone; stuck like air-bubbles in glass beyond hope of rescue. He got up slowly and walked up the steps into the house.

The Enemy's Grave

His farewells completed Baird squared his shoulders under the old service pack and walked down the rocky road; he felt that they were standing silently watching him as he skirted the cherry grove, crossed the little circle of cultivation, and disappeared up the familiar cliff-path. He did not turn round and wave good-bye—the preoccupation with his mission was complete, creating a solitude around himself. His heart, however, was beating rather fast and he felt a trifle out of breath as he progressed along the ridge of the mountain with a taciturn and dogged persistence. Oddly enough it was not the familiar associations of danger and sudden death that came back to him as he entered the familiar scene of so many actions; rather was it the cumulative memories of days dedicated to boredom, to apathy, to waiting. Here, by this very myrtle bush, they had waited, the Abbot and he, for the mules to catch up; they had been arranging an ambush, and were doubtful of its success. He remembered with utter clarity the face of the Abbot as he shredded up the packet of cigarettes and moistened the tobacco into a chewable quid—for smoking had been forbidden during an operation. He remembered every word of that last conversation. They had discussed the illness of Koax and his possible death. A little higher up where the hill-side jutted he would smell the familiar scent of almonds and oranges from the little grove at the crown of Penthali.

He crossed a rock-torrent by the much-worn stone bridge, over which all their supplies had come; the water still gnashed as it leaped through the sluice and into the stony bed it had carved for itself the other side. At the last corner before he

turned west he repeated the familiar action which had become
a habit-pattern with them all—stopping for ten minutes under
the oak tree to see if anyone followed him along the path, and
then lighting a cigarette. He could hear the thin beat of his
heart in the crisp mountain air—a small tedious noise as of
knitting needles at work in his breast.

From here on it was along the level crown of Nanolithos;
the road turned and twisted under frowning limestone cliffs.
He walked it with an emphatic certainty, imitating in his own
mind the thousand and one journeys he had made along it in
the past. Yes, here was the tiny pink shrine to St. Nicholas
with its battered ikon and broken lamp; and near it on the tor
the rubble left from the ruined Venetian tower.

He skirted them both and passed steadily on until the massive front of dark rock divided itself into a ravine, with a solitary pathway running down the centre. He had reached the
entrance to their operation-headquarters, and for a moment he
stopped to watch the shadows playing on the surfaces of rock.
He felt stirring within him, deeper than his disease of mind,
something like alarm—as if somewhere among those balconies
of rock a watcher was sitting and observing him with invisible
eyes. Wherever he turned his gaze, however, his eyes met
nothing. A bush waved in the wind for a second and frightened him with its resemblance to the camouflage of a sharp-
shooter. He slung the pack on to one shoulder and mopped his
forehead with his handkerchief. In the khaki pack he carried
his lunch and the old bent entrenching-tool which, for some
reason or other, he had been carrying about for so many years.
He remembered now Hogarth's explanation of the reason, and
smiled. Had he really been reserving it for this moment, this
time and place, on a mountain-range in Crete?

He walked steadily down the causeway and through the
archway. It was with a kind of numb incomprehension that he
saw once more the exact site upon which Böcklin had been

killed; somehow he had expected to find it disappeared, transformed, perhaps removed altogether by a landslide. Yet here it was completely unchanged: the familiar orange seams of rock, the knot they had used as a target for their pistols, even the waterlogged shreds of the old ammunition box upon which Böcklin had been sitting when he died. The sweat had started out upon his head; he could feel its coldness in the breath of the wind that played around the ravine. He stood staring stupidly at the rock, which at this point was full of caves and foxholes. In them the wind whistled shrilly. Familiar debris still lay about, broken matchboxes, bandages, a torn sock, some exhausted revolver bullets. He stopped and picked up an empty case, turning it over and over in his cold fingers. Then once more he had the feeling that perhaps he was being watched, and looked up at the frowning sills of rock above, but all was still as death. The wind moaned in the central cavern which was set like a sinus under the cliff. The marks of their fires still dirtied the walls. Outside there was nothing. High in the cloudless blue an eagle sat its chariot of Greek air; the grass rustled quietly around his boots. This was the exact spot, in the shadow of the cliff, where Böcklin's grave had been; the winter rains had washed out any depression in the ground.

It was almost absently that Baird began to dig; but before he did so he sat down close to the grave and ate ravenously. Somehow his agitation had translated itself into a devouring physical hunger. The bread and cheese tasted delicious in that cold air. He had filled an empty beer bottle at the rock-spring. Now as he ate and drank he asked himself what he was going to do with Böcklin's body when he had exhumed it. The monastery was half an hour off; he would have to notify the Abbot and the sacristan of his desire to bury him in consecrated ground. And if they objected?

Putting these vexatious afterthoughts aside he took up his

entrenching-tool and began the work. Somewhere out of sight
a bird was singing softly, complainingly, in that cold air. He
dug with circumspection, gently as an archaeologist afraid of
damaging a trophy. The earth was not hard, for it lay in the
dense shadow of the cliff where the dews could reach it. He
paused for a moment to roll up his sleeves before resuming the
work. How would Böcklin look now?

It was only after an hour's work that it suddenly became
clear to him that *Böcklin was not there.* The idea was borne in
slowly upon a long train of evidence, and for some time he
refused to countenance it. But by the time the sun had passed
its zenith he had dug himself a hole large enough to prove the
point conclusively. At first he felt his back and shoulders con-
vulsed by a kind of shiver—as if the chill air of the mountain
had suddenly affected him. He went on working, however,
long after the probability had become a certainty. It seemed
somehow imperative to find the body; and yet there was not a
single trace of it to be found. He walked up and down the
edges of the burrow he had dug, smoking and thinking furiously. Was it possible that a War Graves unit had removed the
body to a military cemetery? It was most unlikely, for they
would have their work cut out on chartered battlefields—like
those near Canea and Retimo. Besides, who could have reported Böcklin's death? Or had the body decayed? He kicked
around in the pit for a while, sifting the rich clayey compost
through his fingers, searching for traces that would give him
some clue: tunic-buttons, rags, medals. There was absolutely
no trace of his victim, and he suddenly sat down on a rock
with a gesture of acceptance and began to laugh. Agitation and
relief mingled with a confused amazement. It suddenly
occurred to him that perhaps Hogarth, in order to complete
the pattern of symbolism, had deliberately removed Böcklin.
"That's it," he said to himself, still laughing, "that old bastard
Hogarth has done it." He had a long drink of water and sat

for a while soberly on a rock, smoking, his eyes fixed upon the grave. Then they wandered to the mouldy remnants of the ammunition box. Somewhere, in the depths of his mind, he felt that a corner had been turned; and yet after a while he was so overcome by his thoughts and the oppressive silence that had descended upon the place that he got up abruptly and moved off, tossing his spade into the hole he had dug with it.

He soon found himself sitting in a grove of ilex and arbutus on the opposite hill-side, enjoying a sensation of relief and deliverance—as if he had conquered a grave hazard. Through the waving fronds he caught sight of the sea from time to time. Its broad candid blue tamed his anxiety. He drank in the keen air with a heightened delight.

The shadows were already lengthening when he rose and followed a rocky bridle-path downhill. He had decided to walk across to St. George and see whether the old Abbot was indeed still there; in Canea they seemed to think he was. Perhaps he could throw some light on the question of Böcklin. And over and above all these things there was the question of finding out what the good Abbot was doing with the smuggled ammunition that Whitehall were so anxious about. It would be the best policy of all to call direct on the Abbot John before his arrival had been announced; Baird's experience of Greeks had taught him that boldness was the only method to obtain his ends.

In a little while he came across a man in blue trousers goading a small laden hill-donkey along with sharp objurgations. He was able to ask the question that lay uppermost in his mind after the usual exchange of civilities. "Up at the monastery—is the Abbot John still there?" The peasant had a broad but starting forehead with a widow's peak of hair. He spat with unction. "They are always there," he said. "Thieves, blackmailers, priests." Baird smiled. "Greece", said the man, "carries the priest in her skin like a dog fleas."

"Greece could do with more patriots as fine as her priests," said Baird shortly, thinking of the marvellous actions of the old Abbot, his joyousness and insouciance; craziness and humour, childishness and resolution; that kaleidoscope of emotions which is forever turning in the Greek's brain, defying logic. The man looked at him with a grudging pleasure. He had simply wanted a grumble—the natural conversational form of Greeks. "Well," he said, "the Abbot John is a swindler."

This Baird did not doubt for a second. He turned the subject towards a more congenial exchange of information. The man had two children. He was a fisherman (which was synonymous with pirate in Baird's vocabulary). He was from the village of Nesboli—two hours away. Baird could not resist telling him that he had been there when the Germans had burnt down the village. "The Abbot John saved your kinsfolk then," he said. "What has he done to make you speak like this of him?"

It was clear from the conversation that followed that the man was in the habit of unloading caiques at the coast and bringing up loads on his donkeys to the monastery. Baird did not ask him what the caiques were filled with. Instead he professed indifference and at the next corner of the road they parted.

He was almost down to the sea-line again as he skirted the cliff-path above St. George. Below him, perched on the irregular hill-side he could see the red belfry and the white wall of the monastery glowing in the light of the afternoon sun. It had been built at a point where a shallow stream made an issue through the rock to reach the sea. Thus, in all that wild landscape it seemed to be an oasis of greenery, for the fresh water had thrown up cherry and walnut trees to cluster about it. Seen from above, the little building seemed to float upon this dense green sheet of foliage. A narrow shaded path led to the great oak door over cobbles; Baird fingered the familiar burns in the wood, remembering the occasion when Germans had conducted reprisals here on captive guerillas. Then he caught the massive knocker in both hands and knocked twice.

There was no answer. The door yielded slightly to his shoulder and opened, admitting him; he was standing once more in the little white courtyard paved with coloured sea-pebbles. The sunlight was white and lucid on the rock. Flowers were growing in pots along the sea-wall and he noticed that in some of them grew sweet basil, the Abbot's favourite plant. He stood quite still and looked about him. Somewhere from the back of the building came a noise as of a pot being scoured with sand. The door of the little chapel was open. Inside the gloom was intense as that of a cave. Baird stepped inside, crossed himself, and waited for his eyes to begin printing the remembered picture. Gradually they emerged like a developing photo—the savage ikons with their tinsel haloes, the swinging lamps, the garish ironwork and plate. Presently, too, St. Demetrius swam out of the gloom—his eyes great boring points of blackness. Baird saw a bottle of olive oil on the ledge and, taking it according to custom, he tipped a little into each lamp to replenish it.

Now he crossed the dazzling courtyard and looked over the sea-wall. Withes of brown fishing-net lay spread upon a rock to dry. A small coracle of wood and straw was drawn up under the stairs leading down to the water. Several brown gourd-like lobster-pots lay beside it. Not a breath stirred the sea as it stretched clear from that white wall to the coasts of Africa. He watched it quietly swelling and subsiding, replete in its trance of royal blue. Once it gulped and swelled a few inches to carry back with it the limpet-shells left behind by some rock-fisherman.

Baird skirted the main building, struck by a sudden idea. The sea-wall ended in a small white balcony and a pergola of grape-vine. Here lay the Abbot fast asleep in an old deck-chair, his noble beard lying upon his chest, his brown wrinkled hands with their short nails lying folded in his lap. His stove-pipe hat stood beside him on the ground, and his feet were stretched out, one on either side of it, clad in heavy hob-nailed boots. Baird came up quietly and sat down upon the white sea-wall, facing him, looking eagerly at that venerable and inno-cent old face. Here he sat, waiting for the Abbot to wake, and feeling himself sinking insensibly into a doze, little by little; sinking through the floors of thought and action to that level in which one becomes suddenly one with the passive, accept ing sea and air. It was as if all the contradictions and questions which had been filling his mind had suddenly been spilled into this broad and gracious quietness. He felt his eyes closing and his head falling upon his breast.

Once or twice the Abbot stirred in his sleep and seemed to be on the point of waking, but each time he settled himself deeper into the honey-gold quietness of the afternoon, into his own contented slumber. At last, when Baird was almost asleep himself, the old man spoke, without opening his eyes. "Well, my dear Baird," he said; and now he looked up. "We all knew you would come back. It was simply a question of when."

He rose groaning from his chair and they embraced ten-derly. Then he sat down again and closed his eyes for a moment, before taking a packet of cheap cigarettes from the folds of his stained gown and lighting up. He yawned prodi-giously and said: "I was aware that someone was sitting silently before me. I thought perhaps I was being covered by a revol-ver. You see? We haven't shaken off our old habits yet. I just had a peep through my lashes to see what was what. Have you noticed that it is quite impossible for one to murder a sleeping man?"

"I knew you'd seen me," said Baird.

"And so, my dear fellow," said the Abbot, his face wrinkled

shrewdly into a smile, "you have come back at last to revisit the scene of so many adventures." He got up and put his arms round Baird, giving him a great bear-hug. Then he brushed the ash out of his beard and stretched again, yawning. "I cannot think of anything better," he said.

"And what's going on in the great world?" he asked, with that typical Greek passion for news from abroad.

"It is all exactly as you prophesied."

"The nations are quarrelling?"

"Yes."

"I knew it. About possessions?"

"Pipe-lines, spheres of influence, trade. . . ."

"Did you expect anything different?"

Baird saw once more the shrewd hawk-like cut of the Abbot's features, the curly rings of his beard around his wry mouth, and remembered those endless conversations with which they whiled away their inaction and solitude on the White Mountains. "I did," he admitted at last. "I thought everything would be different once the basic revolution in property had been accomplished. I was wrong."

"False premises, false conclusions," said the Abbot John, and passed his hand slowly through his great beard, brushing away the cigarette ash which had a habit of clinging to it. "But console yourself. You are not the only person who is wrong. Wait until I introduce you to Brother Mark. Brother Mark is one of us—probably the most diligent. He believes that it is we who are building the new world—the new heaven and earth; here in this monastery. He believes that the invisible propaganda of our lives here is somewhere registered to our credit—to the credit of all humanity. Now surely that is just as bad as any business man? It proves that Brother Mark has not learned his own business yet. Virtue, and the practice of it, is its own end."

"That is why", said Baird, "you spend the intervals in

business? You must be a rich man by now, both spiritually and financially."

The Abbot looked slightly discountenanced. He coughed and examined the sky for a moment. "It is true", he said in a faraway voice, glancing at Baird out of the corner of his eye, "that I am engaged in rather a profitable business at the moment."

"It's causing alarm in London."

"What?" said the Abbot. "Do they speak of it in London? Is it so widely known?"

Baird could see that in his mind's eye he was seeing a picture of London—a town slightly bigger than Megara—in which the citizens spent the day sitting on chairs outside their front doors and gossiping; an occasional shepherd passed with his goat, and sold the milk direct from the udder to the customer, milking it into any receptacle that was handy and receiving his payment at once; occasionally a lord in a top-hat passed in a car. "So they speak of me in London?" repeated the Abbot, registering something mid-way between pride and alarm. "What do they say?"

"That guns are necessary for revolutions."

The Abbot giggled and hid his face in his sleeve. "Are you hungry?" he said, and, without waiting for an answer, clapped his hands twice and shouted: "Calypso."

A small girl came round the corner of the house with quick lithe steps. "Bring whatever we have to eat. Your godfather is here," said the old man. She embraced Baird rather self-consciously and brought them food; some bread, black olives, onions and wine.

"Will you stay long?" asked the Abbot John, obviously working out in his mind the estimated time of arrival for a shipment of smuggled goods.

"I am at Cefalû," he said, "staying with Axelos. Perhaps I shall stay some time. I am so glad to be back." It was on the tip of his tongue to say something of Böcklin, to mention his visit to the mountain hideout, but the Abbot had embarked on a new line of thought. "All the world", he said, "is coming to Cefalû. It seems there is something wonderful about the statues and things we found in the caves. Now here is something I don't understand." He paused.

"What?" said Baird.

"Old Axelos," said the Abbot, "is he right in the head? He wishes me to pretend that I helped him *carve* some of the things in there. What do you make of that? He has given me a hundred pounds to swear it, and not to tell anyone that we *discovered* the statues together." He stamped his foot. "There," he said. "I've done it again. It was supposed to be a secret. First I accept his money and then I tell someone about it." He struck his forehead twice with the knuckles of a huge gnarled fist. "The cursed garrulity of us monks—it is sinful. May the Creator punish us all." He made Baird promise that he would not repeat the story. The Abbot relaxed and said: "But, after all, why should I not tell you everything—you are one of my oldest friends? Why should I not tell you also that that peasant woman Katina—he is married to her? I married them myself. Then why does he keep her as a servant in the house and never give her her dues as a wife? No, there's something wrong with him."

They walked together up and down the still courtyard. Baird admired the new lamp in the chapel, the pots of basil, and the vegetable patch. The three other monks who shared the old man's monastic solitude were asleep. "I am very happy," said the old man. "So very happy. I have never spent my time to better advantage. I see no one. I think of nothing. I pray a little and sleep a lot. As for the guns you mentioned, I will tell you about it so that you can reassure the citizens of London. There is no thought of revolution here. It is business only. I buy them cheap from the Jews in Palestine and sell

them at a profit to the Jews of Tripoli. We are happily placed
for communications here and recently some of the bravest sea-
men have come back to their villages. It is not a great profit,
but it is a profit—and, of course, it is always a pleasure to make
a profit from the Jews. Are you satisfied?"

Baird was glad that the whole subject had come into the
open; it enabled him to compliment the Abbot on his honesty,
when the old man knew well enough that for ten pounds
down any peasant would have furnished the required information. They walked, their arms amiably linked, and Baird found
himself once more admiring those eagle's features from which
every trace of earthly grossness seemed to have been purged,
listening to that musical-assured voice. The Abbot was a
philosopher whose judgment occasionally foundered in his
cupidity.

The old man's daughter came and handed him a bunch of
spring anemone and kissed him.

"Come," said the Abbot. "You must stay tonight at least
with us. We have a lot to say to each other. You shall have
Niko's little room."

Together they mounted the long white staircase of wood to
the terrace. Baird could hear snoring from behind a closed
door. Brilliant dragon-flies scouted the flowers. The sea shook
itself and settled into sleep once more.

The small white cell was spotless. It contained a bed, two
vivid oleographs, a table and a chair. The window looked clear
out on to the sea. "I will send you a couple of blankets. It must
be very primitive after what you are used to, but it is all we
have."

Baird lay down on the bed and said: "Thank God, Abbot,
for the Mediterranean basin. Do you still bathe at the point? I
should like to try and get brown all over again."

"After you have slept," said the old man tenderly, shaking
hands with him again and smiling. The little girl came in bear-

ing a pitcher of fresh water and a bowl. "Ah, Calypso," said Baird, "you are becoming a woman of the house." She smiled and withdrew again, but not before the Abbot had pulled her pigtails and called her a werewolf-child. "In ten years' time," he said proudly, "there won't be a prettier girl in Crete."

"By that time", said Baird, "we shall be fighting the Russians or the Chinese."

The old man sat upon the chair and threw one leg over the other. He gazed earnestly at Baird for a long time without speaking. "There's something else as yet," he said at last, with all his old shrewdness. "That is in your mind to ask me. Something you have come to find out."

"Yes," said Baird. "It's not important."

"At the heart of the honeycomb lies the sweetness," said the Abbot oracularly. "What can it be?"

He listened attentively while Baird told him of his dream; of the reappearance of Böcklin in his mind; of the visits to Hogarth. Somehow he found it very simple to express the basis of Hogarth's teaching to the old man. He nodded all the time. It was surely the first person he had met, thought Baird, to whom Hogarth's peculiar doctrines were not unfamiliar or downright insane. When he spoke of Hogarth's suggestion that he should return and dig up Böcklin and lay his body in consecrated ground, the Abbot John slapped his knee heavily and said: "This man is a very wise man. A very wise man. In this way your conscience would clear itself and the dream would lift."

"But it has lifted anyway," said Baird excitedly. "In fact, it has lifted by a miracle. For Böcklin is not there—is not anywhere, unless you have moved him."

The Abbot shook his head. "Unless", said Baird, "this sudden feeling of liberation is false. Unless I dream of him again. But I feel as if a miracle had happened; as if he had never existed."

The Abbot leaned forward and patted his arm reassuringly. "You will see for yourself in time," he said. "Now I am going to leave you for an hour's sleep. Then we shall walk down to the sea together like in the old times."

Baird fell asleep as he was leaning down to undo his boots.

In the Darkness

For a time she sat in the darkness and tried to shake Fearmax awake, but after a while it became clear to her that he must be dead. The dampness of his clothes conveyed the horrible suggestion of blood flowing from serious wounds. His hands were cold and clenched. Miss Dombey had lost her little torch in the confusion, and she groped at his bony face in the darkness, uttering little wails of terror and supplication. "Mr. Fearmax," she cried. "Mr. Fearmax." There was no response. She got up at last and walked slowly down the narrow corridor; she was beginning to feel the staleness of the air, to wonder whether they were not bricked into a tunnel from which there was no escape. She was still moaning under her breath. Her hands outstretched like a sleep-walker she proceeded step by step. When she had gone some twenty paces in this manner her fuddled wits came to life and she remembered that there was a box of matches in her coat. With trembling fingers she cast back her tweed overcoat and took the little box out. The first match shone for a second along an empty black passage-way and went out. The second burned a little steadier. The corridor seemed to have become larger, the ceiling higher. Strange reverberations still shuddered through the length and breadth of the stone honeycomb; dust hung in the unbreathed air. The light went out.

Miss Dombey's mind was filled with a confusion of panic-stricken images in which all continuity was lost; past and present mingled freely. Perhaps *this* was the Second Coming she had been so assiduously advertising for so long? She saw the Guardian's face, with its pale attenuated lines, engraved upon the darkness before; saw Mr. Sowerby peering through his steel-rimmed spectacles at the Wigmore Hall. She struck another match in her nerveless fingers, and then another. She had concentrated so completely upon the death of the world and its summary judgment that she was totally unable to decrease the compass of her thoughts enough for the contemplation of her own personal death. Numbly, with chattering teeth, she went forward, without a plan, lighting match after match until the box was empty. Then she sat down in the darkness and began to weep. What would Andrew, her brother, say? She had not seen him for years. He had been in Quetta with the Army.

Growing up in her mind there came a feeling that perhaps some sort of summing-up, some sort of clue to her whole life's activities, might be disentangled from this terrible accident which had befallen her. Yet what? She saw her life stretching away, incidents appearing and dissolving before her eyes as meaningless as Chinese idiograms. She was back in the mission-house at Hwang-Tu. Her father was talking about the mystery of the Cross to a group of Chinese children. "To settle your differences with your own soul," he was saying in that rich deep voice. His clothes smelt of cheroots, his silver hair played on his neck. Her fingers closed absently upon the little phial of sleeping-tablets in her pocket and she remembered Dr. Andrews, looking over the top of his glasses at her, warning her not to take more than . . .

She heard the dull roar of the minotaur sounding in the depths ahead. The noise passed her in the damp heavy air, almost like an object of weight and substance. She opened the bottle and shook out the little tablets into her palm. Something at the farther end of the corridor moved, a vague shape of darkness upon darkness. She shouted "Hullo! Anyone there?" but her empty voice was flung back at her from the stony throat of the tunnel in little flat echoes.

She swallowed them one by one, remembering how adept she had become at swallowing pills without any water. Malaria had taught her that during the last visit to Egypt. It was with something that bore a recognizable resemblance to relief that she lay down on the cold stone of the corridor wrapped in her coat.

Now she was walking once more across the paddy-fields, hand in hand with her father. Small clouds of thistledown floated in the sky above the river. At the door of the temple a little old man was sitting very softly carving upon a peach-stone; the brooch was one that her father had given her. She lost it one day walking across the wet meadows near Horsham. Search as she might, she could never discover where. It was like the severance of a link in time; she had been cut off from her father by that far more completely than by his own death in China years before. Cut off from her own childhood, that term of happiness and tenderness which she was never to know again once the sea was crossed and Dover reached. She remembered the silent reaches of the lock, the convoy of swans sailing upstream, the yellow kingcups standing attentively by while she walked backwards and forwards, searching and weeping.

Miss Dombey sat up for a moment and opened her eyes. She knew now, for the first time, with complete accuracy, that she was going to die. The familiar sluggish throb of her heart, its strange drugged rhythm had conveyed the information to her. In a sense she was no longer afraid of the labyrinth, since it was no longer the labyrinth that was killing her. Ah, but this was not the martyr's death she had dreamed about; it was something small and irremediable, lacking even the small logic of her faith and beliefs.

She did not wish to think of God, yet she supposed that someone in her position ought to be praying. "Oh God," she began accordingly, repeating the formulae that stretched

away on all sides of her like well-trodden paths, "Why have
I never really believed in You?"

Even through her drowsiness she recognized this as a very
remarkable beginning to a prayer; yet the sense of something
lacking, even in this confession, persisted. Father, Son and
Holy Ghost—what did they mean? They rattled about inside
her mind like nutmegs in a tin. Yet over and above it all she
felt the emanations of her father; her father reading from the
big black book; her father preaching; climbing on to his knee
to let him cherish her and rub his warm palms upon the back of
her small neck. In some vague way the Second Coming had
been designed as a plot to bring him back. It was in the shadow
of this immense Imago that Miss Dombey fell asleep at last. . . .

Fearmax, for his part, awoke with a large lump on the top of
his head, and the feeling of having been involved in an earth-
quake. For a long time he lay quite still, moving his arms and
feet gently to see if they were intact. Apart from the contusion
upon his head, and the feeling of sickness he could trace no
other infirmity due to the adventure. He had fallen sideways,
so that his body rested upon his mackintosh, in whose pockets
he felt the hard edges of the carton containing his lunch. He
lay for a long time staring into the blackness, every nerve relaxed, wondering what he should do next. His last coherent
memory was of the guide planing through space towards him
astride an enormous boulder. What had happened? The debris,
perhaps, had pushed him to one side, down this stone chute.
Slowly he sat up, groaning more in anticipation of broken
limbs than in any real discomfort. His head, however,
throbbed from the blow; but did not appear to be bleeding.
His feet were chilled to the bone from the large pool of water
in which he had been lying. He picked up the sodden mackintosh and groped for the box of matches he knew he had been
carrying. In the little yellow spurt of flame his eye caught the
glimmer of something on the ground not three paces away.

It was his torch, and picking it up with trembling fingers, he pressed the button, relieved to see once more the powerful yellow beam without whose aid he would have been as helpless as a blind man.

He turned it first upon the blocked passage-way behind, examining the great mound of stones and mud which had been forced like a cork into the neck of a bottle; before him, however, the corridor stretched away into infinity. What was he to do? Fearmax felt a strange calm descend upon him, a sense of well-being and relaxation. It was as if there were nothing more to wish for, and nothing to fear—a resolution had been made in terms of destiny. He must walk as fast and as far as he could, in the hope of finding an issue. But first he sat down and ate, balancing his torch on his knee to do so. It was a welcome pause, too, for he had not fully collected his wits. He noticed the wet footmarks leading from the puddle with a sudden start; he had not been alone, then. But who had left him like that, without a word, and walked off down the corridor? The footprint was small enough to be that of a woman.

Fearmax bolted the rest of his food in his excitement and set off down the corridor, stopping at intervals to shout "Hullo!" Hope sprang up in his breast at the thought that he was not alone in the labyrinth. But as the corridors multiplied and ramified, stretching away into infinity, he became despondent. How could one find anyone in this maze? It was possible, too, that he was only going in a circle.

He passed through a cavern into which the blinding blue sky peered and threw up startling images of volcanic rock, blue, gold and green, which covered the walls like dried sealing-wax. Fearmax looked longingly at the sky, raising his thin arms and shouting until the echoes wheeled down over him like a flock of exhausted birds. Ten feet of rope was all he needed to gain his liberty. Yet it would be fatal to linger.

He started off once more at a great pace. At least if he could reach the river they had crossed it would be something, but cavern led to dry cavern, tunnel to tunnel, until he felt completely dazed and bewildered. Several times, too, he stumbled and bruised his ankles, for the going was rough and the surfaces uneven.

Now gradually his pace slackened and he became more composed. He had found a battered cigar in his coat-pocket and the rich smoke soothed his nerves. In his mind he found himself composing sentences which, if he were to escape from the labyrinth, would find a place in the book he planned to write. The theme was a simple one and owed a good deal to Hogarth; he was writing a treatise upon the psychic mind—its predisposition to epilepsy and schizophrenia. It was to be a guide to the mediums of the future. "To deal with evidence that cannot be reconciled to the body and canons of everyday science has been the task of all independent minds since the beginning of history. It is no less the task of the individual in whose experience must inevitably arise emotions or thoughts which are neither rational nor commonplace. The body of work left us by men like Blake or Nostradamus. . . ." He bumped his head on a ledge and stopped to swear. "Madness, therefore, must be a conditional term in our judgment of them." His torch picked up arch after arch, corridor after corridor. The labyrinth seemed to have no end.

Suddenly Fearmax thought of "French Marie". He thought of her with a sudden pang of anguish, and halted in his tracks. Could it be that the footsteps he had seen near where he lay . . . ? Or was he losing his mind—that it should entertain so fantastic an idea. Yet try as he might he could not rid himself of its seduction. Perhaps among these corridors he would come upon the real "French Marie", the partner and wife he had been searching for for so long. He was sitting upon a stone idly watching the smoke from his cigar trail off down the corridor. A sudden idea struck him? *Where was the smoke going?* Surely it must be naturally drawn off down a current of air? And a current of air pointed the direction of an issue? He laughed hoarsely. Was the smoke leading him, then, to the surface; or perhaps somewhere ahead "French Marie" was waiting for him, waiting to be sought out and recognized.

Fearmax started off once more, following the smoke from his long cigar, pausing every few paces to blow another puff into the sterile air of the tunnel; it moved sluggishly but perceptibly away, leading along tunnels which seemed to descend, across galleries of rock with vaulted arches, for all the world as if they had been designed by human architects. Fearmax followed, one half of his mind still grappling with the problems of composition. "Their work constitutes, therefore, as does that of the medium, deliberate evidence of states of being *not communicable* in linguistic terms."

Could she really be there, waiting for him? The idea both delighted and terrified him. What would they speak of when they met? The smoke led remorselessly onward; once it led him through a cavern where stalactites dribbled noisily, and he thought he had found the river. But he was disappointed again. Had it been the river, he thought, he might have floated down it to the sea, and yet it would be horrible to be lodged in some cranny too small to admit the passage of his body— lodged like a tea-leaf in a tooth and suffocated. He tried to reconstruct a long quotation from Mysers with which he had intended to end his book. It was about materializations; it reminded him suddenly of the bubbles of paraffin drying—inside them the invisible plump and shapely hands of "French Marie". Why had she suddenly deserted him? And why had he come all the way to Crete to get lost in this hideous labyrinth? Was there a pattern, a design about it all?

Hogarth would have first asked him to question himself as to the dramatic justification for such a situation. He remembered him saying: "We act our inner symbolism outward into the world. In a very real sense we do create to the world around us since we get it to reflect back our inner symbolism at us. Every man carries a little myth-making machine inside him which operates often without him knowing it. Thus you might say that we live by a very exacting kind of poetic logic —since we get exactly what we ask for, no more and no less."

Fearmax wondered now whether he had "asked for" this damp gloom, these caves with their melancholy sound of water falling, and the blank bottomless silence which drank it all up at last—to the very dregs?

Before he had time to answer it he heard it—that shapeless echoing roar which memory made familiar to him as the voice of the minotaur. He stopped irresolutely. It seemed to come from some distance away. His torch which had been so bright had become all of a sudden very dim—perhaps the damp had affected the cells of the battery. He took a corridor indicated by the slowly-travelling smoke and hurried on a dozen paces. What kind of animal could make a sound like that?

The corridors sloped gently down to a sort of natural *rond point* from which other corridors jutted, scattering through all the points of the compass. Here the air still vibrated with the passage of the monster's roaring.

"What is reality?" said Fearmax aloud, and recognized it as one of those questions whose import had troubled him for as long as he could remember. His feet—the same feet that had walked backwards and forwards across the damp pavements of Exeter—what were they doing here? Or was this whole place merely a mad exteriorization of his inner confusion; his feet walking slowly down metaphoric corridors of his own subconscious—in which only the roar of the sleeping monster gave him a clue to his primal guilt? It was a pretty fancy. If he ever got out he would have the pleasure of sharing it with Hogarth. The work of Rank on the symbolic significance of labyrinths, and their connexion with divination by entrails.

Olaf's observations upon the corridors of the Great Pyramid; was it possible that the place he was traversing had been hollowed by the hands of men to suit some occult purpose? That in coming here he had been sent with a purpose: to make his own observations and deductions upon cults and sciences long since dead—or else only preserved in the esoteric forms of alchemy, or the Tarot pack of cards? It was a proposition. His feet had begun to hurt. Fearmax began to talk to himself aloud with complete freedom; it was as if the last barrier between himself as an individual and himself as a personality had been dissolved. He could hear his muffled tones glancing from the archways around him. He blew out a long tape of smoke and watched it slowly quest, like a pointer, until it at last found the right corridor and vanished down it. He followed slowly, cautiously, talking aloud.

"Suppose, then, that all this were simply an apprenticeship."

"Towards what possible end?"

"A novitiate towards a new degree of self-knowledge."

"My poor man, you are raving."

The roar of the minotaur sounded again. "No," he cried suddenly, apprehensively. His torch had dimmed down to a dim circle of yellow light, incapable of piercing the farther end of the corridor. Fearmax sat on a stone and took another puff at his cigar; of the two corridors facing him one was clearly indicated. The smoke quickened as it was sucked noiselessly into it. Somewhere, vaguely, it was as if he could smell something, something like scent. And yet it was not really a smell, for when he concentrated he could smell nothing beyond the dampness and the smoke of his cigar. Somewhere beyond the shadows, perhaps "French Marie" was waiting. He got up and advanced upon the two corridors that faced him; his smoke dawdled slowly ahead of him. Yet it was from the second, the one down which the smoke had not gone, that he heard the steely vibrations of the minotaur's voice—a dull jangling like strings out of tune, like dusts being washed backwards and forwards in a confined space.

It was not a question of conscious choice, it was rather as if all activity save this devouring and overmastering curiosity in his mind had been suspended. He turned aside from the smoke and entered the other corridor; it was now that a curious thing happened. He began to feel that it was all a dream—as if he were lost in one of those dreams which confuse our childhood. He felt fear, yes, but at one remove: as if through the clouds of a morphia injection. He was supported now by the vertical clear flame of this overmastering curiosity to know what exactly the minotaur could be. Perhaps it was only one of "French Marie's" disguises, one of her voices or aspects?

A faint odour seemed to have grown up in the corridor he was traversing; it was somehow unpleasant and yet familiar. His feet began to scrape against objects on the hard stone floor; he picked them up and examined them in the last wavering flicker of his torch before it gave out completely. They were twigs of wood. They broke dryly between finger and thumb. Was he then moving towards the lair of some animal which carried twigs down into the underworld to line its nest?

He halted for a second to get his breath, wondering whether he should not turn round and retrace his steps; it was however in the same direction that he found himself moving, his feet scraping against twigs and branches, his nostrils full of an odour he had already begun to recognize as that of putrefaction. What was it? He drew several deep breaths of the foul air and suddenly his memory provided him with a clue. Once as a boy he had found a heron's nest as he was walking across the marshes. The bird was sitting upon a structure of filthy twigs, surrounded by the half-chewed and decomposing remains of its feasts—fragments of fish and gobbets of field-mice. Now it was the same odour of decomposition that he smelt, only greatly magnified. What kind of animal would have so deep a burrow, and live upon carrion? His imagination simply could not supply an answer.

He sat down upon the stone floor and rested his face in his hands, thinking furiously. Somewhere an obstinate thought seemed to divine the presence of "French Marie" behind it all; a nerve of misery and disquiet in himself which could not be quietened without the promise of her. And yet this terrifying odour of rotten flesh filled the close air of the corridor, and he trembled so violently now that it was as much as he could do to control his limbs. His fear seemed to stretch away on either side of him, filling the hollow sinuses of rock, overbrimming them. His breathing had become harsh now and stertorous. Was he about to enter the trance-condition so long denied him? Was he about to hear that window open abruptly in the air above him, and the voice which so long had tantalized him by a half-uttered word, *speak*?

Even as he was thinking this thought he heard, at the farther end of the corridor, a faint noise—like the dim and paralytic shuffling of some very aged person. He was reminded of the harmless shuffle of carpet slippers across the wooden floors of the museum library. Presently there came a gust of tepid air— as if the displacement of some large body farther down the tunnel had driven it towards him. He called out, and as he did so tasted the impure, fetid breath of the Thing. It moved slowly in his direction—so slowly that the anguish was unbearable. It moved towards him at the speed of ice-crystals forming upon the stalactites, of the ash growing upon his cigar, of the nails growing upon his ten fingers. As yet he could see nothing, but the vague swollen promise of the darkness ahead. His torch lay expiring on the floor beside him.

Then, at last, the immensity of darkness seemed to thicken, to ripen, to swell out towards him and he saw what appeared to him to be a pair of small bloodshot eyes moving towards

him. Fearmax put his hands over his face and mentally sur-
rendered himself to it. His lips moved but no sound came
from them. He felt himself picked up at last in a soft wet
mouth of enormous dimensions and carried, half-senseless,
down the long damp corridors of the labyrinth.

At the Monastery

It was still high afternoon when Baird awoke and washed his face in the cold spring-water from the enamel jug. The Abbot was tending his vines. "Bravo," he cried, "I'm glad you're in time to bathe." Together they walked across the woodland paths to the little spit of shale which formed the promontory's butt. With them went the faithful Mark, carrying the towels and a basket of fruit to refresh them. The sea was an ineffable blue; as if, thought Baird, our bodies would turn Tyrian blue from dipping into it. A dolphin leaped for the sun about four cables' length out, hitting the water with the smack of a football squarely kicked. Baird took off his clothes as one might take off the soiled and ragged clouts of this world and lay down upon the hot pebbles. "Come," he said, "I know you Greeks never find the water warm enough till August. Make an exception." The Abbot pleaded old age and all its infirmities, and carefully tested the temperature with his finger. "It's terribly cold," he said, turning pale. "I could never bathe in that." But under the lash of Baird's teasing he finally slipped off his robes and hob-nailed boots, and did up his back-hair into a tidy bun. Brother Mark reverently took the stove-pipe hat and sat on a point to observe. The old man entered the water uttering groans of rage. His large flabby body was like oak. Baird saw the bullet-marks in his shoulder and thigh—purple scars that looked like knots in old wood. "Here I come," he said, and they swam slowly out into the icy blueness.

"Mark. Wash the grapes," called the Abbot, and the little

monk obeyed. "Mark's contributions to our researches into theology and morals are wonderful," said the old man, doing his jerky dog-paddle out to sea. "He moves from prejudice to prejudice like a logician from premises to conclusion." Baird turned on his back and saw the little monk washing the grapes tenderly and drying them on his master's towel.

They walked back, all three arm in arm, to the monastery garden, where Baird and the Abbot, reclining in deck-chairs, the sea at their feet, spent the rest of the afternoon in idle innocence, eating and talking bad philosophy. Brother Mark sat discreetly in earshot, drinking it all in. "Mark," said the Abbot suddenly, "what is goodness?" He nudged Baird and invited his amusement at poor Mark's answers by wrinkling up his nose. Brother Mark shook his evil-looking forelock in their direction and raised the hand from which an exploding depth-charge ill-fused had removed two fingers. "Goodness", he said, "is doing right. Doing what the book says."

"Which book?" said the Abbot.

"The good book," said Mark darkly. He knew he was being made fun of; he moved his jaws with a queer chewing motion.

"And if you cannot read?" persisted the Abbot.

"The Abbot John is my eyes," replied the monk with the air of having scored heavily. The Abbot roared with laughter and slapped his knee. "Was ever a man so focused on goodness?" he asked. "He would disembowel his mother if I told him to. I don't think he's a real Greek—he is not argumentative in a sunny obstreperous Greek fashion; but in a gloomy way, like an Englishman or someone suffering from interior stresses." Baird closed his eyes and stretched out his legs towards the sea. In the gutter two scorpions copulated like watch springs. Bees droned in among their conversations, and almost palpable waves of heat came off the stone wall of the terrace. The Abbot caught sight of Brother Mark, sitting unhappily on the edge of the parapet, looking at his own fingers; he recollected that it is bad manners to make fun of a countryman before strangers. "Go to Brother Mark," he said. "You are a holy man who would delight the heart of John the Baptist if he were here." The little man looked up gratefully. His smile was like that of a small girl—a transfiguration.

"Idolatry," said the Abbot John, shaking his head. "Simply idolatry. It makes you despair of the world."

They dined that night on the great oaken table in the courtyard, under the plane trees. There was red wine in plenty, and in the soft candle-light the old Abbot's face glowed with recaptured memories as they talked. Finally he went up to his room and brought down his little account book, and explained to Baird some of its mysteries. He had entries for every cargo of arms bought across from Palestine and smuggled into Tripoli. "You see," he said, indicating the quantities, "there is not much. And I am serving your cause, my dear Baird, since I am removing arms from British territory and sending them into French; in both cases at the expense of the Jews; isn't it wonderful? It is good patriotism, *and* it shows a good profit. I have bought a large farm in the south for Calypso's dowry when she grows up. Perhaps an Englishman will come from London and marry her."

The news of the disaster in the labyrinth was brought to them after dinner by a passing shepherd. It cast rather a gloom over their gaiety. A search-party had been into the tunnel leading to the "City in the Rock" and had reported dangerous falls of rock in many places. The Abbot was pessimistic about the possible escape of the others. "It's a terrible place," he said. "Even the corner where we had our headquarters was dangerous. But this place of Axelos's . . ." He waved his hands expressively.

They sat for a time in silence, watching the moon rise out of Africa, bronze-brown and beautiful. Somewhere out of sight the pure scroll-like sound of a flute could be heard and the chipped noise of sheep-bells.

"Sleep early tonight," said the old man. "I am sure that the dream which troubled you has gone at last."

Baird smiled and said, "Good night." In his little cell he blew out the light and climbed into the narrow bed, lying for a moment to hear the gentle swish of the sea upon the sea-wall, and the chaffer of fishermen putting out with their cargoes of lobster-pots. Then he sighed and went forward candidly, joyfully towards the sleep that fell upon him like a benediction out of tomorrow.

The Abbot John, however, could not sleep. He turned and tossed for a long time in his narrow wooden bed, and finally gave it up. The fleas were biting tonight. He made a mental note to tell Spiro, the novice, to rub the floors with paraffin and plug the seams. The wood throughout the whole monastery was rotten and cankered. In his own bedroom there were several knots upon which he was always catching his foot in the dark. He lit his small night-light and took up a book of medieval sermons. The light shone upon his narrow bookshelf, his robes hanging upon a hook in the corner, the great Bible which stood upon a lectern in the alcove—an English Bible. He was getting a very old man; he had reached that age when the body seems to develop small distempers—a heart beating over-loudly, or a lung that wheezes—and in the stillness of the night he would lie and, as he put it, "listen to himself dying in pieces". Tonight he was filled with a vague melancholy. He got up and put on his embroidered slippers. From the bottom of the cupboard he took a bottle of mastic and poured himself a tot, noticing as he did so how slack and flabby the skin of his hands had become. Soon he would be seventy. "And so little accomplished," was the mental thought that accompanied the reflection—though precisely in which field his accomplishment should lie he could not tell. Had he

wasted his life? Those years in Asia Minor, in Athos—had they
borne fruit? Had he approached a complete holiness through
the exercises of the Orthodox Church? A faint smell of incense
wafted from the cupboard. It was of Athenian manufacture.
Ah, if he could only get some of the pre-war Damascus incense, rich and pungent. He sighed as he sipped his mastic.

Lighting a cigarette, he said to himself: "If you had told
him the truth would he be happier or less happy? Would
Böcklin's disappearance as a miracle have more effect upon
him than as a question of scientific fact? It is hard to say."

In his experience it was the miracle that usually counted; and
the more enlightened the person the greater the power of the
miracle. He inhaled deeply and combed out his beard with his
fingers. Somewhere above him Baird slept—his slumbers
lulled by the prodigious snorings of the novice. The Abbot decided to take his problem to the sea-wall. He blew out the light
and left the room, closing the door gently behind him. All was
still in the courtyard. A bright bluish light from the risen moon
deepened the shadows to the colour of ink; the sea sighed
from time to time as one turning in a deep sleep. The darkness
was fragrant with the scent of wallflowers. He sat himself upon
the parapet close to his beloved pots of sweet basil, and consulted the glimmering tip of his cigarette. It was absurd really,
he found himself thinking, that he should make a moral problem out of what was merely a kindness done to a friend. After
all, he had loved Böcklin in a sense as dearly as anyone. Was
there any need to reopen the whole question of his death and
their guilt in making him die? "It was as much I", he said to
himself, "who fired the shot."

He put out the cigarette and shuffled across the courtyard
to the outhouse where Spiro kept the pots of tar and linseed
oil, and all the tackle and gear of fishing. He lit himself a dark
lantern, muttering to himself as he did so, and by the light of
it unearthed a pot of dry tar. Over a small fire of shavings he

melted it and then made his way once more across the courtyard to the chapel.

Here the darkness was absolute. He locked the door behind
him with the great key, setting his lantern and his pot of tar
upon the ground. The tinsel nimbus of St. Demetrius glim-
mered at him from the shadows of the altar. Mice chirped in
the rotten woodwork of the pews. Other features of ikons less
visible swam out at him upon the absolute darkness.

He sighed deeply, for what he was about to do would cost
money to repair. Taking his pot of smoking tar he advanced
into a corner and faced a small sandstone plaque standing
above a slab of the paving. Through the soles of his slippers he
felt the damp flags exuding their chill. He took up the stick
with the rags tied to its end, which served him for a brush,
and began to paint out an inscription in Greek which read:

UNDER THIS SLAB LIE THE MORTAL
REMAINS OF G. BÖCKLIN, A VERY
GALLANT OFFICER OF THE GERMAN ARMY,
KILLED IN ACTION 1944

He lingered for some time after he had successfully removed
the inscription, reflecting with irony that his effort of age had
been made on behalf of someone who did not believe in
miracles. At any rate now Baird would never know the truth!

The Abbot fell asleep almost at once after reaching his
room again, and did not wake until Brother Mark tiptoed into
his cell at dawn with a crust of bread and a glass of goat's
milk. He slept very well, so there was no excuse for his drowsiness the next morning when Baird found him sitting half-
asleep on the white parapet, fishing-rod in hand. The sun was
shining brightly. Baird approached on tiptoe and peered down
into the blue. "Your bait has gone," he said pleasantly. The
Abbot groaned. He was holding a book in his other hand and
trying to read between naps. "I hate fishing," he said. "I

don't really know why I do it. Self-discipline, I suppose."
Turning his head he roared: "Calypso. Come and change my
bait."

The little girl came and with expert fingers crushed the shell
of the hermit crabs and fixed their limp writhing bodies on the
hooks, while the Abbot averted his face. He could not bear to
see them wriggle. "How they move," said the little girl in her
faraway voice. "Don't," said the Abbot, "don't tell me. I hate
inflicting pain." She gave the signal and he cast the line errati-
cally out into the blue again.

Baird sat down on the wall and tossed pebbles into the sea
absently, waiting for his friend to catch something. "In half
an hour", he said, "I must walk over to Cefalû. Will you
come?"

The Abbot John said he would. "But promise", he said,
"that you will say nothing about the City in the Rock being a
real discovery." Baird promised.

Campion

Campion and Virginia Dale were pushed bodily into something that was not unlike the flue of an old French chimney; the girl had fainted, and Campion had put his arms round her and managed to stagger a few feet into the gap, while the stones and earth poured into the opening behind them. Their faces were brown with dust, he noticed, as he climbed slowly up what seemed to be a flight of irregularly-hewn stairs towards a broad band of daylight. The girl was heavier than she looked; he was carrying her over his shoulders after the manner approved by firemen in rescues from fourth-floor windows. Campion was spared the anxiety of Miss Dombey—spared everything except thoughts of merciful deliverance, for almost from the beginning he could see the encouraging whiteness of daylight at the other end of the hold into which they had been blown. He climbed slowly, pausing to place Virginia gently on her feet and shake her; he did not think she had been hurt, as she had been standing behind him, and might, at the worst, have been flicked by the passing splinters of stone, one of which had lodged in his eye and temporarily blinded him; at least it felt as if it had blinded him. How magnificent the daylight looked, streaming softly into the entry above them. "Virginia," he called, wiping the sweat from his forehead with the back of his hand. "Virginia." The girl seemed inclined to come round. He blew into her nostrils and saw her eyelids flutter. "Are you all right?" he said, but she subsided once more into what seemed to be more like a troubled sleep than a faint. Campion dragged her a few feet higher and paused. To his left there was a hole in the rock, a panel as large as a small bathroom mirror. It pierced several feet of solid rock and gave him a dim aquarium-like view of a cavern, in which, to his surprise, he saw the diminishing figures of Mr. and Mrs. Truman; saw them, briefly, for perhaps a second—for all the world as if he were looking at them through the wrong end of a telescope. He shouted hoarsely, putting his mouth to the opening, but there was no response. The grey-green sub-aqueous light shone steadily in a little group of stones. They had been (unless it had been an optical illusion) perhaps fifty yards away. His eyes were beginning to trouble him again; he could feel something stuck to the cornea when he closed it. Virginia stirred and moaned. Pausing from time to time to shake her, Campion mounted the last twenty paces, and collapsed with her upon the ledge, half-blind with sunlight. Here they lay for a long moment breathing the welcome scents of sage in the rare mountain air, and listening to the distant drum-beats of the sea. Presently Virginia sat up and looked round her. She was still pale and seemed about to be sick. Campion peeled off his coat, turning his body as it lay on the ground, to disengage first one arm and then the other. Thank God, he had managed to bring their lunch. "Virginia," he said, "are you all right?" The girl gave a little cry and pointed to his face.

"Your eye," she said. "Come here."

In the cornea there was embedded a small fragment of stone —like the tip of a lead pencil. He sat patiently while she removed it between finger and thumb. It was not painful. He could still see out of it. Campion thanked her and lay back once more.

"What a merciful deliverance," he said, with unusual piety. He lit a cigarette, deeply inhaling the smoke, and letting it gush from his nostrils; his hand still shook from the exertion and the fear of the last few moments. He thought of the others, trapped down there, and as he did so noticed that the girl was crying. Perhaps the same thought had visited her; Campion

hated women to cry. He lay back and closed his eyes. In a little
while they would have such food as they should find in their
little cartons, and then slowly climb down to Cefalû to bring
the first news of the disaster—if indeed the absence of the
guide for so long a time had not already given the alarm. He
settled himself more comfortably on the hard rock, feeling the
wind flutter his hair, and ruffle the leaves of his small sketch-
book which protruded from the pocket of the discarded coat.
Idly now he took out the little packet of pastel crayons; they
were all smashed up in their carton ridges. "Virginia," he said,
"do you feel better?"

She tossed her hair back out of her eyes, and sniffed. "Yes,"
she said stonily. She had been thinking of the tender, the considerate Graecen lying down there smothered in earth and
boulders. Who knows what declarations he might not have
made if they had had the time; or even if he had been here with
her instead of Campion. She dabbed her eyes and moved back
until her shoulders were pressed to the wall of the natural stone
balcony upon which they found themselves. "We'll have a
spot to eat," Campion was saying, his voice still squeaky with
fatigue, "and then work our way down the cliff to Cefalû, to
tell them what has happened." He did not mention his sudden
half-second vision of the Truman couple crossing a rickety
gallery of stone; what would have been the point? He could
not rescue them. Besides he was relieved to see that the girl
had stopped crying at last. "Unpack the food," he said, anxious
to give her something practical with which to occupy her
mind, while he himself reconnoitred.

Walking to the edge he found himself looking down upon
the broad upturned face of the sea, several hundred feet below. The balcony upon which they stood was simply a narrow
cockpit thrust out from the cliff-face over the water. His face
grew anxious, and then all of a sudden very pale. The rock
stretched away in a clear cleavage of limestone, sheer to the

sea; not a foothold or cranny could his eyes pick out as they travelled frantically backwards and forwards over the surface of stone. Campion hoisted himself upon the ridge and tried to climb upwards; he found one foothold and hoisted himself a few feet, only to see that it was hopeless. Smooth and un-broken except by major cleavages the cliff swept up into the sky.

He returned once more and gazed out at the sea, moving from side to side, his whole mind furiously engaged by this new problem. Behind him the girl had removed the battered sandwiches from their wrappings and was calling him to eat. Without speaking, he motioned her to join him and, drawing her down by the shoulders, lay beside her for a long time staring down into the insolent blue of the waters below. She gave a little cry as she understood.

It was perhaps three hundred feet down, he told himself. Could they jump? A kestrel whistled and dived from a ledge just below them, flattening out into a glide before touching the surface of the sea. He could feel the dry island wind playing upon his forehead. Faintly, very faintly from the outer world he could hear the music of trees and the singing of birds. A small ragged strip of coastline was their only prospect. The sea looked deep. Nearer inland it became shallower; he could see the yellow freckles of light moving across the sand bar. If they jumped they would have to clear the fringe of rocks beneath. How far *was* it? Campion knew he was hopeless at factual calculations of any sort. He closed his eyes and tried to recall the height of the eight-metre board at Villars. An airman had once told him that the resistance of water made it as solid as concrete for anyone attempting to jump into it from above a certain height. What was the height? He could not for the life of him remember. They lay there side by side for a long time, hardly moving. The sea rocked below them, its savage noise coming up in the little lulls of wind from the land. Campion opened his eyes very wide and carefully, elaborately lit another cigarette. His fingers were shaking again. The girl said nothing. They turned back to where she had unwrapped the sandwiches. Campion was thirsty, but they had brought no water with them. Lunch would, in the normal course of events, have been eaten near some fresh-water spring under an olive tree. . . . He made a grimace and said, "I suppose you're thirsty too." Virginia sat down, drawing her legs up under her. Her face was flushed as if she had been running. Campion guessed that tears were not far off. "We will have to jump for it," he said, and undid the little box of crayons, while he held his sandwich in the other hand. It soothed him to scribble on the smooth rock. They sat for a while in silence, he drawing and she watching him as she ate, slowly and tidily, like a cat. After he had done a series of small men in bowler hats, an eagle, a train, and the *Europa*, he dusted his fingers and said, with something of the old mordant truculence: "It's just as well, really. I'm not sure I want to go back."

The girl put her head on one side and examined the statement of his with an expression of gentle impartiality. "I mean, if one could live how one wanted," pursued Campion, "and not be at the mercy of a silly world that cares for what is ephemeral and neglects everything that is essential." His silence was only a grace note. He had begun to sketch a little landscape, a house, some olive trees. "At twenty", he said softly, "I thought I knew what was wrong. I was a Marxist. A redistribution of property was all that stood between us and heaven. The last few years have been an eye-opener." At twenty a *fumiste*, at twenty-one a *pointilliste*, and twenty-five a Thomiste; at thirty a potential Trappist. Campion scribbled away as he talked partly to himself and partly to Virginia Dale. As he did so much of his life came back to him—without form and order, but with a new marked coherence. The girl he met on the Strada Balbi in Genoa; the broken-down room over the wineshop with its cracked and peeling cherubs on the ceiling, and the red-curtained four-poster bed; a broken mirror and a soap-dish with a lottery ticket lying on it. Is it possible that but for the accident he, Campion, might have spent the rest of his life with her between those dirty sheets—entangled in long rich-smelling dark hair? Or Nanteaux, where he had suddenly woken one morning to see the blue Mediterranean gleaming like a stained-glass window, and realized that there was nothing more he wanted to do, nowhere he wanted to go? What had ejected him from these situations if it had not been this restless voracious self with its *groundless* fears and fantasies about happiness and order? Now perhaps if he should find his way out of this impasse, what could he devise for himself as a way of life that would fulfil the potentiality that he felt about to realize—now experienced only as a gaping hole in his *moral* outlook. "Stay like that," he called out. The sun was striking sideways on her face. He began with his nervous deft fingers to draw her.

"I suppose", said Virginia, "you are a Jew?"

This surprised Campion. It was a charge he had never been able to bring himself to admit. "Why should you say that?" he replied in as off-hand a tone as he could muster.

"No reason," she said. "I was talking to Richard about you only yesterday. He says you are a great painter."

"Did he say I was a Jew?" said Campion sharply.

"No. I did. He didn't think you were."

Campion put down his pastel and rubbed his fingers on the stone. "And what makes you think I am?" he said.

"I met a lot of Jews in the city," said the girl. "They all had the same sort of attitude to the world."

"What attitude?" Campion was getting out of temper with her monotonous delivery.

"That the world is not good enough for them."

He smiled grimly and picked up his small stub of crayon

again. He began to shade in those anaemic but rather gracefully equine features. She sat obediently with her face turned away from him so that the afternoon sun threw into relief her throat and the high cheek-bone.

"Yes," said Campion, "I am a Jew." He stubbed out his cigarette and added: "If you really think that Jews have a common psychology."

Virginia Dale stifled a yawn. "When are we going to jump?" she asked. She seemed to have recovered a great deal of her composure. Campion said rudely: "You can jump whenever you like. I was trying to find out whether I *wanted* to jump back into the world or not."

She considered for a long moment. "I suppose you're afraid," she said, and added hastily, "I don't mean of the jump, but of the world. You oughtn't to be. A great artist should have some control over the world. Not be bowled over by small worries." Campion listened with fascination to this small Cockney child lecturing him in her flattened Golder's Green accent; the presumption of her made his hair stand on end; and yet he could find nothing to say in return. He went on drawing with an over-elaborate concentration. It was as he was giving her permission to have a few minutes' rest and a cigarette that a small bedraggled object emerged from the tunnel behind them, whimpering softly. "Spot," cried the girl, "however did you get up here?" Miss Dombey's dog looked as if it had been set on fire, its coat was black with dust. It crawled whining into Virginia's arms and buried its head in her lap. "It's trembling all over," she said, becoming soft and receptive and motherly. Campion watched with fascination the endearments, the petting, the cuddling. English women, he reflected, being given to this kind of generalization, only really yield to their pets—to their dogs. Never would the girl register such melting sympathy in the arms of a man. His thoughts turned with regret to the sanguine and lovely Francesca, with her plump, well-modelled buttocks and fig-like breasts. When she kissed it was as if she were burning to print some indelible message on one's mouth; her whole being ached in her kisses. They hurt her to give and to receive. Campion sighed and ate a bit of bread, feeling steadier.

The girl, too, was happier with a child-substitute to fuss over; fawning, Spot accepted some food and wagged his tail. He must have believed himself safe from peril at last. Neither of them speculated aloud upon the possible fate of Miss Dombey, yet both wondered whether she were alive or dead.

Once more Campion hung over the edge of their eyrie and stared down upon the sea, trying to measure the distance with his eye. It was hopeless. He tossed a large boulder over and it seemed to take ages to reach the water, settling slowly in the viscous blueness with barely a splash. Suddenly he had an idea.

Turning, he called the dog to him, wheedling it with the promise of food. Then, taking it in his arms he stood up and was about to pitch it over when the girl rushed at him. "What are you doing?" she shouted, and half-dragged him back. Campion disengaged himself from her with fury. "Idiot," he said. With her scuffling he might easily have been pushed over himself. "Can't you see we must find out?" She protested indignantly against the use of Spot as a guinea-pig for such an experiment. "Don't be a fool," said Campion again, and grabbing the now struggling dog he advanced to the parapet once more. Spot squawked loudly and struggled. "Shut up," cried Campion, and gave a sharp exclamation as the dog bit him.

Spot pitched out into space, and for a second seemed to hang in the air before he began his slow parcel-like flight towards the sea; Campion lay sucking the wound in his hand and watching. The little dog turned over and over, and finally melted with a small white feathery scar, into the sea's blueness. For what seemed centuries Campion lay, his eyes fixed on the spot. Presently something rose slowly to the surface, and after lying still for a few moments began to weave slowly towards the shore. Campion shouted.

The girl was sitting where she had originally been, with her back pressed to the wall, examining her fingernails. "He's all right," said Campion again, and at his cry she rose and came to his side. Spot was out of sight now round the edge of the headland, but moving under his own steam. Campion lay back and breathed a sigh. "Well," he said, "that gives one some indication." Virginia was suddenly elated. She clapped her hands together and said: "What a wonderful chance." Campion lay still blowing smoke softly into the air above his face and thinking. It was, of course, not certain that a human being weighing twenty times as much as an animal, would escape as lightly.

"What are you thinking?" she said, noticing his preoccupied face.

"There's only an hour of sunlight to go. I think we should wait until tomorrow morning. Even supposing we get down safely and crawl out on to the land we may find ourselves miles from anywhere, wandering about in the dark with wet clothes."

"Yes," she said slowly, as if unconvinced.

They sat together and watched the sun sinking ponderously into the sea. Somehow the very act of sitting there, without speculation and anxiety, quietened and soothed their nerves. Gulls wheeled with anguished cries below them upon the great mauve expanse of water. The wind had crept up to pencil its strange hieroglyphs on the southern half of the bay. Slowly, very slowly the great golden drop touched the horizon, and the blue meniscus of evening ran, a crack of nacreous red, from one end of the sky to the other. They had no light, save the box of matches in Campion's pocket; but there were plenty of cigarettes. The wind was not blowing directly into their balcony of stone. The night was warm. They settled themselves as comfortably as they could against the stone, he placing his arms round her shoulders. The darkness came on, blue and dense, and the stars put up their high malevolent lights, winking like the eyes of so many needles. "Campion," she said drowsily, "I'm sorry if I hurt your feelings just now." Campion pretended ignorance of any slight, but he knew quite well what she meant. "I mean about being a Jew," she added. Campion smoked on in silence for a while. "I think you are unjust to me," he said at last, "in assuming that my idiosyncrasies are racial; I do belong to a race—but the race of artists: the Jewish part is what is personal in my nature, but there are other difficulties which belong to my other racial inheritance. As a matter of fact," he went on with a chuckle, "I am not a Jew at all. I am just one of the others." He began to talk slowly and without emphasis of what the artist was, what his peculiar needs were, his fears, his ambitions. It was only when he realized that she was asleep that he desisted.

They dozed fitfully that night under his coat, and rose at the first light of dawn. The air was cold and they were both cramped. A heavy dew had settled over everything. They ate the remains of the food left over from their lunch the previous day, and smoked the last two cigarettes left in Campion's case, waiting for the sun to warm the rock upon which they sat. "So you do want it all," said Campion at last. "Golder's Green? The rain? The damp tubes? The last bus?" The girl stopped her ears in mock horror. "Please," she said. "Don't spoil it. It isn't that I want. It's other things, can't you see?"

She took out her pocket comb and balancing a strip of mirror in a cranny, made up her face as well as she could, combed out her hair, and smoothed down her eyebrows with her finger. "I'm ready," she said quietly. Campion stood up with a sigh. They took off all their clothes except their shoes, and made them into one bundle. Then, naked, they stood hand in hand upon the last jutting foothold of the balcony. "When

I give the word," said Campion. His voice had gone flat and calm and without emphasis. She leaned forward, bracing her toes against the stone. "Wait," she said suddenly and leaned forward to kiss him on the mouth. Campion smiled and called: "One, two . . ."

The rushing of wind struck the last word from his lips, and he felt himself turning over and over as his body was poured down the ladder of blueness. A red roaring seemed to fill the horizon. Frightened kestrels fell with them from ledges of rock for a few metres and then planed out, whistling their curiosity and terror. The sea turned up its expansive shining surface and waited for them.

The Roof of the World

Truman dragged his wife clear of the chute of rocks and earth, dusted her down with many a violent oath, and suffered her to cling to his arm as they stood side by side, and watched the corridor fill up until the pile of dirt had completely sealed it off. The sound and fury of the fall was gradually sealed off too until at last they stood, as if in a padded cell, hearing the concussions and rumblings upon the other side continuing. Sound had become soft and distended—so that what they knew to be boulders falling beyond the wall seemed to be merely the noises off of some celestial pillow-fight. He was still panting from the effort of having to drag her away from the fall to a point of safety. "Listen to it," she said shakily turning away and sitting down upon a rock. Truman listened grimly, his hand groping in his pockets to feel the comforting bulge of the lunch-carton and cold edges of the little torch.

They were standing in a corridor illuminated by the faint greyish light from a slit in the roof of a nearby cavern. The blocked mouth of the tunnel from which they had retreated still trembled under the landslip, whose echoes ran away in all directions, repeating themselves from all points of the compass. Truman listened carefully, hoping perhaps that some information might be gained from the noise. It still rang in his head, but soft and muffled, like a pulse; like the tapping of a finger upon the bone of the frontal sinus, or upon the mastoid. "Well?" said his wife anxiously, watching him. He sighed and turned to her. "I'm afraid they've caught it," he said darkly. "Not a sound from them."

He sat down beside her and mopped his forehead. Then he

examined his cigarette-case, and the crumpled pouch in which
he carried the coarse tobacco for his pipe. "Well," he said,
"there's a smoke or two left." He lit a cigarette and handed it
to her. They smoked together in silence for a time, their faces
turned upwards to watch the dense beam of dust-motes turning and twirling in the light from above. Truman was thinking
frantically as he smoked, his jaw set at the angle necessary to
register absolute determination. His wife had produced a
pocket comb and was slowly combing her hair. She had recovered a good deal of her composure now. "What are you
thinking?" she asked in a whisper; the dank gloom reminded her
of a church and made her whisper. "What are you thinking?"
she repeated again in a normal tone. Truman was thinking in
a confused sort of way that there must be some exit, some
opening of the corridors which would enable them to regain
the daylight. He looked at her quietly and reflectively for a
moment, saying nothing. She went on combing her hair, and
then with a little smile got up and retreated to the farther end
of the tunnel for a moment. He watched her as she squatted
down, gathering up her skirts. "You've got a smut on your
nose," he said absently. He was trying to calculate how far
they had come into the labyrinth, but the task was a hopeless
one. In the darkness a journey of a few moments felt like a
journey of hours—or even days. It seemed useless to speculate,
to plan. They could only wander on and on until they ran out
of food. His wife came back to him, brushing a cobweb from
her mouth. She perched herself once more upon the rock beside him and said: "What do you think of the chances, eh?"
The question was more rhetorical than anything else, yet
Truman felt impelled to answer it. He coughed and stamped
out his cigarette on the cold stone. He cocked his head and
listened for a second as a small tributary series of bangs told
him of landslips in other corners of the labyrinth, before speaking. "It's like this," he said at last forcefully, placing the fore-

finger of one hand in the palm of the other in a gesture of
determination. "We have enough food for perhaps a day and
a half if we're careful. We should be able to walk about twenty
miles before we have to pack up. Now this place *can't* be more
than a couple of miles long at the most. I think with a bit of
luck we have a very good chance indeed." It was a master-
stroke, and she smiled her pleasure at the proposition, putting
her hand in his arm and giving it a squeeze. "Let's just go on,"
he said, pleased at his own reorientation of a desperate situation in terms of probable success. "As if we were walking . . .
in Devonshire." This was an even happier illustration, for they
had once been lost for a day on the moors above Tyre Basin,
and had enjoyed the memory of that hazardous adventure ever
since. They stood up and faced one another for a few moments
while she smiled lovingly and brushed some of the dust from
his lapels. "Now", he said, "take it easy. Every hour we'll rest
for fifteen minutes. We won't eat until three o'clock today.
Got it?" While Elsie Truman was grateful for his masterly
presentation of the fiction, and glad that their plan of action
had been so intelligently developed, she could not resist a little
banter—if only to let him know that his optimism had not
completely taken her in.

"One important thing," she said gravely, "is the old minotaur. You forget that." Truman gave her a pat on the behind
as she turned. "Well, let's deal with that when we meet it," he
said equably.

They crossed the lighted area of the cave hand in hand and
began the long walk which was, unknown to themselves, going to lead them out on to the Roof of the World. Slowly they
bored their way from vault to vault and chamber to chamber,
buoying themselves up with private jokes against that ever-
growing feeling of unreality which comes to those who spend
too long in the darkness. Yet the routine of their march, by its
very strictness, seemed to have a purpose, a meaning. It was

difficult going, for Truman used the torch as sparingly as possible, and the surfaces were widely different in structure, the faults and abruptions of the rock-face frequent. From time to time their hopes were raised as they passed abruptly into some dimly-lit cavern in which the shafts of sunlight, distilled and diluted in that green air, turned languidly in spirals or shuddered into activity as they passed and disturbed them.

Elsie Truman was heartily grateful for her stout shoes and the coat. She talked a good deal, partly because the sound of her own voice was something she could not do without, partly to show her husband that her morale could answer every demand made upon it. He, for his part, hardly bothered to answer her, except with an occasional grunt. His whole energy was concentrated upon the journey itself, his mind, so to speak, was always ahead of them forearmed against possible pitfalls and disappointments, against dangers and disasters which might at any step overcome them. And wherever the track seemed wide enough he came up beside his wife and took her arm, unconsciously re-creating those thousand and one walks they had taken together, in comfortable familiarity, arm in arm; contributing to her own optimism and courage a sense of plausible continuity, a hope for the future. In his own mind, however, Truman was re-living those exciting films of his childhood which always ended with a chase across the underground cellars of Paris, or across the crooked roof-tops of London. They constituted the only poetry he had ever known, and now, as they toiled from cavern to cavern, from gallery to crumbling gallery, he could not help but imagine himself as a character in *The Prisoner of Zenda* or *Toilers of the Sea*, battling his way up towards the daylight. His mind was absolutely without fear, because he was convinced that his time had not yet come—as convinced as he had been during the bombardments of the late war. And this conviction seemed to place a merciful veil between himself and the reality in which he had become involved. Somewhere, quite near, was the real world where flowers blossomed and trees grew; there were human beings like himself obsessed with small problems, small responsibilities. Truman was quite determined not to lose his hold upon this world which, it seemed to him, he had hardly had time to get to know. So deliberate was this certainty that his wife impelled herself to test it from time to time with a remark like, "I've had enough of this. Why don't we sit down a bit?" or "What about lunch? Don't want me to die of hunger, do you?" He treated these reservations upon an agreed attitude as meaningless interruptions to a continuity of purpose he was determined to maintain. And regarding him, seeing his set and resolute features, and the way his neck had drawn itself into his body—the watchful, condensed approach of a boxer to an opponent—she was at once revived and restored in her own feminine resolution.

They stumbled and crawled through a network of caves and galleries filled with this delusive half-light which reminded her, as she said, of the Aquarium of Brighton; in which she half expected to see the vast and gloomy forms of fishes dawdling through the crannies and corridors around them. In the centre of one of them, scooped clear in the cold stone, lay what at first seemed to be a miniature lake—its black surface untouched by reflections or movements. She gave a little cry of interest and pleasure and advanced towards it with the intention of washing her face in it: but as she stopped, taking off her hat, her husband caught her arm. He was staring keenly down at the polished surface. They were aware of a faint sour smell, like that of slightly burnt milk. "Wash your face in that, would you?" said Truman softly, more to himself than to her, and, reaching down, picked up a twig off the floor. "Look." He dipped the twig into the liquid and drew it out, letting the bitumen run sluggishly from its end, smoking like black sealing-wax. "Well I never," she said, "it's tar. How did it get down here?" It provided her husband with an excuse for a homily upon feminine irresponsibility and the evils thereof. He did not spare her, and she listened to him, outwardly very meek, but inwardly smiling in fond amusement at this oft-repeated performance. His concern was flattering, even if his opinion of her intelligence was not.

They took a turning now, and followed a slowly-descending gallery to a network of caves in which, as in a sea-shell, they could hear the distorted sighing of the sea. "It sounds so near," she kept repeating painfully, "so very near"; but the rock offered no egress except in one place where they could stare down through a narrow trapdoor of stone, upon a patch of darkness broken from time to time by a small iridescence, a trembling as of sequins in a dark ballroom. "The sea," he said, with longing suddenly breaking through his reserve. "If we could only reach it." They sat for a time and smoked there. From time to time he stared down through that narrow shaft at the water coiling and uncoiling, and seemed to be trying to work out some way of climbing down to it. His wife watched him, blowing the cigarette-smoke through her nostrils. "I bet", she said, "the others found a way down." Truman looked at her in silence. "Into the sea?" he said at last with polite irony. "Why not?" she said. She had not been thinking of the sea at all, but since he chose to offer her a ground for argument, she saw no reason why she should not take the opportunity to talk a little. "I can just see Campion nipping into a tunnel like that and out into the sea in a moment." Campion had become associated in both their minds with the qualities of deftness and cunning. Her husband put out his cigarette and said: "Lot of use that would be if he can't swim a stroke." He recalled a conversation with Campion about the length of time a man could stay afloat if he fell overboard. Campion confessed then that he was unable to swim. Mrs. Truman looked crushed, though the same affectionate amusement stirred in her as she heard the broad unconcern, the male superiority of his tones. She was getting really hungry now, but he would not let her eat, saying that it was not time.

The tunnels led them upward now, through crumbling arches and over pits and crannies, away from the soft walled-off sound of the sea bursting against the cliffs. They hated to leave the sound, so closely did it match those other sounds of the everyday world from which they seemed now to have been parted for centuries. A vague sense of gloom and unreality had descended upon them. They came at last to yet another nexus of corridors—a "terminus", as she called it. While she sat upon a stone and rubbed her ankles her husband set off methodically to examine the various tunnels for clues by which they might guide themselves back towards the world. Three of them became, after a few yards, narrow and impassable. The fourth looked more interesting. It mounted steeply, and in the yellow beam of his torch, revealed a floor of limestone. There seemed to be traces of brown earth about, and this itself absorbed him, since so far they had passed through solid rock for the greatest part of the way. He walked on a few paces when his eyes fell upon some twigs lying near his feet. He picked them up. They were dry and brown. It was as if they had fallen from a head of a birch broom. Truman blew his nose carefully and methodically, switching off his torch as he did so. A vague excitement possessed him. Ten paces farther on the corridor narrowed considerably; here stopped and examined the wall-face with intentness and concentration. His patience was rewarded at last. He gave a grunt of interest and picked from the wall a few small tufts of hair, measuring their height from the ground by spanning the distance, like a builder, finger to thumb. His wife was sitting waiting for him. She had found a pencil in her handbag and was scribbling on the rock. Truman sat down beside her and fell to studying the tuft of hair in the light which filtered in through the roof of the cavern. Absorbed in her game she did not look up. She was busy drawing hearts with arrows transfixing them, over each of which she wrote, laboriously and carefully, her own name and that of her husband. "I shall do this all the way along," she said. "In case other people come this way." He was sitting quite still, whistling softly through his teeth, abstractedly examining the clue from the tunnel, his mind working on possible solutions. "Well," he said at last, "it can't be a bear. Unless bears have browny-white hair. It's pretty big though."

His wife turned round to see what he was doing, and as she did so the cavernous voice of the minotaur sounded, this time close at hand. Its resonance in that narrow place was deafening. It was accompanied by a rushing noise, as of dead leaves stirring in the empty caverns before a whirlwind. Dust began to trickle down from the balconies of stone. They jumped to their feet in alarm, turning their heads this way and that, responding to the tremendous echoes which multiplied the sound and flung it back at them from different corners of the place. "Christ," said Truman. "There it is." His eyes were wide and shining now, and she could see that he was having difficulty in continuing to convert his fear into resolution. The echoes passed them, banging away down the tunnels. He leaned forward and said quickly: "Give me the knife, will you?" He was glad to feel the smooth handle of his old bowie-knife in his hand. Taking off his coat, he draped it over his forearm in the manner of a bullfighter, explaining as he did so: "Its burrow can't be far from the top, Elsie. Maybe if we find it, it will show us the way out." Too fearful to answer him she stood with her back to the cold stone and waited as he made his preparations. "Now," he said at last, pausing to listen to the vague explosions of sound sinking away behind them into the stone network. "Now then. Quietly, see? Follow me." She heard the small sound of the blade as it clicked out of its case.

He took up his torch and moved towards the tunnel quickly but with circumspection.

Their feet seemed to make a prodigious noise among the stones. They traversed a dozen low-roofed corridors without mishap. Nothing stirred around them in that damp air save the sound of their own progression, small, perfunctory, meaningless as the scratching of moles under the earth. Truman was nursing his failing torch, using it only in small spells, in order to see the way ahead. They would form a picture, so to speak, of every stage, snap off the light and accomplish it in darkness. His hand contracted lovingly about the blade of his knife, as he thanked God for its long sharp blade. Pen-knives had always been a mania with him, and he never travelled without one. The present bowie had been a present from a G.I. in the late war, a marvellous strong piece of workmanship, which he had re-ground himself before they left England. Now as he went forward to meet whatever reality chose to offer him in the way of chimeras—or obstructions more substantial—he felt the warm currents of his own life flowing through his bull-neck and powerful shoulders.

Some way along, the corridors suddenly became damp and clammy. They noticed that their floors had become of stone no longer, but of earth and rubble. The air exuded damp which mingled with the cold sweat on their foreheads. The last march had been upwards, along corridors leaning up at an angle, cutting diagonally through the honeycomb of caves and galleries. Hope mounted in them as they saw, here and there, the roots of trees struggling through the walls, their white frilly roots showing like clusters of worms. Truman felt his own breathing become thinner, easier, as if fresh air were already coming down to meet them, to buoy up their failing lungs.

They stumbled at last into a small natural amphitheatre in the rock and were about to cross it and enter the corridor beyond when they were startled by the blundering crashing sound of some heavy body in the darkness before them. A gust of sweetish breath seemed to swirl into the little cabin of rock and earth. Truman recoiled and switched off his torch. They stood hand in hand, trembling and waiting for the minotaur to reveal itself; and as they stood, their uneasy silence in that half-light was broken by a coarse grunting and slavering noise which reminded them irresistibly of a horse in its stall. Their eyes had already become accustomed to the dark monotonous light, and fixing them upon the tunnel ahead, they saw something move in the shadows behind a coign of stone—a parapet shaped not unlike a byre. Truman took ten paces forward very swiftly and silently, and pressed himself to the rock. Then, turning on his torch, he craned his head round the corner to stare speechless into the terrified eyes of a cow. For an age he continued to stand thus, his body pressed to the wall and his heart contracted into an icy lump in his breast. As he stood, letting the breath come slowly back into his body, his mind ranged over every available expletive in the English language which might express some of his relief—a small part of that overwhelming, overmastering relief that had bereft him of word or action.

Seeing him standing there, and imagining perhaps that the sight of whatever lay behind the rock had been so hideous as to unman him, his wife picked up a boulder and rushed to his side; she too found herself staring into the blood-red eyes of a cow. The stone fell from her hands. She could feel his body trembling with laughter now, and as she opened her mouth to speak, the cow turned tail and, letting fall an alarmed pat of excrement, bolted down the tunnel. "Quick," they both shouted incoherently, and ran, screaming with laughter, in pursuit. They blundered down a series of arches, composed apparently of the roots of trees and then suddenly, absurdly, into the light of day.

Between laughter and tears they sat down and covered their eyes from the blazing radiance of the light, sitting thus for at least two minutes, during which through their parted fingers they caught glimpses of the world of familiar shapes; a sloping hill-side studded with swart green grey olives. They had emerged from between the roots of a huge plane tree. Somewhere water gushed. Lifting their hands from their eyes by small degrees they stared into the blue Aegean sky, and let it stare back at them, uncompromisingly, utterly blue. Trees were stirring faintly, as if in an awakened interest. Bees hung, slowly frying, in the flowers. The Roof of the World had revealed itself to them, in all its pristine novelty, as if by a razor-stroke. No extravagance of gesture or exclamation could do justice to its beauty. Elsie Truman kicked off her shoes and stretched her toes, lying back slowly in the grass. "It's like being reborn," she told herself as she lay, unspeaking and felt tears fill her eyes, and run slowly over her cheeks. Her husband, too, lay down and let his head rest upon his forearm; the coarse inhalations of his cigarette seemed delicious beyond expression. Life, which had seemed to offer them so little beyond a death by hunger in the labyrinth, suddenly crowded upon them both, not only with the blessings of movement and feeling, but also with those hundreds of memories and plans which they had not allowed to occupy their minds while their realization had seem remote. His lips moved silently from time to time, but he was not praying. He was talking to himself.

"And now," she said, "let's eat."

"Eat away," he said, lying motionless, feeling the unshaven flesh of his cheek between finger and thumb. She rose slowly, still weighed down by that marvellous convalescent sense of weariness and unpacked the by-now-battered sandwiches, peeling the damp paper from them with distaste. "Here," she said, "eat something." Her husband sat up and stretched, taking the bread from her fingers as he did so. "All the best," he said, taking his first bite, and looking round him to trace the sound of running water which had been running like a musical accompaniment to his thoughts, along a parallel track. "It's cold, you know," she said, feeling the air upon her lips and throat as she sat down beside him. "I wonder where we are?"

The landscape in which they found themselves was startlingly wild and craggy, thought Truman, as he looked about him between mouthfuls of food. At each of the four points of the compass he could see the necks and shoulders of tree-denuded mountains butting up into the afternoon light. Their summits, topped with snow, caught the glittering rays of lights and flashed them back at one another—a thousand diamond-flashes against the grey bony twilight which was reaching up towards them from the lower slopes. Yet despite the gauntness of the further prospect they found themselves upon the declining edge of a bowl—perhaps a quarter of a mile round—in which fruit, trees, flowers, everything seemed to flourish. Faintly in their nostrils they smelt the cool rotten smell of vegetation which hangs about a snowline; yet the little bowl could only boast of one clump of firs upon its farthest edge. It was clear too that the backdrop of mountains was in some way divided from this small formalized territory, which fell away so steeply into space.

"Those mountains are a long way off," muttered Truman in a puzzled voice. "And we don't seem to be very high. I wonder where the sea is?"

They continued to eat with deliberation and enjoyment, hardly speaking, and when they had done Truman buried their scraps methodically in the ground under the plane tree.

"I wouldn't," said Truman slowly, still looking round him. "I wouldn't be too optimistic, Elsie. We can just as easily starve on a mountain as in a cave, you know. There's no road I can see and no houses."

She dusted the crumbs from her dress and said: "There's bound to be a farm about somewhere. Besides, look," her eyes had lighted upon a rock whose surface looked smooth and polished—as if with resin. "What?" said her husband. She got up and went over to it. "It's a 'greaser'," she said, recovering the old Derbyshire word, with its memories of holidays spent on farms during her childhood. "That means some sheep or goats."

They walked down into the little valley, hand in hand, looking about them curiously. The prospect looked, with all its cultivation, like the park of some great house—the result of deliberate labour and intention rather than the casual handiwork of Nature. A stream blundered over gravel. Birds sang. A walnut tree nodded its pronged branches in the wind. Farther down beyond the last bluff of rock, puffs of colour stood out against the grey, hills—peach-blossom. Warm, verdant, and unself-conscious the meadows seemed to have been tended and mown, lying in the shadow of the sun-burnt mountains. They were filled with a gradually growing sense of incredulity and amazement, comparing the richness of the amphitheatre in which they stood with the brooding hulks of stone which raised themselves in the air at every point. Their feet trod grass. Yet everywhere they turned their eyes picked up the formidable crests of mountains plunged in snow. "I can't make it out," he said slowly, "it seems queer somehow. It's so warm." His wife walked silently beside him tasting the purity of the air as it entered her lungs and was expelled from them. The mountains looked grandiose and beautiful rather than menacing. She was full of that light-headedness which comes upon all who walk upon the mountains of Greece, and feel the scent of thyme mingling with the pure cold air. Immense pearl-covered clouds hung in one corner of the sky, like canopies of silk. The gestures and manœuvres they had set out to rehearse had degenerated into this immobile stillness. Occasionally one of them would throw a damp splash of shadow on the mountain-side. "It's wonderful," she said, unpreoccupied by the problems which he was turning over in his mind. "Simply wonderful."

A tree knelt above the rocky pool into which the mountain water spun and curdled—a tree white to the lips with cherries. Small birds frisked in the branches. "Did you say we'd starve?" she asked mockingly, reaching up and pulling the ripe cherries from the stalk. "Come," he said, and locking his arms about her thighs, lifted her towards the ripest clusters. He stood, his head against her thighs, and absently heard the words of an old song running in the back of his mind: "If you were the only girl in the world." It stretched so far back into the past that he could no longer identify the incidents and localities connected with it. His wife wriggled as she tried to reach higher and higher. "Steady on," he said, and as she leaned down to stop his lips with the cold fruit, "Where do you think you are? The Garden of Eden?"

They sat side by side on the bank and bathed their feet in the icy water, eating cherries and smoking one of his last cigarettes in alternate puffs. The shadows of the pine trees were growing longer. "You know", he said, "we shouldn't hang about much longer. It's just as well to find out where we are before taking it easy." She stood up and dusted her dress. Her feet were still cold from the icy water of the torrent, and she skippered up and down to stretch them and start the circulation. "Well?" she said, "after the minotaur I can stand anything." He was wrapping up his raincoat once more and the thought seemed to strike him with some force. "You don't think that *was* it?" he said incredulously. "What else?" she asked. Truman shook his head and puzzled over the problem for a moment; it was as if he were unwilling to admit that they had domesticated, so to speak, the minotaur; domesticated their terrors in the shape of a brown cow whose mooing could be picked up and amplified in the bowels of the earth. "I don't know," he said at last, and rising, joined her.

"I think we should get up those trees," he said, "and look down the slope. Maybe we are on the hill above that village— what's it called? Cefalû? Yes, Cefalû."

They crossed several small dry river-beds where winter torrents would run, and plunged into a dense grove of myrtles. As they mounted, behind a neighbouring hill, they caught sight of some sheep grazing. "You see," she said, "I told you. There must be a farm hereabouts." But the terrain offered no signs of paths or other cultivation beyond the well-kept appearance of its trees and woodland. It was as they took the final gradient and mounted the hillock towards the clump of pines, that they saw, below them, a stranger. He was sitting at the edge of the bank, where the stream suddenly grew deep and turbid, carving for itself small pools and marshes in the limestone. In his hand was a fishing-rod. His back rested against the bole of an olive tree. His head was covered by a bright handkerchief, and he appeared to be asleep. "At last," said Truman with relief. "Our troubles are over," and cupping his hands he shouted: "Hullo there!" as they started to descend towards the solitary figure. "Better try repeating that in Greek," said his wife ironically. "He doesn't seem to hear." Indeed, the stranger still sat with his back to them, unheeding. It was only when Truman shouted a second time that he turned, and they saw that it was a woman. She stood up, dropping the fishing-rod, and stood, as if uncertain whether to fly or to await their approach. Truman and his wife marched happily down the slope, arm in arm, and, noting her attitude, felt called upon to justify their presence in the valley by shouting: "We're lost." But the woman gave no sign beyond the half-suppressed temptation to fly which was obvious in her attitude. She was dressed in brown trousers, and an old patched woollen sweater. A scarf was tied under her chin.

As they approached her, Elsie said in an undertone: "Doesn't seem much good. She doesn't understand. Doesn't look Greek though somehow, does she?"

It was when they got much closer that they saw she was an old woman, with a slight boyish figure, and a short-cropped head of silver hair. Two brown eyes, set in her puckered face, and surrounded by a network of fine crowsfoot wrinkles, regarded them with distrust and a certain alarm. She stood and faced them across the stream, one hand reaching nervously behind her to touch the olive-bole, as if to take confidence from the feel of it. Elsie was reminded of a child shyly holding the edge of its mother's skirt. She nudged her husband. "Go on. Talk," she said. A look of comical indecision came over Mr. Truman's face. He concluded from the silence of the old woman that she had not understood their remarks in English. Of Greek he had none. However, squaring himself and opening his mouth he said haltingly: "English. We English. Ingleses," pointing first to himself and then to his wife.

The woman smiled now for the first time—a smile of relief mingled with enlightenment. "Thank God," she said in a voice which was harsh, but which carried in it some quality of distinction and self-possession that reminded Truman at once of Graecen. "Thank God. I thought you were from Evan—you'd come to take me back." She relaxed all of a sudden, and bending forward the better to accommodate her body to the laughter, laughed aloud, patting her thighs with her hands. "You speak English, then?" said Truman, rather nettled at having been forced to debase his tongue with pidgin. "Well," she said, taking up the fishing-rod, and drawing the handle of a wicker pannier over her arm, "I am American actually. My name is Adams, Ruth Adams." She walked downstream for twenty paces in order to ford it upon a series of stepping-stones, talking as she did so. "I haven't seen a stranger in years," she said, with the small harshness of tone, but with the same note of authoritative self-possession that made her voice pleasing and musical to listen to. "You must forgive me. When you don't see strangers you forget how to be polite to them." She crossed the stream and walked down the bank towards them. Elsie Truman saw that in place of shoes she was wearing a number of pairs of khaki stockings, with the soles padded in some way. At close range she looked even older; and yet in some curious way the proportions of her face retained an almost childish smoothness of contour. Yet it was deeply wrinkled. She stood before them now in her brown corduroy trousers much patched, and stretched out a shy hand as they introduced themselves. Her wrists were small and finely formed, but her finger-nails were unkept and broken, and her palm was as hard to the touch as that of a ploughman. "Ruth Adams," she murmured to each in turn. "You must", she said, "have come up through the labyrinth." The word restored to Truman the sense of urgency and danger which the last few minutes in this landscape had all but dispelled. "Yes," he said quickly, "and there are several others down there. We want to get help to them as quickly as possible." The stranger turned and walked slowly beside them, saying: "You must be tired out. Come along with me and we'll see if I can't fix you something to eat." Elsie Truman walked beside with a feeling that something was wrong; she had shown no trace of hearing her husband's words about the others. "There are," she said carefully, with an almost academic correctness (she felt that perhaps the difference in American and English idiom might have led to a misunderstanding), "there are no less than four or five people lost in those caves." The stranger looked quickly up at her for a second, smiling, and then said: "I'm sorry. I did hear your husband. But there's nothing we can do, you see. There's no other way up here except through the labyrinth."

"No other way!" Truman tripped himself—by the very

force of his own exclamation it seemed—recovered and halted to confront her. "What did you say?"

"No other way," repeated the woman, pushing her hands into her pockets, having first placed the pannier on the ground carefully so as not to displace the three small fish which they could see, peeping through a screen of fig leaves. She made a vague gesture at the horizon and carried it round until it all but circumscribed the whole visible landscape. "It's all enclosed," she said vaguely, her voice a little off-key; and then, seeing the incredulity on their faces mixed with the consternation, she added: "Please listen to me." She said it with earnestness, but with the faint note of self-assurance that made it almost a command. "Listen to me."

"No other way," repeated Truman angrily, as if the words had been an insult to him, to all the energy and determination he had put into their escape from the labyrinth.

"It's true," she said stubbornly.

"Well, what happens over there?" He pointed vaguely ahead of them to where the mountains rose, turned rose-red and bitumen-coloured in the waning sunlight.

"Cliffs," she said. "All round. I know you can't believe it easily. I couldn't when I first came here. We tried so often to find a way down."

She walked on a few paces, having picked up her basket, and then called over her shoulder: "Follow me and I'll show you the house."

The Truman couple exchanged glances. Once more that feeling of unreality, of having become entangled in a web, took possession of them. "Do you think she's all right?" asked his wife, making the vague gesture of screwing a nut into her temple with her forefinger. He did not answer. "At any rate there's a house," he said. "Come on." They walked on, like characters in a dream, and caught her up as she reached the corner of a meadow.

Beyond the brow of the hill they saw for the first time the signs of conscious cultivation—a small vineyard in a bowl, sheltered from the north by a low wall of rocks. "Yes," said the woman catching Elsie Truman's eye, "our tenderest care is that little vineyard. The wine is indifferent, but that's because we are not experts in making it." Truman came up beside her and said: "Who is 'we', Mrs. Adams?" She turned up her grotesquely lined yet so childish face and smiled apologetically at him. " 'We' *was* my brother and me. But I'm alone now. I haven't talked English since . . ." She turned suddenly and walked on, without saying any more.

Several promiscuous hedges of cactus now came into view lining a rough track. To their surprise as they passed into a grove of dwarf-olive and holm-oak they caught sight of a small house, crudely made of stone, standing in a paddock from which, faintly, came the lazy slurring of bees. "There it is," said Mrs. Truman, whose relief at this evident example of domestic architecture was manifest in her smile. "And you have bees," she added.

"Yes. For honey. I'm afraid the bread hasn't been very good since Godfrey went. It's hard work grinding the grain up fine enough, you know, and I'm getting an old woman." She nodded and smiled as she spoke.

Truman's face still wore an expression of troubled incredulity. He simply was not convinced. They approached the house, walking abreast, and he examined its workmanship with a careful professional eye; it was built of roughly-pruned rock laid together in blocks. Its corners were unpointed and the joints of the stone empty of any mortar that he could see. The porch was held upon saplings, and roughly boarded over with the grey wood of old ammunition-boxes. He could read the serial numbers and specifications in some places. The woman led the way in. "It took us six years to build this house. And, of course, Godfrey did a lot of work on it putting in im-

provements. He was a marvel of inventiveness. It was frightfully hard work. We were living in a cave up the hill before.
But it's quite solid, and look how nicely he has finished the
interior." She threw open a heavy door and showed them a
long low room, floored with crude staves of pine and cypress.
The walls had been washed with some kind of crude earth-
pigment to an uneven grey upon which somebody had drawn
several large cartoons of human faces in charcoal. "Isn't it
nice?" She crossed to the stone hearth in which a log fire was
smoking and stirred it, placing some more logs upon it. On
the hob stood a tarnished petrol tin half full of warm water.
"Come in, do," she said, turning to them with such pleasure
on her face that they felt their constraint to be something chur-
lish. "I never thought I should have the fun of showing
strangers Godfrey's work. Godfrey is my brother." She
pointed to one of the faces sketched on the wall, a turbulent,
good-looking face topped by a head of wavy hair, and smiled
again.

Truman's eyes widened in admiration. There were no chairs
in the room, but several simple cushions stood about, stuffed
with some coarse grass. They were covered in what he recognized, after a moment, as fine parachute-silk. Two tables of
smooth wood stood nearby, whose feet were contrived from
roughly-pruned logs of wood. Warm in the mounting firelight gleamed three Red Indian blankets. The whole interior
looked bare and clean—and yet, at the same time, essentially
complete and inhabited.

"Before you wash", said the woman softly, "I think I'll
make you some tea—not real tea but almost as good. Cretan
tea—*salepi*—you've probably heard of it. I won't be a
moment." She left them standing irresolutely in the middle of
the floor, and they heard her busy in the next room. Elsie
Truman sat down on one of the cushions and stretched out her
feet to the fire. "Well," she said, "what do you make of it?"

Truman did not know what to make of it. He reserved judgment. Presently the woman returned again with a look of anxious expectancy on her face. "Excellent," she said, seeing Elsie Truman sitting before the fire, "I'm so glad." It was as if she had been afraid that they were only figments of her imagination, waiting until her back was turned to disappear. She pressed upon them enamel mugs and poured the boiling water in a metalled pot. "Swamp orchis," she explained. "Another piece of Godfrey's cleverness. I think you'll enjoy it." Handing them their cups she apologized for not having any sugar to offer them. "Neither sugar nor salt can I get on this mountain," she said, sitting down and peeling off her several pairs of socks before turning a pair of finely shaped feet to the fire. "There is a sugar-beet patch up the hill, but I don't know how to extract it, and it's tiresome just to chew it. But perhaps you can help me?"

Truman disclaimed any professional knowledge of the sort, with a preoccupied air. He was still convinced that it was possible to find their way back to Cefalù, and consequently resented the faintly proprietary air with which the stranger seemed to include him in her own activities. "Tell us more about Godfrey," he said, feeling suddenly hopeful, for surely she had said that Godfrey was no longer with her?

"Godfrey," she said, and sipped her tea. "After the other two had left, Evan and John, Godfrey stayed on with me. He was my only brother. He was nearest to me in resignation, at least, so I thought. He was happy when he was constructing things to make life here more tolerable. His house, his porch, his kitchen sink—you haven't seen it yet. Almost every good thing was Godfrey's. But somehow he began to get upset when year succeeded year and there seemed less and less to do. He was a victim of activity. At first he used to call this place a heaven; but he was the kind of man who would get discontented with heaven itself. He was in love with mountains—and well known as a climber in his day. To be marooned here and surrounded by unclimbable mountains was too much for him. He tried to climb out, back into the world, but lost his foothold. He fell a clear seven hundred feet. I'll show you the little pennant on the end of his pick. You can see it from above—we call it Ibex Point because John, my husband, once saw an ibex there. It waves when there's a wind—the pennant. Gives the oddest illusion of him being alive still—as if he were calling for help. He fell between two great slabs of granite. It was his own fault. There was a high wind. I was sitting watching him when it happened. It must be several years ago. I've been awfully lonely since he left, and sort of helpless too. Godfrey was never at a loss. But now you're here it's different. Perhaps your friends will find their way up too and join you. It's so much more fun with several people. That reminds me, I shall have to get you some blankets from the hollow. The nights are cold now." She stopped all of a sudden, seeing the expression of discomfort and disbelief upon Truman's face. "I see you don't believe me."

"Well," said Truman, "you must admit it's a queer story."

She put her cup down and rose, saying: "We still have an hour of light. Walk round the whole plateau with me and see for yourself that there is no way back. I'm sorry. I know how you feel. But it's useless."

Elsie Truman settled herself like a cat before the blaze of the fire and drained her mug of *salepi*. "I can't believe it," she said, in a voice so innocent and friendly as to be empty of any suggestion of insult. "I simply can't."

"I have been here since 1926," said the woman quietly. "It's written on that wall there; when we built the house we put up our calendar. It is now . . ."

"Nineteen-forty-seven," said Truman.

"Twenty-one years."

"A long time."

"We came first," she said, sitting down afresh beside his wife, "we came first to Crete because there was a dig my husband wanted to try—at Castro. He is, was, an archaeologist, and Evan was a student who was then his assistant. Godfrey came out for a holiday from England and joined us. We were staying at the village—Cefalû—you must know it. And for a joke Godfrey thought we should try and chart the labyrinth. He was so confident that it was safe. We went quite far in when one of the small tunnels fell in and so we couldn't turn back and follow the line we had laid. Fortunately we had food with us. It took us a week until we came out here."

The Truman couple sat quite still listening. "But where's your husband," said Truman at last, "and the other man?"

The woman put her hands up to her face and slowly rubbed her cheeks with her palms. "They went back," she said absently, her voice now flat and without colour. She began to pull on her coarse stocking and thrust the padding which served her for soles into its proper place.

"Went back where?" said Truman sharply.

"Down the labyrinth?" he repeated in a voice of mingled perplexity and amusement.

"Yes," she said. "You see, my husband got very upset at being locked up here. He hated it. He and Evan began to quarrel frightfully. It was only Godfrey that kept the peace. I don't know what would have happened if he hadn't been with us. I think Evan—no, that's a lie: I know Evan was in love with me. One day they decided to take a chance, to enter the labyrinth again and try to find their way through to the other side. I have never heard if they did. That was years ago." She stood up and pointed to a date on the wall, and, with the other hand, opened the door. "Come", she said, "and see it for yourselves."

Half an hour's walking was all that was necessary to prove to them conclusively that they were marooned. It was still hardly credible, yet it was true. At every point of the compass the hill was dropped away sheer, and fell hundreds of feet towards the verdant but unpeopled valleys. It was no longer even possible to tell in which direction Cefalû lay. Dimly in the distance Truman made out the forms of orange trees. The sun was ebbing fast now, and the mountain peaks around them gleamed with melting jewellery. Nowhere was there an outlet to this girdle of hills; nowhere was so much as a hamlet visible; nowhere shone the sea. The landscape might have been part of a crater on the moon's surface.

The old woman walked beside them, silent for the most part, and thoughtful. She no longer seemed so pathetically anxious to prove to them the truth of her story. She led the way to the trout stream, and across the meadows to where the five sheep and the cow stood passively contemplating them. At different times, she explained, they had found their way up through the labyrinth. "So far", she said, "they are the only ones who have shown no anxiety to get back." Between the beauty of it all and the weariness Elsie Truman felt her eyes fill with tears. "Do let's go back," she said at last, "I am so tired."

Already they felt as they entered the little house a sense of familiarity and pleasure—almost as if they themselves had been its owners. All their preoccupation as to the fate of the rest of the party vanished too, now that it was so clearly impossible to do anything for them. Together they helped the old woman brew some more tea, and build up the fire until its flames threw their dark shapes upon the farther wall where the three faces of the men who had grown tired of this Eden looked at them, incurious, thoughtful—each wrapped, it seemed, in the impenetrability of a vanished pose. "Past tense, present tense—what does it mean?" said the old woman at last, drawing up a cushion to the blaze. "And yet I would like you to give me an account of the world outside. Tell me what has been happening."

With many hesitations the Trumans began to answer her eager questions. Yes, there had been a war. "I thought so," she exclaimed. "I thought they'd had another." She rose and leaned against the wall, adding: "You know one day a series of parcels began coming down out of the sky, attached to parachutes. Massive bundles of equipment—medical supplies, clothes: things I'd never seen before. You must tell me about them. There are about fifty rifles in the clearing: Godfrey stacked them all there. He wondered whether we could use the barrels for a system of piping. Godfrey made a nice little stone bath, but he didn't suggest any way of heating water."

"Now, if you had an old Primus", said Truman, "and some piping, I'd fix you a bath-heater."

The conversation became animated. At some time during the Cretan campaign a mass of German equipment had fallen, by some misdirection, on to the plateau. They agreed to go out together in the early morning and inspect it in the light of Truman's specialized knowledge. "And clothes," she said, "you shall have lots of clothes—warm ones. Trousers and tunics of wool. Lovely things. Some of them look English."

Their conversation prolonged itself throughout dinner, which consisted of soup, trout, cream cheese done after the Greek style, and a glass of hot goat's milk swimming with yellow beads of fat. The cooking was excellent despite the lack of salt. As they ate they saw the great candent peaks of the mountains slowly lighted up by the moon, like massive pieces of theatre machinery. A tremendous stillness reigned between their sentences. Elsie Truman could feel it seeping in, dissolving the words she uttered, reducing them to unimportant noises in the face of its huge ponderous tranquillity. She was possessed by something like fear; yet something less defined, less immediately comprehensible, for what was there to fear save the anticipation of being cut off from the known world?

"Godfrey, Evan, John and I," said the old woman. "We

fetched up here in a state of complete exhaustion." She was looking into the fire as she spoke, summoning up the forgotten scene. "Yet we made a tolerable life for ourselves out of the few elements which fate had left us. A burning-glass, some blankets, a small saw, a hatchet, and shotgun and so on. For months you know it was only fires that kept us alive. We put down the first northern wall of the house during a winter of exceptional bitterness. We worked like mules under Godfrey. He took charge of everything so naturally. There are still a lot of essentials lacking, as you see; glass for the windows is one of them. Those grey silk screens are pretty, but very rough; I dare say you feel the draught coming through them. They give a sort of Chinese feeling to the room, don't they, 'specially when you see the mountains slowly develop on them like photographs? It was so quiet after they left, and yet everything changed for the better. Something inside me seemed to change, too, though I don't know how to express it properly. Perhaps living alone did it. Or perhaps I only imagined it; but Godfrey said that in some way we had become allied to the forces of Nature instead of against them. He had studied philosophy and used to say that the whole of the western civilization we knew was based on the Will: and that led always to action and to destruction. Whereas he claimed there was some thing inside us, an element of repose he called it, which you could develop, and alter your life completely. Sounds rubbish, doesn't it?"

It did. (Lumme, thought Truman, stifling a yawn, have I struggled so far and so hard, first with life and then with the labyrinth, in order to have nonsense talked to me on a plateau in Crete from which there is no escape?) His wife, however, seemed interested. Her cheeks became pink as always when she was excited, and she leaned forward, saying: "Do go on."

The stranger sat before the fire cross-legged and looked before her, stretching out a small hand from time to time to catch the warmth. "Godfrey said that one could even have a physical effect on the world around you. Now, here's a funny thing. I began to notice since he left that the axe was not wearing out. You can't imagine how important it was to us in the early days of house-building; we used it with great care. Even then it had to be ground once every so long. Godfrey did that. But since he left it has remained sharp and bright as ever; and you can see that I've done quite a lot of cutting with it. Just put your finger to it. Sharp, isn't it?" She smiled up at Elsie Truman and said: "You are looking distressed. Please don't. I'm not mad."

Mrs. Truman disclaimed the impeachment. She would have liked to hear more, but the stranger rose abruptly and said she would light them to their room. Picking from the corner a spill made of twisted reeds dipped in resin she led them to a small room with two beds in it. The window was boarded up, but the walls were whitewashed after the fashion of the living-room. It was bitterly cold. Elsie Truman began to cry. Her husband made no attempt to comfort her; he lay beside her staring at the ceiling and repeating in a perplexed voice: "You can say what you like, it's a rum go. No doubt about it." And fatigue triumphing at last over perplexity, he fell asleep, his hands under his armpits for warmth. His wife lay there for a long time listening to the graduations of the silence which came, it seemed, from the heart of some huge sea-shell; broken now and then by small noises, as of a mouse stirring, or as of ice-crystals being crushed beneath small feet. She could feel the presence of those icy peaks outside the window, standing up nude in the light of the moon, buried in their own snowy preoccupation. It was as if she had lost her way in one of her own dreams; yet underneath her growing sense of terror lay the feeling that perhaps it was only the unfamiliarity of this world that seemed inimical.

In the middle of the night, in order to relieve the demands of Nature, she picked her way by memory to the large living-room with the fireplace in it. The moon was high now and its blinding dazzle played upon the silk screens covering the windows; a faint breath of wind moved them from time to time. She was about to open the front door when she saw, to her surprise, the silhouette of the woman, thrown by the moonlight upon the nearest screen; she was seated upon a three-legged stool, facing the panorama of mountains, her body wrapped in a rug. Her head was cocked up at an angle, as if she had heard a sound, and yet her whole attitude was one of repose. "Don't be afraid," she said. "Come out if you wish.'

Elsie Truman felt rather like a small child caught on an escapade. "I just came down for a second," she said, lifting the latch and stepping out on to the porch.

The stranger did not turn round or say any more. So rapt was her expression that it seemed for a moment as if she might be praying. Elsie Truman went about her business, for the night was cold, and she was in no mood to hang about in that icy air. On her way back to the porch she heard the other say: "Elsie." She did not turn but still looked upwards, her eyes fixed on the snows. "Yes," said Mrs. Truman.

"I suppose", said the stranger, "you'd think me mad if I told you that I *never sleep*." She emphasized the words with slow pleasure. "I spend every night here and feel perfectly refreshed. Here, sit beside me for a moment and I'll tell you something."

"It's cold," protested Elsie Truman.

"Just for a moment." She obeyed, perching herself uncomfortably on the balcony wall. "Now then," said the stranger, her eyes fixed upon the great range of snowy mountains whose ragged fissures glittered black and baleful in the moon's light. "Feel my pulse. Normal, eh? Feel how warm my hands are, and my feet. If you were a doctor you would mutter respectful things about my arterial system." She still spoke in a dreamy, abstracted voice as if she were employing the greater part of her faculties elsewhere. "Sleep", she said indistinctly, "was invented for the tired. People are tired because their style of body or mind is wrong, just as athletes get tired if their position is a cramping one." Elsie Truman blew on her cupped hands impatiently. She had once taken a biology course at the London Polytechnic, and nothing of the kind had been suggested. "There is no more need for sleep than there is for death," said the woman slowly. Then she added with more emphasis: "I wish I could tell you what happened to me. When Godfrey had gone, between tea-time and dinner, without warning, with no premonition—a very odd, almost disagreeable sensation, but somehow one that I recognized inside as being useful. How can I put it? On a dark night you try to find the keyhole in the front door. You cannot. That is what our lives are normally like. Then at last your key suddenly slides into the groove and you are master of your house again. A half-second of relief and power. And another thing. This experience I felt was not an extraordinary one. It came out of ordinary faculties, through repose. I had never been still enough before. Here I got as still as a needle. Elsie, are you listening?"

"Yes." She was, all of a sudden, listening with great attention. It was as yet obscure and muddled in her mind, but something about the phrasing struck her with a sense of familiarity; reminding her of the occasion upon which Campion had revealed the existence of a beauty in her quite independent of her prettiness.

"I remembered how life was before," pursued the old lady quietly. "I was outside everything in a certain way. Now I participate *with* everything. I feel joined to everything in a new kind of way. Before I lived by moral precepts—for morality is an attempt to unite ourselves to people. Now I don't feel the need for religion, or faith in the old sense. In my own mind, inside (not as something I think or feel, but as something I *am*) inside there I no longer prohibit and select. I include. It's the *purely scientific* meaning of the word 'love'. Does it sound rubbish? Do you understand a word I say?"

Indeed a strangely disquieting sense of familiarity had begun to grow in Elsie Truman's mind. It was as if the conversation had outlined hitherto undescribed blocks of experience lying within her. It was as if a part of herself had been an untenanted house, with all its huge furniture covered in dustcloths of accepted prejudice, vague and shapeless. "I don't know," she said, afraid of making a fool of herself. "I feel uncomfortable and foolish."

"It is not important", said the other, "to anyone but yourself. I thought I would try to explain why it is that I never sleep. And also why it is that I shan't die until I really want to —until I've really explored this world to the full. Until I'm used up and, so to speak, emptied out of this world into the next."

Elsie Truman stared fixedly at a chip in the masonry and said: "I would like to know more about it. I feel I know what you mean, but I can't express myself. How do you . . . did you . . . find it? I mean the feeling?"

For a long time the woman said nothing, she arched her brows as if she were trying to locate within herself the sources of the spring. At last she said: "I don't know." She closed her eyes. "There's no positive way. It's rather a negative business —becoming still enough inside to be receptive to it. You can't seek for it, but if you prepare for it it will come and settle on you like an Emperor moth. In fact, not 'seek and ye shall find' as the Bible says, but 'prepare and ye shall be found'. Oh, I can't hope to make it any clearer."

"There was a man on the ship," said Elsie Truman slowly. "A painter; he is lost too, by the way, in the labyrinth. He painted my portrait, and said a lot of things which sounded as if they were the same sort of feeling. I thought I was a bit in

love with him. I went to his cabin one night and we slept together: he was furious afterwards because he said it was a betrayal of this thing. I thought it was silly, myself, but he main-
tained that it was not love I was looking for but that other
thing he had got. And that by letting him make love to me, he
was simply producing it in an inferior way. There was some
truth in it for I soon found out that I did not love him. But he
had a queer kind of life in him, and I was interested in that: he
said I had duped myself by pretending it was love, and he had
duped me by letting me think it was. Altogether it was very
confusing and I felt miserable."

The woman said nothing. Elsie Truman suddenly felt as if
she had committed a solecism. "I simply felt", she said lamely,
"that he was talking about the same sort of thing as you are."

"Yes," said the stranger. "Obviously."

"He was furious with himself and me."

"It was silly of him on one plane."

"That's what I thought."

"He was right about it on another."

Elsie Truman stood up and dusted herself down. "Well,
which plane is one to be on?" she said peevishly. "One is in
life after all, which is full of people and things and situations.
There isn't room for everything, you know."

"Perhaps not."

She did not turn her face away from the snows. "Perhaps
not," she repeated softly. Yet looking at that smooth childish
face with its wrinkles, and the deep repose of the expression,
Mrs. Truman felt a sense of inadequacy and panic: all the limitations of urban man in the shape of nails, clothes, teeth,
seemed to press upon her as she stood in the shadow of the
porch to say good night. As she climbed into bed a strange
sense of anger and joy took possession of her. "It would take
a helicopter exactly an hour to get us out of here," she repeated
to herself triumphantly, though from where she expected the

helicopter to come, she did not specify. She lay awake for a long time, however, thinking of the silent figure outside the porch, in the light of the moon, awake.

The adventure did not in any sense become real to them until they had been several weeks on the plateau. It was as if the shock had been delayed. They still carried in them, so to speak, the taste of their former lives: the only thing which constituted a term of reference to this elegaic existence among the ferns and the fruit trees on the little plateau that Godfrey had called Eden, and which Truman himself had called "The Roof of the Bloody World". It was some time before Elsie Truman felt, with a sense of panic mixed with pleasure, that there was indeed no further continuity between all she had left and all she had inherited. How remote the past seemed: memories of a smoky house and garden in England, memories of holidays at Clacton, rides by bus or helicopter in the damp highways of the capital. Even the heavy battledress with its familiar shaggy cut of shoulder and bust (as a transport driver in the late war, she had been used enough to uniform) seemed now to be a new costume, a new treatment of her personality in terms of . . . what precisely? She did not know. Something vaguely connected with growth, development. Helping to lift out the crude wooden frames of the beehives, or to select salads from grass by the river, or to select edible mushrooms from the plot below the pine-wood, she would stop for a moment and try to bring the realization more clearly into focus, wiping her brown face upon her arm where the fine golden hair testified to the heat of the summer which was upon them. It was as if her nature, the inner elements of her nature, were composing themselves kaleidoscopically into some new pattern.

Meanwhile, around the three of them the aerial landscape drew in neat formal shapes: supple strokes of cypress and pine, greeny grey parasols of olive. In the smaller life of the house things were also taking shape according to a plan. Three people eat more than one. Truman's enjoyment at expending his energy and skill upon the crude little olive-press was something new to him. It was as if the work came from new centres of feeling. Happiness had been something positive before. It had become something negative now, but lucid, far more satisfactory. It made him more comprehensible to himself. Yet his energy was repaid only in olive oil from the frugal crop of last year.

Ruth Adams was obviously glad to have them with her, to temper her solitude. "I am so glad", she said, "that when I die you will inherit it all. I like to think of the house being kept up, and things still going on. Don't look like that. I have a feeling you won't go away. You will pass through the restlessness and irritation you feel now. Evan and John were different. They were worldly in a weak way, they had nothing to learn: or perhaps I should say everything. They went off into the labyrinth to find the way back. They wanted me to go with them but it was too late by then. I often wonder whether they got through or not. It seems unlikely. And yet from time to time people and things get through from the other side. Once a donkey came loaded with geological equipment. Now you. But you are exactly right for this place." They were sitting together before the fire after the midday meal. "Most people," she said, warming to her favourite topic, and yet showing by the diffidence of her smile that she was at any moment ready to drop it in favour of anything more interesting to them. "Most people's characters are like badly done-up paper parcels. And the outlines of the good personality, or the balanced one, are as simple and geometric as a problem from Euclid. I wonder why the world goes out of its way to drug itself—to retain the confusion? Of course, it's easy to pronounce judgment when one is out of the world as we are: but surely things like pleasure and work should be dithyrambic? Not narcotics designed to retain the turbid confused state of one's inner man.

The things you were telling me, Mr. Truman, about the growth of the state as a concept, and the beginning of social conscience—all this is only a detour, a long and vicious detour through the material amenities towards a happiness that will continue to elude men just so long as they continue to elude themselves and each other. Look at those faces." She pointed to where the firelight danced upon the charcoal portraits of her vanished companions. "Godfrey's face is the only one which retains any traces of a noble human animal. His despair and suffering were of a fine order. There was literally nothing else for him to do save to fall to his death—indeed in one sense his false step was deliberate, as deliberate as his olive-press and his bath. He belonged neither to the world outside, where he thought he preferred to be, nor even to this little heaven. There have been great spirits of discontent like him before. But as for the others, John, my husband, and Evan." She waved her small hand idly towards them. "Look at their features. They had to forfeit their place and start again at a lower level of growth. Like snakes and ladders. Accident brought them here, and all their energies went in trying to get back. Of course, in a sense they did belong outside. I feel released by their departure. I suppose there is a special world for them and people like them—it must resemble one of those mock-Tudor road-houses you used to see on the Great West Road. But in a sense Godfrey is always with me. He taught me what to recognize in myself: I learned from him that death doesn't exist except in the imagination. Thus I was hardly sad when his discontent carried him through to the other side— like stepping into a mirror. I was sorry on another plane altogether. I missed his tea-time conversation: his flag still flutters from the rock—but I showed you. Ah, but I fear you think I'm talking nonsense again."

Very often it sounded like absolute nonsense; yet in the course of time the very boundaries of language themselves seemed to fall away, so that the meaning of what she said seemed to render up overtones and distinctions more clear to either than had seemed possible. It was as if they were being initiated into an entirely new vocabulary.

One day while they were standing, paddling in the little basin where the icy water from the trout-stream curled about their ankles and whispered in the cresses they picked, Elsie Truman asked curiously: "Ruth, is there nothing you miss from your old life?"

"Everything. If I were taken back tomorrow by force—if Evan came for me, I would go without a murmur. But that's because I really know how to live anywhere now. I think I'm a person now, not a fog. Perhaps my influence would be helpful, beneficent. But when you say 'miss' you really mean 'long for'. I don't long for anything—not even for lunch, which is going to be late unless we hurry . . ."

"It's odd", she said on another occasion, "that we live between the two accidents which might alter our lives completely. If we broke the burning-glass one day, for example, where should we be? If a helicopter such as you describe, Mr. Truman, were to come and settle on the meadow: we should have to choose between going and staying. Either accident is possible. Death or Life? Life or Death?"

"Think of them all," said Truman. "Cities, manganese mines, governments, clubs. India, China, Russia—makes you wonder what it all means. Cotton, iron, steel . . . where does it all lead?"

"All parts of an unco-ordinated pattern. Man as a person looking for what I think I've found. The search throws up bright bits of gold and information which catch his attention and prevent him from looking deeper into himself. Yes, a staggering spectacle of a *genus* engaged in a wasteful way of living. And yet every activity leading back like an arrow on the map to central metaphysical problems of the self. The wars of factories, of diplomats, of concepts—all hopelessly entangled in the opposites that created them."

"Could you teach them any different?" Truman spoke piously, enviously, as if there were nothing he himself might wish to do more than to alter humanity.

"I would not try: any more than I try to alter you."

"What would you do then?"

"Nothing. Pay my rent like everyone else."

Truman grunted with disappointment. He had hoped for something more simple: a formula, a maxim. "I bet", he said, "you'd find a little hill covered with gorse and olive-trees and heather. And build yourself a house and some beehives. And keep a goat."

"Yes," said his wife. "And wait for us to come along, with new ways of making hot bath water and milking the goat. I bet you would fetch up here just the same. It suits you."

"It suits you too, but you haven't fully realized it yet."

"Well," said Truman, "I never was one for grumbling. And the life is remarkably healthy in spite of the cooking."

He made his way slowly from the house whistling softly and crossed the meadow. "I have no more idea of what everything is all about," he said to himself gravely in an undertone. "I'm fogged. That's what it is. Completely fogged." Yet he felt remarkably clear-headed in that blue air. "Fogged," he insisted from time to time as he milked the goat and wandered off for a walk. "Bloody well fogged."

He stopped upon the bluff and stared across the vast bluish plains towards the distant hills tremulous in mist. "Someone must come out one of these days," he thought, "to prune those orchards. I wonder whether we could signal." He put the thought carefully aside as if it were something fragile and breakable. In the kitchen Elsie had already lit the wood fires. She was about to start cooking some wood-pigeons for lunch. "Hunger," said Truman trenchantly, "that's all I feel. Hunger.

You keep your philosophy, my girl, for after meals."

His wife was smelling her hands carefully, inhaling the faintly musty odour of the dead birds. "You go away," she said. "It won't be ready for hours yet."

He stood irresolutely and watched her moving about. "Are you happy?" he said at last with peculiar diffidence, standing on one leg and folding his arms across his chest. She looked at him smiling.

"I never stop to consider," she said. "I mean, really contented," he continued.

"I don't know," she said slowly. "Are you?" "I'm fogged," he said, exploring his teeth with his tongue. "I'm absolutely fogged. I don't know what I feel about anything any more. I feel as light as a feather. I feel absolutely fogged." It gave him a peculiar sense of relief to confess himself; and at the same time he was irritated not to be able to define his feelings more clearly.

He left her and went for a walk by the stream, with his hands thrust deeply into the pockets of his battledress. He had intended to carry this feeling of confusion with him and to try and clear it up, but his hand closed about his beloved knife, and soon he was whittling at a branch of walnut, whistling through his teeth as he worked. He presumed that this must be happiness. He raised his eyes and looked across the valley. Below them he saw birds making their short elliptical flights, busy upon errands whose purpose was like his own, but more mysterious, more beautiful. An almost damnable sense of the mysterious nature of the world took possession of him. He would have smoked if he had had any cigarettes left. Instead he went, still whistling, and mended the rough parapet of the little trout pool into which the stream overflowed, working slowly like a beaver. Looking down into the wrinkling water he saw the sunlight freckling the smooth pebbles of the stream's bottom; it reminded him of the freckles upon his wife's nose. She had become swarthy and more beautiful, with brown face and arms always bare to the sunlight. He had changed also: was bearded now. He regarded his image in the flowing waters with curiosity and humorous indulgence. His eyes stared back at him shining with strange watery lights. "It's rum", he told himself, "for an ordinary bloke like you. Very rum."

The season moved towards its centre—towards autumn and the pressing of the little grape yield: towards winter with its rude terrors of wind from Tartary. Their function became more absolutely defined by the work demanded by the season. Yet there was no sense of calendar time left in either of them. They gathered the barley and the wild corn; they gathered the burst vessels of fig from the trees, full of the cloying honeyed richness of summer. Day after day the great fireplace had to be stacked with logs against the cold. There was work to be done. Ruth Adams, gentler, less communicative now, shared these labours with them, working in a quiet enjoyment of the time which as yet neither knew properly how to share.

The small orchard gave them fruit. The old woman taught them how to make wine from flowers. From the little marshy hollow below the cliffs—the last point at which the stream bent suddenly in upon itself and rushed through a sill of rock —they gathered the bulbs of swamp orchis for their tea; or nearer the house camomile, sage, vervain. It seemed as if very little were lacking—though both wine and bread were of a crude quality as yet.

Autumn came and with it the first rain—millions of silver needles bounding from the rocks and concavities around them. They worked on in a peasant frenzy of determination not to let the rain steal their barley, or to let the old woman find them inferior to herself in the tasks of existence. They were learning. Elsie Truman's hands had become hard and

calloused from the work, but her face and her carriage had
been improved. She was serener, yet more alive. "You're like
a gipsy," her husband told her, as she lay in bed beside him.
Her body had filled out, become firm and round. "I almost
feel as if I were going to have a child," she told him. "Doesn't
seem likely somehow or possible at my age, does it?" She did
not add any reflections upon her private conviction that the
child, when it came, would be Campion's. That could wait for
futurity—the futurity of comprehension and tranquillity when,
by the terms of self-knowledge, such small offences against
defined loyalties could be added up and probably forgiven.
The child, too, in a sense, still belonged to the old world of
troubled relationship; had as yet no place in this quiet house.

Tenderly he put his arms about her shoulders and laid his
bearded face beside hers on the pillow. Their love too had
suffered a metamorphosis, for he regarded her now with something like admiration and surprise. She had changed; was less
approachable, more withdrawn into herself—and by consequence infinitely more desirable than the shadowy companion
whose journey through the labyrinth he had made easier by his
jokes and his courage. "A savage," he said sleepily, thinking
of the easy naturalness of her demeanour, her warmth: as if
passion itself were the last point of communication between
them. As if in everything else she had become possessed by
herself, gradually excluding him—her dependency on him
—for something richer, deeper, more intimate.

For days now their world was circumscribed by clouds
which closed in on them like wet washing, grey, green, blue,
according to the angle of the sunlight shining through them.
They walked every afternoon to the bluff and sat watching the
landscape below shine up in sudden rifts: watching the wind
tear aside a corner of the veil and show them the pristine sky.

Softly "whewing" they heard the storks passing overhead
all night long, moving towards Egypt, their necks and wings

straining towards the warmth. The torrents were swollen, too, and the crying of the birds mingled with the musical enunciation of water on stone, on wood, water on moss and lichen.

There was nothing, in the deepest and most vital sense, to be said; no summing-up, no judgment to be passed upon what had begun to travel through them—time in its pure state—as water will run noiselessly through fingers trailed from a boat. Even the snow, when it came, seemed part of the order and style of the little universe which hemmed them in. Its soft drifts mounted against the walls of the house they lived in, sparkling with a thousand dewy points in the sunlight. It climbed up the sides of the byres which Truman had built for the sheep and the cow. These animals too had found their way up through the labyrinth. Happiness for them also had become an idle proposition.

Dawns came now with an immensity and terror that staggered them: the first raw burst of colour in the east spreading upon the snow-capped mountains around them, like blood swelling from wounds. As the season deepened they could hear the roar of avalanches where the higher snow melted upon the desolate face of stone. The wind strummed fitfully in the pines. They might have been in Asia.

When spring came they took to walking on fine evenings to Ibex Point and sitting there upon the mossy network of stones which seemed almost to be the remains of some old fortress. Below them Godfrey's pennant still hovered in the breeze. Beyond, the valleys curved away towards the final foothill, fitfully blue and peaceful. It seemed to them at such times that they had reached the meridian of human knowledge. The luminous landscape echoed, in its tranquillity, the thought. If there was no way back there was at least no way forward: the discovery of themselves was itself complete enough to prevent them wanting, hoping, striving. "I feel," said Truman, struggling with the inadequacies of his vocabulary. "I feel O.C.

Universe," and his wife lying down with her hands behind her head, smiled up her content and happiness as she chewed a grass-stalk. She had realized that the roof of the world did not really exist, except in their own imaginations!

At Cefalû

All night long the falls of rock in the labyrinth continued. Graecen heard them through his dreams—as if through some thick curtain—and imagined they were part of them; but some time before dawn he awoke and realized that they were not: and shivered, drawing the bedclothes over his head as he settled himself to sleep. It was full daylight when he awoke once more. Sunlight was glancing through the trees; raising himself on one elbow he could see, beyond the green lawns of Cefalû, the glittering enamel-shining sea. He seemed to have completely recovered from the shock of the day before—it was irritating in a way, for he had planned to spend perhaps a day in bed, resting. Yet one felt so confoundedly well in this blue atmosphere, this Greek morning which seemed to hold in it exciting premonitions like poems unwritten, poems balancing upon the edge of one's tongue. He got up and stood at the window for a while staring down at the sea, and the clutter of painted boats beside the mole. Somewhere a bird was singing out of sight. "Where birds like arrows glide, upon the resistless Grecian tide, and ships like swans upon the lawns . . ." It wouldn't do. He lit a cigarette. The chink of teacups made him crane forward and peer down through the wine-wreathed pergola. Axelos was seated at the breakfast-table in his pyjamas, cracking the top of an egg. "Silenus," called Graecen; "any news?"

Axelos raised his dark countenance. "Hullo, Dickie, how do you feel?" How did he feel? Graecen had half-hoped for an excuse to feel ill—well, indisposed. He had planned a day of rest. A bit of fuss over him: his food on a tray: visitors. "My heart *seems* all right," he admitted cautiously if unwillingly. In the panic of a spasm he had told Axelos about his condition, and had found, to his surprise, gentleness and anxiety where he had expected something like Hogarth's irony and disbelief. "Don't get up unless you feel like it," said Axelos. "I'll send your food up." For a moment Graecen was tempted. "No. It's all right," he said at last; the day was too beautiful to waste. "I'll come down."

Soon he was sitting on the terrace above the dew-drenched lawn feeling rather hungrier than seemed right or proper for a man in his condition. "What news", he said, "of the others?"

Axelos finished his third egg and wiped his mouth. "None, I'm afraid. I think they don't stand much chance, you know. And there are falls still going on. The City in the Rock has gone, I'm afraid, unless the Museum can put up the money to dig it out. I went up again early this morning; and Baird hasn't come back. Spent the night up at the monastery. You don't know what he's up to?" he added with a trace of anxiety. "What is he trying to find out?" Graecen did not know. He ate his egg in silence, thinking of Campion. "Poor Campion," he said; "I must do a little essay on him for *The Times*. A great artist, you know, but such a beastly little man. Unconventional, troublesome, pompous—no, not pompous, affected. But what a painter." He wondered if perhaps all great artists, from whose company he reluctantly excluded himself, were not absolutely revolting as human beings? Dostoevsky writing about Christian meekness while he browbeat his menservants, Lawrence saying nasty things about one when one wasn't there—even when one was trying to place his stuff for him. It was very odd. "He simply wasn't a *gentleman*," he added reluctantly, with no trace of snobbishness, but using the word in its exact sense. Campion had been lacking not so much in gentleness of birth, as in gentleness of nature; nothing was beneath him. Nevertheless he was a great spirit and something must be done towards the memory of him. He troubled and enriched (that was rather good), he troubled and enriched the world: the world was the richer for his passing through it. "Sir, may I draw the attention of your readers to the passing of one whose presence troubled and enriched the world, during his all-too-brief passing through it? I refer to . . ." That was a capital beginning. Graecen cracked his egg with a magisterial air, happy to feel the seeds of composition stirring in him once more.

"You know, Dickie," said Axelos, "I have a feeling there's nothing wrong with your heart. I had a friend once who was told the same thing. The doctor had swopped his name in the card index with someone else. You ought to check back."

"I say," said Graecen flushing, "do you really think so?" It was a straw, but he grasped it. "It's just possible, I suppose." He knew as he spoke that it was not possible, but the idea buoyed him up. He would write to those London brutes and ask them to check the diagnosis. "It's just possible," he repeated, dipping deep into the buttercup-coloured heart of the egg.

"Oh, and another thing," said Axelos, "I think I've laid the minotaur. You see this chap coming up the path with the policeman? He has the secret I feel sure."

The village policeman was advancing across the lawn dragging a fisherboy by the arm. He was a stern old man who looked like a discharged sergeant-major, red-faced, moustached. "This is the boy," he said, springing to attention and saluting. The boy was about fifteen years of age, clad in tatters, with bare feet. He looked very frightened and his lip trembled as Axelos addressed him in his most formidable lord-of-the-manor voice. "Your name?"

"Peter, son of Karamanos."

"You were found blowing a ram's horn down one of the tunnels of the labyrinth?"

"Yes."

"Why?"

"Because it makes 'boom-boom'."

"And why do you wish to make 'boom-boom' in the labyrinth?"

"I am poor, sir."

"You are paid for it? By whom?"

"Oh, sir." The boy burst into tears and fell blubbering on the grass, repeating between snorts: "I must not say who. I must not say who."

"Get up, wretch," said the policeman, still standing to attention. "Get up, werewolf, pigsdroppings. Rise." He delivered a surreptitious kick at the boy's posterior and became immediately rigid again.

Axelos selected a peach from the dish in front of him and began to eat it. The boy's sobs diminished in volume. "Take him away", said Axelos mildly to the policeman, "and cut his legs off at the ankles. Perhaps he will speak then."

The boy set up a howl. Axelos waddled across to him and lifted him up in one huge hairy arm. "Speak," he shouted suddenly, so loudly that the crockery jumped and Graecen was all but precipitated out of his chair. The boy spoke.

"Mr. Jannadis," he said.

"The tourist one?"

"Yes."

"You may go. Wait." Katina had appeared on the balcony, attracted by the noise. "Katina," said Axelos quietly, "give this boy a hundred drachmae and tell him not to do it any more." He settled himself in his chair once more and bade the policeman good-bye. "There," he said. "You understand? A tourist stunt. What is one to do?"

Graecen called to mind the terrible groans and bellow of the beast in the darkness of the labyrinth. "We live in a rational world," he said sadly, "I suppose everything has a rational explanation."

"Well," said Baird's voice behind them, "nearly every-thing." He appeared on the terrace and shook hands all round. "It's a long time," said Axelos. "A very long time. I'm happy to see you."

"By the way," said Baird. "Some news. Virginia is safe. She apparently found a way out and jumped into the sea." Graecen turned bright green. Axelos stood up. "She's broken her leg," said Baird, "but she'll be all right; I saw her comfortably tucked up in the monastery. The Abbot has set the break. Afraid it'll be some time before she can be moved."

Axelos hovered irresolutely. "She must have a doctor. I'll get through to Canea. Her people should be notified. Have you her address?" Baird had forgotten to take it. "Never mind," said Axelos, "I'll try and ring that journalist fellow." He hurried off into the house.

"A woman falling out of the sky," said Baird, lighting a cigarette. "We had just started off, the Abbot and I, when the mad novice jumped in the air and said he'd seen a woman falling out of the sky. As he is given to visions most of the monks thought it was a personal visitation of the Virgin Mary. The Abbot turned back and was about to shout some insults at them for their superstitious nature when, by God, we saw an arm sticking out of the sea. 'A woman,' yelled the Abbot and, behaving like a man who hasn't seen a woman for some time he dashed into the sea followed by all the monks who could swim. Those who couldn't brought out the fishing boat. It was a wonderful picture, Graecen. You should have seen them all in their wet cassocks and stove-pipe hats swimming about shouting at the tops of their voices. I thought she was a goner when we got her into the boat. But we filled her up with warm tea and got her settled into warm blankets and, as I say, the Abbot has put her leg in splints. Apparently she was with Campion."

"Campion?" said Graecen, startled.

"Yes. I didn't press for details as she seemed so weak and done up. She said she wasn't sure whether he jumped with her or not. They've got the boats out now looking for him. So far no trace, however."

"Campion," repeated Graecen. "Well. What do you think of that for a story? I hope they find him." But he felt a pang of regret.

They walked together across the lawn and sat in the patch of sunlight under the plane-tree. Axelos could be heard off-stage shouting into the telephone. "Hullo; Hullo; Canea? Hullo . . ."

"It doesn't sound as if it works," said Graecen.

"I say," said Baird suddenly. "I found out some funny things about old Axelos. Is there a peasant girl here called Katina?"

"Yes," said Graecen. "The servant."

"He's married to her."

"Rubbish," said Graecen. "How could he?"

"The Abbot married them himself. Then another thing. This City in the Rock business."

"It's gone, by the way. Fallen in."

"The Abbot says it was quite genuine. They found it one day when they were looking for a smuggler. Then, he says Axelos gave him money and told him he should say that they built the damn thing, carved it and all that. What do you make of all that?"

Graecen was thinking how nearly he had proposed to Virginia. His scalp tingled at the nearness of his escape. He must get away before anything silly like that happened to him. "Eh?" he said, aware that Baird was staring at him.

"What do you make of *that*?" repeated Baird.

"I knew it was genuine the minute I saw it," said Graecen loftily; "I have no idea why he should pretend it isn't."

"Let's ask him," said Baird, all curiosity; but Graecen got up and took a stroll up and down the lawn. "You know," he said, his natural tact revolting at the idea of prying into other people's secrets, "I think it would be better if we didn't really. He's a very old friend of mine indeed. And I wouldn't like to embarrass and hurt him. Besides the whole place has disappeared now. Let's leave it."

Axelos came out from the house in his straw hat and pyjamas. "It doesn't work," he said, sitting down beside them. "What a country."

"What a country," echoed Graecen, his eyes fixed on the moving sea, and the dazzle of white buildings on the cape.

The three of them sat quite still and felt the sunlight soaking into them. Birds were singing in the planes. The summer had begun.

"I'm only sorry about the minotaur," said Graecen sleepily, as Katina came out towards them in her bright clothes bearing a flask of wine and some glasses. "You could have spared me that Silenus, at my age."

But Axelos silently contented himself by pouring out the dark sweet wine into the glasses and sighing.

Author's Note

Not only the characters depicted in this story, but the events also, are fictitious. Even the island of Crete may rest assured that no libellous motives suggested its choice as a *locale*. The following fragment from *The Islands of the Aegean*, by the Rev. Henry Fanshawe Tozer, M.A., F.R.G.S., Oxford University Press, 1875, must be held responsible for suggesting the story:

"Our object now was to recross the island on the Eastern side of Mount Ida to the town of Megalocastron, or Candia, on the northern coast; but before doing so we determined to make a *detour* to visit a place which is known in all the neighbouring district by the name of 'The Labyrinth' (*Ο Λαβύρινθος*). Our host, Captain George, undertook to be our guide; and accordingly the next morning we started in his company and, fording the stream close under the Acropolis of Gortyna, ascended the hills towards the north-west and in an hour's time reached the place which bears the name. It is entered by an aperture of no great size in the mountain-side where the rocks are of clayey limestone, forming horizontal layers; and inside we found what looks almost like a flat roof, while chambers and passages run off from the entrance in various directions. The appearance at first sight is that of artificial construction, but more probably it is entirely natural, though some persons think it has served for a quarry. We were furnished each with a taper and descended by a passage, on both sides of which the fallen stones had been piled up; the roof above us varied from four to sixteen feet in height. Winding about, we came to an upright stone, the work of a modern Ariadne, set there to show the way, for at intervals other passages branched off from the main one, and anyone who entered without a light would be hopelessly lost. Captain George described to us how for three years during the late war (1867–1869) the Christian inhabitants of the neighbouring villages, to the number of 500, and he among them, had lived there, as their predecessors had done during the former insurrection, to escape the Turks, who had burned their homes and carried off their flocks and herds, and all other property they could lay hands on. He pointed out to us the places where the stones were piled up so as to form chambers, each of which was occupied by a family. When I inquired, half in joke, where their refectory was, he replied that far, far within there was a large and lofty central hall, capable of holding 500 people together, to which they gave the name, and that there they used to meet from time to time and dance, sing and enjoy themselves. They had brought a provision of bread to eat and oil for light; and water they obtained from a spring in the innermost part of the cavern, which appears to be the only one, for we saw no stalactites or dripping water in other parts. After wandering in different directions for half an hour, during which time we had not penetrated into one-tenth of its ramifications, we returned to the open air.

"Notwithstanding the modern name, and the opinion of some scholars in favour of this place, there is no reason for supposing that this was the original Cretan labyrinth. The place was in all probability a mythical conception, like the stories attached to it, though like many other Greek legends, it may have been attached to some geographical feature, such as a cavern; but all Greek writers localize the story at Cnossus, besides which the coins of that city bear as their emblem an idealized representation of the Labyrinth.

"Ascending the hillside, we crossed a plateau, the ground beneath which is mined by the Labyrinth, and at one point

Captain George pointed out to us the position of the refectory underground. Higher up we obtained a view of the snowy mountains of Crete together, comprising the Dictean Mountains, Ida, Kedros, and the White Mountains."